A New Collection of Women's Erotica

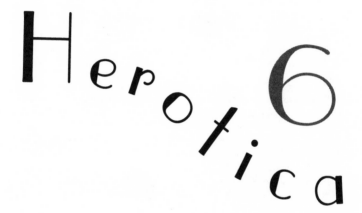

Herotica 6

Marcy Sheiner
Editor

Down There Press • San Francisco, California

Herotica 6. A New Collection of Women's Erotica. Compilation
© 1999 by Marcy Sheiner
Individual contributions © 1999 by their authors

"Herotica" is a registered trademark of Open Enterprises Cooperative, Inc.

Library of Congress Cataloging-in-Publication Data

Herotica 6: a new collection of women's erotica / Marcy Sheiner, editor
  p. cm.
    ISBN 0-940208-25-3 (pbk.)
      1. Erotic stories, American. 2. American fiction—Women authors.
    3. Women—Sexual behavior—Fiction. I. Sheiner, Marcy. II. Title:
    Herotica six.
    PS648.E7H4781999
    813'.01083538'082—dc21   98-50893
                                                          CIP

We offer librarians an Alternative CIP prepared by Sanford Berman, Head Cataloger at Hennepin County Library, Minnetonka MN.

Alternative Cataloging-in-Publication Data

Sheiner, Marcy, 1946-
    Herotica 6: a new collection of women's erotica. Marcy Sheiner, editor.
San Francisco, CA: Down There Press, copyright 1999.

    Twenty-one short stories, "each exploring aspects of women's sexuality in explicit and uncompromising scenarios," by Red Jordan Arobateau, Deborah Bishop, Kate Dominic, Mel Harris, Maria Mendoza, Mary Ann Mohanraj, Carol Queen, Cecilia Tan, and others.

    1. Erotic fiction, American. 2. Women—Sexuality—Fiction. 3. Women's erotica. 4. Short stories, American—20th century. 5. Women's fiction, American—20th century. 6. Commitment (Psychology)—Fiction. I. Title. II. Title: Her erotica 6. III. Title. Women's erotica. IV. Down There Press.

813.5408 or Fiction

Additional copies of this book are available at your favorite bookstore or directly from the publisher:

Down There Press, 938 Howard St., #101, San Francisco CA 94103

Please enclose $17.00 for each copy ordered, which includes $4.50 shipping and handling.

Visit our website: www.goodvibes.com/dtp/dtp.html

Cover illustration: "Blue Fern" by Jody Hewgill
Cover design: Gail Grant Design
Book design: Small World Productions

Printed in the United States of America   9 8 7 6 5 4 3 2

Again, For Marco

Contents

Acknowledgments

Thanks to the powers-that-be for being right;
to Shar for seeing me through yet another collection;
to Leigh for her persistent efficiency;
and to all the writers who showed me new ways to be
sexually creative within committed relationships.

Introduction

When the powers-that-be first suggested that we center the sixth *Herotica* collection around a theme, I went wild with ideas: Sex in Uniforms. Chicks with Dicks. Hairy Heroines. Orgies. Said powers considered all my suggestions and then came back with their own: Committed Relationships.

Huh?

It was a theme, they said, that would appeal to the large number of women seeking erotic fiction to share with their lovers. Women were looking for stories that would serve to enhance their sexual relationships with long-term partners — stories that might give hints on how to keep the home fires burning beyond The Seven Year Itch, Lesbian Bed Death, kids, careers and hectic schedules.

The *Herotica®* series is known for being eclectic: in fact, *Kirkus Reviews* noted that the stories in *Herotica 5* "have little in common with one another beyond their use of explicit erotic material." The comment was neither unkind nor inaccurate: The *Herotica®* books have always contained a mix of raunchy and romantic, hard-core and soft. I worried — unnecessarily, as it turned out — that the seeming confinement of Committed Relationships might lead to a homogenous collection that would be anything but eclectic.

Although in my personal experience sex has always been better within the safety of a committed relationship — as trust builds so does my willingness to expose my quirks, fantasies and desires — my professional experience has been quite the opposite. Having edited two previous *Herotica* books, screened fiction for *On Our Backs*, and taught sex writing, I thought I'd pretty much seen how erotic writers handled this subject: They'd invariably set up a hot scenario in a hotel or bar or dark alley, and in the end would deliver the "surprise": "It was actually my husband/lover/girlfriend giving me the best birthday present of my life!" Hell, I'd even written those kinds of stories myself.

I also worried that I'd be deluged by flowery paeans to heterosexual monogamy, and that the sex would read like a romance novel. I fully expected it to take years to accumulate enough hot quality stories to constitute an anthology.

I was in for an awakening when, months later, I sat down with a box of 200-something manuscripts, reached inside, and pulled out "Neighborhood Round Robyn," the first story in this collection. I laughed out loud reading this clever tale of a suburban housewife innocently causing a chain reaction that arouses and transforms the whole neighborhood; I was amazed that a story revolving around an ordinary heterosexual couple managed to convey an almost pansexual sensibility.

I reached into the box again — and came up with "The Album," a story of genderbending and fantasy play between two long-term partners. Talk about pansexual sensibility! "We've acted out a lot of our fantasies," says the narrator. "We've been girlfriends and boyfriends. We've traded genders. We've done bondage and S/M in exotic scenarios. But it's always been just the two of us. When we're brutally honest with each other, we need and want the security of monogamy."

By this time I was thoroughly jazzed; I picked up a third manuscript and sat transfixed by the heartbreaking — and ta-boo-breaking — "Mourning the Peasant."

I'd read just three stories and they were all in the "Yes" pile, an unprecedented occurrence. I went for a walk and ruminated on this unexpected development.

I am prone to a psychological process that shrinks refer to as "globalization:" I tend to draw vast philosophical conclusions from a small sampling of information. On the basis of these three wildly different and unique pieces of fiction, my overac-tive mind began spinning an entire philosophy about the role that love, commitment and longevity play in peoples' sex lives. I realized I should not have been surprised to find creativ-ity and hot sex permeating stories about committed relation-ships: Such partnerships do, after all, provide the stability that enables people — particularly women — to explore their sexual-ity within the context of safety and security. As the narrator says in "June's High Holy Day," "This trust was a big deal. I'm really not inclined to put myself in vulnerable positions; in fact I've only done so with June, and only in our most intimate moments."

That committed relationships can provide deep and satisfy-ing sexual experiences should not have come as a revelation. As I said, this has certainly been my own personal experi-ence — I'm more likely to share my most elaborate, secret fan-tasies with long-term lovers rather than with one-night stands.

And the stories in this collection aren't only about couples sharing fantasies, but about acting them out. Now, this is fic-tion, and we don't know what, if anything, is based on real experience — nor does it matter: The point is that these writers are able to imagine and portray sexual relationships in which committed partners have as much or more fun than bed-hop-pers. They don't make the assumption that diminished passion is the inevitable price we pay for comfort and companionship. They don't think that sustaining a life-enhancing partnership and fucking like slut bunnies are mutually exclusive.

Of course, not every story in my pile of manuscripts was wonderful — there were those that didn't fire my imagination and/or libido; there always are. But by the time I'd finished reading through the stack, I had a respectable "Yes" pile.

Admittedly, some of these stories employ the old "Surprise, I knew him all along!" ending, but that was inevitable. And, yes, many of the stories are romantic — another inevitability — but let's face it, a healthy dose of romance is a turn-on to most women. There are more birthdays and anniversaries celebrated within these pages than in previous *Herotica®* collections, an interesting commentary on commitment. And a couple of the stories deal with the death of loved ones.

I think what surprised me most, though, was an expanded idea of commitment. In "Three Note Harmony," the bonds of friendship are tested and strengthened. "Blue Moon Over Paradise" gives new meaning to what we think of as loyalty. In "Always," the practice of "managed faithfulness," as the narrator calls it, leads to a loving extended family. "Mourning The Peasant" pushes the boundaries of "committed relationships" beyond couplehood, beyond marriage, beyond the traditional nuclear family.

These stories remind us that committed relationships aren't always about couplehood, even when we're talking about sex.

Keeping Sex Alive

So how *do* women keep sex alive in committed relationships? Various self-help books give advice such as playing gimmicky board games to open avenues of communication; exchanging elaborate candlelit massages; spicing things up now and then with an X-rated video; greeting hubby at the door wrapped in cellophane, as the Kathy Bates character did in *Fried Green Tomatoes*. Not one story in this collection relies on those clichés. Rather, they delve into real life experiences, where sex is an expression of abiding love, loyalty or acceptance; they show sex as a tool of discovery, comfort and renewal; they employ sex as a vehicle for working through "negative" feelings like anger and grief. Even those that are strictly about reviving a failing sex life or keeping a good one going are rooted in the dynamics of the relationship. The characters in all these stories test, stretch and deepen their connection to one another through sex. Put that cellophane back where it belongs, honey — on leftovers!

Genderbenders, Pansexuals, and Switch-Hitters

One of the things I like about editing the *Herotica*® books is that when it comes to sexual orientation or preference, we're an equal opportunity series. Every collection has contained a mix of heterosexual, lesbian, bisexual and transsexual stories. As the narrator says in "Three Note Harmony": "Chocolate Chip Cookie Dough. Cherry Garcia. Macadamia Nut Brittle. Which to choose? Isn't it ironic that we're allowed 31 flavors of ice cream, yet only one flavor of sexuality?"

It's notable that this collection boasts five stories I'd call "pansexual," that is, they don't fall neatly into any of the above categories. In "Neighborhood Round Robyn," people with diverse erotic proclivities are aroused by everyone else. "Three Note Harmony" involves a woman and two men, while in "Always" it's two women and a man. "Being Met" and "The Album" are about couples who do "genderfuck," that is, switch gender identity through the use of props or merely attitude. Even two of the ostensibly heterosexual stories, "Snooping" and "Simple Gifts," involve reversal of stereotypical sex roles.

Could it be that, as a society, we're becoming more flexible with regard to gender identity and sexual orientation, that we can slip in and out of roles with the flick of a leather whip? If we choose to look at cultural trends through the prism of women's erotica — as good a prism as any — we find that the species *is* becoming more fluid in this area. True, women who write erotica are a special breed, and those who write cutting edge sex comprise an even smaller group; but while it's always a minority who explore the far reaches of consciousness and behavior, the rest of the culture does crawl along behind. Witness the popularization of S/M, now openly promoted on billboards where a cheery dominatrix pushes Altoid mints as delivering a pleasurable kind of pain. Would such an ad have come into being without the work of Pat Califia and other S/M pioneers, people most mint-chewers have never even heard of?

Similarly, the dialogue around gender fluidity has been pushed forward by the emergence of a transgender movement. Transsexualism is fast becoming the movie flavor of the month. Intersexed people are beginning to make noise: Trust me, you'll be hearing a lot more about this group in the near future. I foresee a time when people will be able to be female for a day, a year, a decade, and then be male, whether it involves surgery and hormones or merely a change of clothing. I don't expect it to happen in my lifetime, but I do expect it to happen.

Gender Identity and Fiction

One of the writers' conferences in an online service I subscribe to is called "Writing the Opposite Sex," a topic in which fiction writers discuss the ways that women write men and vice versa. In all my years of editing erotica, I've always been able to tell when a story came from a man using a female pseudonym. Not so this time: I actually had to ask one contributor who'd used initials for her full name to indicate her gender, despite the fact that her characters were lesbian. Similarly, one of the stories in this collection is written from a male point of view. In this case I know the author personally and can vouch for her gender — but I'm not so sure it would be obvious on a cold reading.

This question of writing as the opposite sex is one that's plagued fiction writers since time immemorial, probably since Lady Murasaki penned the first known novel. Male writers seemingly had no qualms about drawing female characters or even writing as women: Sometimes they hit the mark, but more often they failed dismally. Before the Third Wave of feminism, women frequently wrote under male pseudonyms simply to get published. At the height of the women's movement, there was a burst of energetic fiction from women, often portraying men rather badly as they released a minefield of anger; at the same time, men were criticized for daring to presume they knew how to write from a female perspective. Here in the so-called post-feminist era, we're all calming down a bit, and recognizing that, just as a skilled writer must be able to write about characters who inhabit other times, places and cultures, so too must we learn to write about those who inhabit bodies different from our own.

Erotic writers seem to be moving in that direction — we're all getting better at this. We're getting better at imagining ourselves in one another's shoes, or rather, bodies and minds. Through reading and writing about sex and sexual relationships, we're learning more about how the opposite gender feels and thinks.

I'll go even further and say that writing sex, because it's so charged with intensity, has the potential to teach us a great deal about characterization in fiction. College writing classes and workshops might benefit from the experience and skills of erotic writers. They might even use erotic writing exercises as a way of teaching their students the potential of imaginatiive experience.

Eclecticism Rules!

So here we are, having chosen a theme, and *Herotica 6* ends up being an eclectic mix after all. Some stories are good old-fashioned jackoff material, while others are complex pieces of literary fiction. By offering a variety of stories, we represent the wide range of women's sexual desires and imaginations. Readers of erotica tend to skip around anthologies, to dip and choose and return to old favorites. By remaining diverse, we offer something for almost everyone — and, not so coincidentally, spark new ideas and notions of what is possible and permissible in bed.

And to think that all this came from that humdrum theme of committed relationships.

Marcy Sheiner
Emeryville, California
October 1998

Mel Harris

Neighborhood Round Robyn

Robyn Pearson could not think of his mouth on her body without emitting a little pleasure-filled gasp. It could come at any moment — at the supermarket, driving to work, or getting her hair done. Once it had even happened at the dentist's while she was having her teeth cleaned. The dentist kept asking her if anything was wrong, but all she could do was blush and shake her head. The lingering kiss she'd given her husband Cliff as he'd left for work that day had promised more to come. Ten years of marriage, and she still fantasized about him every day.

Today was her day off and she just wanted to lounge by the pool. The pool had been the selling point for her and Cliff when they'd bought this house six months earlier. They loved swimming, especially skinny-dipping, but they'd had to put it off until they could get a privacy fence erected. It was too easy for their water play to get out of hand; they'd barely made it into the cabana the last time they'd had a late night swim.

Robyn changed into her "tanning" suit — an old, faded two-piece that was stretchy and comfortable — picked up a novel and a mug of iced tea, and headed for the pool. As she positioned the chaise lounge for the best sun, she noticed construction noises coming from the Harolds' house across the street. Shading her eyes for a moment, she watched the handsome construction worker putting the finishing touches on the new sunroom.

Marge and Harvey Harold had a beautiful two-story home and were quite well-to-do, but Robyn wasn't envious. She'd seen Marge Harold wandering around, drink in hand, looking lost and lonely. And she rarely saw Harvey home until late at night. Robyn turned her attention to smoothing suntan lotion over her exposed skin. Satisfied, she lay back on the lounge and picked up her novel.

Derek Collins lifted the piece of redwood siding onto the outer wall of the Harolds' sun room and nailed it in place. He'd be glad to finish this job. Oh, the Harolds were polite and all, and the job certainly paid well. But the hungry look Marge Harold gave him when she thought he wasn't looking made him uneasy. Right now, he was enjoying the relative peace and quiet of the morning. He never saw Mrs. Harold until after lunch; she was probably sleeping off her hangover.

Derek picked up another piece of redwood and laid it out on the sawhorses. Glancing up he saw Robyn Pearson, across the street, getting ready to lie by her pool.

He sighed. It had been some time since he'd been with a woman who really enjoyed herself. Trying not to be too obvious, he continued to watch the sunbather as she stretched out on the lounge and settled back to enjoy her book. Robyn Pearson was the only interesting person in this neighborhood, what with lonely Mrs. Harold and her strange neighbor Perry who lived next door.

Perry Traynor's house was situated just to the right of the Harolds' new sunroom, and he often came out to chat with Derek. Perry was friendly enough — a little too friendly for Derek. He seemed to have that same hungry look in his eye as Mrs. Harold. Derek shook his head. "I guess everybody's got to be some place," he thought. Mostly he just wanted to finish this job and get paid. He returned to measuring the board on his sawhorse.

Perry Traynor sat at his desk in his short silk robe, his head in his hands. He'd been sitting there for nearly an hour trying to come up with an idea for a story he was supposed to write for a gay men's erotic magazine. It was due tomorrow. He wasn't particularly thrilled to be writing those kinds of stories, but it paid the bills and allowed him to stay home to work on his novel. He was going to be a great published author someday, but right now he needed a story, and every idea he'd come up with so far was so . . . *routine.*

Perry stared listlessly out the window in front of him and saw Derek Collins lifting a board into place on the Harolds' sunroom wall. Perry had engaged Derek in several conversations over the adjoining fence, but he could tell that Derek was strictly hetero and only making polite talk with him. Oh well, it didn't hurt a guy to try. He watched as Derek stood at his sawhorse — but Derek seemed thoroughly engrossed in something across the way. Perry followed Derek's gaze until he saw Robyn Pearson settling in by her pool. "No wonder you can't concentrate on your work, Tool Man," he muttered.

Robyn would certainly keep Derek's attention better than that lonely Mrs. Harold. In fact, it seemed to Perry that Robyn Pearson was the only person in this neighborhood who was really happy. Not like that poor Tracy Parks across the street — she came out of her house just long enough to retrieve her mail, and she never looked up or said hello. And no wonder with that husband of hers, Dick. Dick-less was more like it, Perry thought. He could tell from the bruises and occasional swollen lip on Tracy that her husband knew nothing of a tender touch.

Perry sighed again. Well, Derek was a pleasant distraction for him. "If I can't work, I might as well enjoy the scenery," he thought to himself as he sat back in his chair and watched Derek work.

Tracy Parks stood in front of the open refrigerator. She was supposed to be fixing the lunch Dick had ordered her to make before he'd left for work. She leaned over and rummaged around in the vegetable bin — enough for a salad with a sandwich. She took out a head of lettuce and tossed it in the sink. She didn't want to feed Dick Parks lunch, she wanted to feed him poison. A cucumber, two small carrots and a zucchini followed the lettuce into the sink.

Just that morning, she'd decided she was going to leave Dick tomorrow, right after he left for work. She'd had enough of his coarse, disgusting behavior. He treated his truck better than he treated her. He never let her out of the house, even with her girlfriends, always suspicious she'd hook up with some guy. She turned on the faucet, picked up the head of lettuce and slammed it on the counter. Grabbing the core, she yanked it out and threw the lettuce back in the sink to drain.

She knew she wasn't Einstein, but she was decent and hardworking, and she knew she could do better than Dick Parks. She started peeling the cucumber. Maybe she wouldn't even hook up with a guy; she'd had enough of men. Maybe she could find a guy who wouldn't want anything from her except companionship. A guy like that Perry who lived across the street. She knew he was gay, but she saw the sweet way he served coffee to his friends who occasionally slept over. He'd even waved and said hello to her once, but she'd looked away and quickly retreated to her house.

Tracy picked up a carrot and started peeling it furiously as she thought about her escape from Dick. Maybe some day, after enough time, she would find a man like the one Robyn Pearson had. Now *there* was a husband. She saw the way Cliff Pearson looked at his wife and the way he held her before going off to work. She saw the flowers he brought home, too. She threw the carrots into the drainer and picked up the zucchini to scrub. Some day . . .

Robyn put down her book and reached for the mug of iced tea. The sun was definitely doing its job. She took a long drink of tea. Condensation from the mug dripped onto her breasts and ran down her cleavage. God, that felt good. Reaching into the mug, she fished out an ice cube and rubbed it along the length of her cleavage. When that cube melted, she retrieved a couple more and popped them in her mouth briefly before removing them and slipping one in each cup of her swimsuit top. She then got another and slid it into her bottoms. As the ice melted, the cold water trickled down around her nipples and through her pubic hair, finding its way to what Cliff referred to as her "Secret Ridge." Robyn made a mental note to have Cliff do this to her next time.

Still smiling, she lay back and closed her eyes. The reading and the sun had made her sleepy.

Derek was carefully measuring the last piece of redwood for the sunroom when a movement in Robyn's direction caught his eye. Looking up he saw her take a long drink from a mug, beads of water falling on her breasts. His mouth watered from his own thirst and he stepped behind the Harolds' fence. He knew he shouldn't be watching, but his eyes were riveted to Robyn as she smoothed an ice cube over her skin.

His tool belt tightened uncomfortably, and he realized he was swelling. He adjusted the belt, but the swelling continued as he watched Robyn slip more ice cubes into her top and then into her bottoms. He groaned as she patted that last cube just where she wanted it. What he wouldn't give to be that ice cube! Her lazy smile told him she was thinking some very pleasant thoughts.

Derek shifted his jeans, his zipper biting into him, but the more he adjusted, the harder he got. He lifted his tool belt, rested it on his hip bones, then carefully unzipped his jeans. His penis, eager for air, strained at his boxers, and he quickly freed himself from them as well. He looked down at his one-eyed buddy, now waving wildly in the air.

"Jeez, has it been that long?" he wondered aloud. "Pretty soon you're going to jump out and find it on your own!" He reached down and quieted himself with his hand, focusing on Robyn again. By now she had drifted off to sleep, the wet spots dark on her suit where the ice had melted, her nipples pulled taut from the cold.

Robyn shifted and rolled onto her side. Derek's penis jumped in his hand as she revealed the curve where the back of her thigh met her buttock, that tender, dark highway to heaven where her bottoms nearly disappeared. It was the tastiest morsel on the buffet, as far as he was concerned. His buddy was doing its dance in his hot hand, and he knew it wouldn't be long now. He was just trying to hang on . . .

In her upstairs bedroom, Marge Harold stirred. Her head felt like it weighed fifty pounds and her throat felt stuffed with cotton. She went into her bathroom, washed her face and brushed her teeth, avoiding the mirror. Finished, she returned to the bedroom. At least she could swallow now. Sitting at the vanity, she picked up a brush and ran it through her hair. She saw that she still had on the green silk nightie and sighed. She'd intended to seduce Harvey last night, but it had gotten later and later and she'd had too much to drink while waiting for him. She sighed again, and wondered if Harvey stayed at work so late to avoid her. It wasn't that he didn't love her, or so he said. But he was always working.

There was that time, years ago, when she'd made dinner and taken it down to Harvey's office. He'd been surprised, and she'd made him part of the meal. She rubbed her belly remembering the mango and fresh peach she'd eaten off him, finishing with that incredible chocolate mousse that she'd served to his delicate waiting tongue. Marge sighed again. That had been so long ago.

She stood up and went to the window that directly overlooked the new sunroom. She'd hoped the work would have taken a little longer, but she knew from Derek's attitude that he wasn't anxious to linger. Noticing that the hammering and sawing were strangely absent, she wondered if he was through. He'd ring the bell when he was, she concluded, and went back to brushing her hair.

Perry ripped another sheet out of his typewriter and crumpled it in frustration. Three sentences and it was already *dreck*. He threw the crumpled sheet on the floor. He had to get this finished. He picked up another sheet and fed it into the typewriter. As he was adjusting the paper, he happened to notice Derek. Perry's eyes widened. Leaning forward, he rubbed them and looked again. At first he thought Derek was relieving himself in the bushes, but he quickly realized that Derek Collins was holding an erection in his hand. And what a beauty it was, glistening in the sun like the muscles on his delicious back. And that waving thing it was doing. My god, it had a mind of its own!

Perry soon felt himself pulse and, as he looked down, his cock poked out of his robe. He stared at it and it waved back at him. "Oooh, Junior," he cooed, "I'm gonna put you to good use. Just like Hammer Boy and his tool."

Perry giggled and slowly ran his hands down his thighs and then back up again, stopping at his erection. He watched Derek's hand moving along his flushed shaft, sliding it slowly up and down, all the while keeping his eye on Robyn.

Perry looked over at Robyn, but all he could see was the gentle mound of the back side of her hips. He returned his gaze to Derek, who appeared to be having a hard time keeping a grip on himself. Perry's erection pulsated. "You must be looking at something very special, Derek," he crooned.

Tracy had just finished peeling the carrots and was reaching for the zucchini when she looked up and saw Perry Traynor through the open window of the den, sitting at his desk. Something strange was going on; she squinted to get a clearer view. Suddenly her mouth dropped open. In Perry's lap stood a sturdy erection. Perry leaned back in his chair and rubbed his hands up and down his thighs, coming to rest on his penis.

Tracy shut off the faucet, realizing she'd practically scrubbed a hole through the zucchini. Quickly glancing around the kitchen, she spied a barstool and dragged it over in front of the sink. She unfastened her shorts and slid them to the floor along with her panties. Climbing onto the stool, she perched herself, looking out the window. This was one show she wasn't going to miss.

Perry was still in the same position, his hand moving more quickly now. Tracy propped her legs up on the sink, hooking her heels over the edge. Keeping a clear view of Perry, she reached over and picked up the freshly peeled cucumber. It felt cool and delicious sliding in. She tensed her thighs and waves of pleasure ran up her legs and into her belly. By now, Perry was leaning back in his chair, his robe open. His intense concentration and the rippled flexing of his abdomen excited her even more. She slid out the cucumber and reached for the zucchini, which was longer and slightly swollen at one end.

Derek knew that it would only be a matter of seconds before he would be adorning the Harolds' shrubbery. With his free hand, he braced himself against the fence, still staring at Robyn. She shifted slightly, but it was just enough to cause her right nipple to pop out of her top — as if he'd reached over and freed it with his own fingers.

It was all he could take. Derek's abdomen tightened in spasms and he shuddered violently as he spattered the shrubbery and fence, spraying the Harolds' azaleas.

Perry gasped as Derek leaned forward against the fence, giving him an even better view of his full staff. Perry's own erection strained in his hand. That prickly hot rush in his thighs told him he was close on Derek's heels. He pushed apart his robe — no sense in staining good silk — and emitted a long, low moan as he watched Derek lean forward, legs braced, buttocks tight, and erupt all over the Harolds' fence.

Perry reached down with his free hand to cup and massage his velvet pouch, now rippled and tight. "AARRRagghhhh," he cried, falling back in the chair as he shot come all over his thighs. In his intense pleasure, he didn't notice he had leaned back so far that the chair was falling. He landed on the ottoman behind him, which fortunately softened his fall as he continued to orgasm.

The zucchini had been the right choice. Tracy moved it inside her, bringing herself to the edge, Perry's action furiously spurring her on. She spied the peeled carrots and braced her heels firmly on the sides of the sink. Taking the small carrots in her free hand, she slipped one on either side of her tumescent reed, the fresh coolness and the friction causing it to swell. Slow firm strokes with the carrots brought her dangerously close to the edge of that wonderful chasm of pleasure.

Suddenly she laughed out loud. She'd take a vegetable over Dick any day! Just then she saw Perry lean back, reach down, and squeeze himself as he shot into the air. Tracy slid the zucchini part way out and then, in one last stroke, the carrots gripping her clit, she gave the final push over the edge, the zucchini bucking wildly. Oh, how she loved her greens.

Upstairs, Marge Harold had finished brushing her hair. Curious as to why she still hadn't heard anything from Derek, she went over to the window and pushed back the drapes. Where was he? She was about to turn and go into the shower when she gave one last look directly below her window. "My god," she whispered as her hand flew to her mouth. Derek Collins, gleaming erection in hand, was coming all over her redwood fence.

She watched as Derek waited for his erection to go down enough to fit back into his jeans. Straightening himself, he picked up the last board from the sawhorses and nailed it to the sunroom wall.

Marge inhaled sharply; she hadn't been breathing. Without thinking, she picked up the phone and dialed Harvey's office. She tapped her foot impatiently, waiting for his secretary to connect her.

"Hello — Marge?" Harvey sounded surprised. Marge rarely called him at the office.

"Yeah, Harv, it's me," she said breathlessly. "Listen, I've been thinking about bringing you dinner at the office. Something delicious."

"Marge, is everything okay?"

"Oh yeah, Harv. It's more than okay. I was just thinking

about you and the last time we had dinner at your office . . . remember?"

"Mmmm," Harvey moaned softly. "Do I remember? I didn't know you could do so much with chocolate mousse."

Marge giggled. "Well, wait 'til you see the menu tonight."

"I'm looking forward to it. Can you be here by seven?"

"No problem. And Harv?"

"Yeah?"

"I've missed you, and I want to make up for it tonight."

"I can't wait," Harvey breathed softly into the phone.

Perry giggled at himself; feet in the air, erection spent. What a trip! He rolled over, stood up and picked up his chair. Straightening his robe, he sat down and began typing furiously.

Tracy sat there, her heels still hooked over the sink, her legs trembling. As soon as she was able, she got up and put on her panties and shorts. She was slicing the last of the cucumber into the salad when Dick walked through the door and growled, "Where's my lunch?"

Setting the bowl down on the table in front of him she said sweetly, "I've made you a sandwich and here's a nice salad to go with it. The dressing's already on it."

"Salad? Goddamn rabbit food," he grumbled, but he picked up a fork and began to eat it anyway. Tracy quickly turned her back and began washing the dishes.

It was a moment before Robyn realized that something was blocking her sun. Sleepily she opened her eyes and smiled. Cliff was standing there. He reached down and stroked her exposed nipple with his finger. "Looks like one of your girlfriends is winking at me," he said.

She rubbed her eyes and laughed. "The other one wants you

to visit her, too," she replied, holding it up for him.

Cliff looked around. "I wish we had that privacy fence up," he said. "I'd slide the lounge over and let you slip right out of that suit and into the pool."

"Mmmm . . . then what, Mr. Pearson?"

"Well, Mrs. Pearson," he said, sitting on the edge of the lounge and wiggling his finger into the leg of her bottoms, "you'd just have to let me surprise you." Cliff looked around again."Hey, what about that guy over at the Harolds'? I hear he's pretty good with a tool. Maybe I can go over and talk to him about building the fence."

"I don't know," Robyn replied. "I think he might be done. I haven't heard a sound in quite awhile."

Mary Anne Mohanraj

Season of Marriage

She was dizzy with the smoke. The traditional wedding had lasted almost three hours, and the heat and oil fumes from the glowing lamps had combined to make Raji feel queasy. There were kids running around all over the place, dressed in vibrant colors that hurt her eyes. And the chanting. It went on and on and on in incomprehensible Sanskrit.

Raji knew no Sanskrit — she even spoke her Tamil with a New England accent. She was suddenly homesick — for America, for Connecticut, for forests and hills and snow and people you could speak your mind around without treading on some custom you didn't understand. She hungered for cold pizza breakfasts and frozen yogurt lunches, for slumber parties and stolen dates and the friends who had covered for her. Despite the cold heart and the pain that had driven her to this wedding in the baking heat of New Delhi, America was home. And it was too late to go back.

She was married now. The wedding reception was ending, and it would soon be time to leave with this seemingly kind stranger, to go to the house of his mother (whom Raji already disliked), to go to his bed. And all her American casualness about sex, the casualness and experience she had counted on to see her through this ordeal, was suddenly meaningless. She was scared. Why, oh why had she agreed to this?

The answer to that was easy: because she hadn't cared anymore. After she'd found out about Jim and that other girl; after all the broken promises and shattered dreams, it just didn't seem to matter. In the midst of the heat and incense a wave of brutally clear memory washed over her.

They'd just collapsed, Jim on top of her, as he always insisted. He was crushing her with his weight. Raji managed to roll to the side, and then turned to gaze into his eyes, still amazed that this gorgeous man would really want her.

"You were wonderful," Raji said.

"Uh huh." He was still panting, but in a very sexy way, she thought.

"Jim?"

"Uh huh."

"I love you."

There was a disconcerting pause. Before, he'd always responded, "I love you, too." Now, he said nothing for much too long.

"Ummm . . . " Jim said.

"Yes?" she asked, eagerly.

"I should probably tell you something. Now don't get too upset, okay?"

And he proceeded to tell her about Sharmila. Also Indian. Raji remembered her from biology class last semester. Drop-dead gorgeous with unfairly huge breasts. Sharmila, whom he'd been sleeping with for three weeks. His conscience had finally kicked in. Or maybe he was just bored with Raji, and this was the easiest way to make her break up with him. Which she, of course, did.

Looking back, she realized how stupid she had been. Not in dating him, but in caring so much about somebody who had obviously cared so little. She had gotten so worked up about what she had seen as the ultimate betrayal that she had sunken into a black fit of depression during which she had let everyone else make decisions for her. She'd ignored the advice of her friends, both Indian and American, and decided that maybe her parents were right, after all. Maybe American men really were slime. Maybe she'd be happiest with someone like herself.

So she'd agreed to meet some Indian men, and the next thing she knew she was flying to India to meet this man Vivek. And he was gentle. And kind. Rich and generous: He'd given her a lovely ruby and pearl necklace the day after they met. And though she'd only known him for a few days, her parents thought he was very suitable and his parents liked her and it was suddenly all arranged and they were asking her and she said yes.

Now she was remembering all the sweet guys she'd grown up with and wondering where they'd gone. She was finally shaking off the depression that had lasted the four months since Jim; suddenly she knew that she'd have been happier with an American she understood rather than with this stranger from a strange land that she'd left when she was six. Still, it was too late. She was married, and though she could probably get a divorce, Raji wasn't the sort to give up on anything that easily. A divorce would mean that she had failed . . . again. Not to mention that a divorce would break her mother's heart. Her dear, scheming, conniving, thoroughly manipulative mother. Sometimes Raji couldn't figure out whether she loved or hated her mother. Not that it really made much difference at this point.

Her silence was noted by Vivek, who asked her in his perfect, if heavily accented English, if she felt all right. Raji was touched that he had noticed — Jim would never have noticed if she were quiet; he would have been too busy talking. She nodded to Vivek that she was okay, then stood with him as the interminable reception finally came to a close. He gave her a tentative smile; a sort of 'buck up' look that was heartening. Raji wondered what this shy and probably virginal man would think of an experienced American. She'd find out soon enough.

The women took her to the bedroom and helped her undress, giving her fragments of advice in broken English as they helped her into a flowing white nightgown, incredibly demure and perfectly opaque. Raji barely heard them, caught somewhere between tears and laughter. She waited patiently, allowing them to dress her as they chose, and then lead her to the crimson-draped bed. One woman, who Raji thought was her new sister-in-law and recently married herself, touched Raji's shoulder before she left, kindly. Then they were gone.

Vivek appeared, ghost-like in the doorway, dressed in flowing white to match her. He walked toward her silently, carefully; a hunter afraid of startling some strange, wild creature. Raji was determined to try to make this marriage work, and so she smiled, slightly trembling. Vivek returned her smile tentatively and reached up to touch her cheek. His hand was not damp and sweaty as she had feared, but warm and dry, as if lit by some inner fire. He had not touched her before this, in all the days of wedding preparations during the short month since they had met. Even when placing the gold *thali* wedding necklace around her neck, he had taken care not to touch her. She was suddenly grateful for his gentleness: stepping boldly towards him, she stretched her slim brown arms to encircle his thick neck, surprised to find that he was shaking too.

Vivek was not very handsome, but was sturdily built, with hair thicker and richer than hers, and deep brown eyes. Raji had thought them dull and calf-like before, but suddenly she was not so sure. There was a hint of laughter in those eyes, and a sparkle of intelligence. Of course, he was a doctor (nothing else would have satisfied her mother), and so couldn't be entirely stupid. Now, with her hands locked behind his neck and her delicate body inches away from his, Raji found herself bemused, not sure what to do next, or how fast to go. He solved that problem for her.

He placed his arms around her waist, gently. Tilting his head, he kissed her. She was startled, not at being kissed, but at being kissed by him, and she stiffened in his arms. He raised his head questioningly. "Is this not customary in America?"

"Yes, yes it is. I didn't think it was here."

"We are not as ignorant as you Americans assume. We do watch movies, after all."

Now Raji was sure that he was laughing at her, as he leaned down to kiss her again. Despite his claims to knowledge she was fairly sure that kissing was new to him, and so responded gently to the firm pressure on her lips. They kissed chastely for long minutes, until Raji daringly opened her mouth and touched her tongue to his lips. He broke away for a moment, plainly startled, but then returned to kissing her with enthusiasm, opening his own mouth and tasting her lips, her teeth, her tongue. She tilted her head backwards, hoping he would get the hint, and he did — kissing her cheek, her nose, her ear, tracing a delicate line along her cheekbone with his tongue. He went slowly, and Raji stood still, eyes closed, feeling him touch her. This was new to her — this gentleness, this seeming reverence. She had enjoyed sex with Jim, but it had always been hard and fast, a summer storm — quickly started, quickly over. Vivek was twenty-five, years older than Jim had been, but he smiled with the wonder of a child. Raji felt an odd constriction in her chest.

Continuing to explore her chocolate skin, Vivek slid slowly down her neck. Shivers were racing through her now, and Raji tried to hold still, wondering how long she could act the shy virgin, how long it would be before her impatience broke through. His kisses were abruptly stopped by the laces at the top of the gown, and he froze and locked her eyes with his. Raji slowly reached up and, almost teasingly, pulled free the tangled white ribbons and laces. Vivek undid them completely, sliding the white fabric off her creamy brown shoulders, continuing the slow kisses that had fallen as cool rain but now began to burn. Despite a ceiling fan, the room was stiflingly hot to a woman raised in New England winters, and Raji began to sway, dizzy with heat and unexpected passion. Vivek caught and held her, as the gown slid from her bare body to pool on the green-tiled floor. Cradling her against him with one arm, he pulled aside mosquito netting and drapes with the other. Picking her up, he gently deposited Raji on the bed and pulled the sheet over her. All this happened so quickly that Raji had no moment in which to become embarrassed in her nakedness before this almost-stranger, this husband. And then he was undressing too, undoing the wrap of white fabric and climbing in to sit beside her, pulling the mosquito netting around them.

"Are you all right?" Vivek asked.

"Yes, I think so. Are you?"

"Of course I am. I'm a man."

Laughter again, from both of them this time, which trailed away into silence. He looked suddenly vulnerable, Raji thought, as he sat there naked and cross-legged on the wide bed. The silence grew more and more awkward until Raji finally raised herself a little on her elbows, letting the sheet fall down to bare her curving breasts. She puckered her lips for a kiss. He laughed again, and suddenly he was swooping down on her in mid-laugh, slipping his broad hands around her fragile frame. Raji began drowning in a hail of fierce kisses and caresses. In the lamp-lit dimness his hands explored what he could not see, curving to surround her small breasts, which fit neatly into his palms. He fumbled a little, sometimes touching her too softly, sometimes too fiercely, but always kissing as she arched into his touch.

Vivek slid his hands down her stomach, across her hips, gently pushing apart her trembling thighs. She stiffened, remembering what she had not told him, and opening her eyes wildly searched for his, until he, looking up, caught her trapped gaze.

"Don't be afraid." he reassured her, though his voice was trembling. "I'm a doctor, it's all right." He smiled again, inviting her to share the joke. Raji wished it could be that easy.

"I'm not afraid, it's just . . . there's something I need to tell you."

"Shhh . . . don't worry."

Vivek smiled at her confusion, and leaned down to kiss her, at the same moment entering her. Raji was suddenly so hot, so wet and ready for him that she thought she might scream. But remembering his despised mother in the next bedroom, she buried the sound in her throat and only moaned, softly. She curved up to meet him as he began long, hesitant strokes which stretched through her long-neglected body, giving her the attention she so desperately craved.

The world blurred for Raji to a haze of cloudy netting above, lit by the lamp glow and measured by the rhythmic movement of this man, her husband, inside her. Some time during that long eternity it began to rain outside their window, but the thunder and lightning couldn't begin to match the pleasure racing through her. He began pounding faster and faster to match the storm, and came suddenly. Raji was caught in a moment of purest frustration underneath him. She opened her eyes a few seconds later to see his concerned face above her.

"That didn't work very well, did it? I'm sorry," Vivek said.

Raji remembered the numerous times Jim had left her frustrated without even noticing. She decided not to think of Jim again — he didn't deserve to intrude on this, her wedding night. This man, her husband, was thoughtful, considerate. She could have done much worse. Raji smiled up at him, feeling warmth unfold within her. "Shhh . . . it's fine. We have lots of time to practice. But there are a couple of things I don't understand."

"Ask," he said, smiling gently.

"Well, for one, why is it still raining? I thought storms in India were short."

"Usually they are, but this one will last a while. It's the beginning of monsoons, remember? It will be storming for the next three months."

"Oh. I knew that."

Raji had the distinct feeling that he was laughing at her again. Vivek smiled brightly at her, rolling her towards him to rest in the crook of his arm. The storm raged more fiercely outside, no doubt churning the dirt paths to mud, soaking the very air and making it hard to breathe.

"Want to ask one of the harder questions now?" he asked.

"There's just one more. Now you know that you didn't marry a virgin. Do you mind?"

She closed her eyes and clenched her fists against the answer, suddenly wanting desperately to make this gentle man happy, especially happy with her.

"I knew from the beginning. Your mother seemed to feel I had a right to know what I was bargaining for," he said quietly.

"She told you? How could she? She didn't even know . . . " Raji was caught somewhere between anger and relief. Vivek chuckled.

"You would be surprised what mothers know. Mine really

isn't so bad; she's just not looking forward to my leaving with you, so she's a little irritable."

"Leaving?" Raji was now completely confused.

"For America. Lots of work for doctors there. The problem in India is that everyone who can become a doctor does so. There aren't enough jobs. I've been hoping to live in America for a long time, and I could hardly expect my beautiful American wife to be like the innocent girls of the villages here. Not that many of them are really that innocent." He grinned down at her then.

Raji didn't return his smile, suddenly troubled by a depressing possibility. Maybe he had married her only for her citizenship, so he could get a visa and emigrate to America. She had certainly heard of plenty of arranged marriages where that was one of the prime requirements — a spouse with American citizenship. Raji tried to ignore the thought. If it were true, it was too late to do anything about it now, and he had certainly acted as if he wanted her and not just a ticket to America. She didn't want to believe that the man who had been so sweet to her could be so mercenary.

Vivek appeared troubled by her silence. "That is," and he was suddenly hesitant, "if you want to go back to America."

"If I want to?!" and Raji started laughing, smothering her doubts. "Oh, yes. Yes, my husband. Soon, please."

"Soon." he agreed, smiling. "I already have a job offer there, actually. As soon as I get my work visa we can go. I just wanted to make sure that was what you wanted, too."

Now she knew that he could have gone on his own, that he had wanted her and not just any American. Now Raji was free to care for this man beside her, and to acknowledge to herself just how much she longed for apple trees and miniskirts and rollercoasters. India had its own strange beauty, its passion and mystery, but she was an American at heart.

Vivek touched her cheek then and said, "Shall we try that again? My mother will be very upset with me if you continue to be so quiet. She will think that I have been too rough with you and that you are crying."

Raji held herself still for a moment, looking up at the face of her new husband. He was such a mass of surprises. Then suddenly she rolled over so that she was lying on top of him. Raji kissed him wildly, ignoring his startled eyes. She stopped for a moment to tell him, "You're about to find out just how rough American women can be," before she returned to teasing him unmercifully, rubbing her small breasts across his smooth chest. Vivek responded with renewed passion, pulling her close so that her pointed chin rested in his hands and her hair fell forward, veiling their faces. Raji finally left behind all thoughts of mothers and matchmaking, allowing herself to go spiraling downward with her husband, losing herself in the touch of sweat-slick skin on skin.

Any sounds they made were soon drowned in the pounding of the monsoon storms.

Shelley Marcus

A Little Slip

"I've really got to get to the office early this morning, hon," I told Karen, pulling out of her embrace and getting quickly out of bed.

"No problem," she answered.

"This budget has been driving me crazy," I said, more an excuse than an explanation. "I have to finish crunching these numbers and send the damn thing out to the head office by the end of the day. I won't be able to concentrate on anything else until it's done."

"I understand, Joan. Don't worry about me," Karen said lightly, but I knew I'd hurt her feelings.

My timing can be shitty sometimes. What did Karen want? Just to have her lover show a little affection on the morning of their first anniversary. So what did I do? I jumped out of bed as if the mattress was on fire.

I'd been truthful about the budget. It just hadn't been the whole truth. Well, if I couldn't be honest with Karen, at least I could be honest with myself. And the whole truth was, I was starting to feel trapped. Karen and I had been together, really together for a whole year, something I wouldn't have thought possible. I'd always enjoyed playing the field too much. There were too many beautiful women out there to even think about tying myself down to only one.

Then I'd met Karen. The sex was incredible between us, and after a few months of dating we stopped seeing other people. Karen was the one who brought up the subject of moving in together, and I'd finally agreed. I suppose I just lost my head. Hell, I was in love. You know what that's like. Everything is so perfect that you'll do anything you can to make the other person happy.

And I wasn't twenty anymore. I really think getting older is harder when you're gay, and the thought of having someone there to get old with me was kind of appealing at the time. I only wish I'd known then how hard it was going to be giving up all those other women. Some people are marriage material, and I've always known I wasn't one of them.

I swore I wouldn't cheat on Karen while we were together, but she has no idea how close I've come in the last year. One of these days I know I'm going to see some cute young thing, and I'm not going to be able to stop myself.

I felt guilty about the way I'd acted with Karen, so I was determined to make it up to her. Do it up right. I'd take her out for a fancy dinner, maybe to a show, and then when we got home we'd really celebrate. All I had to do was get through the day.

I finished the budget in record time, called down to have the kid from the mail room pick it up, then went on to something else.

"Come in," I answered the knock on my office door, but I didn't bother looking up from what I was doing. "This needs to go out tonight," I said, indicating the overnight mailer on the corner of my desk.

"Yes, ma'am."

I lifted my head at the sound of the voice, unmistakably female. I had been expecting Jimmy, the high school kid who was working in the mail room for the summer, not the young woman who stood before me. I didn't know her, and she was someone I would definitely have remembered meeting.

"Are you new here?" I asked.

"Yes, ma'am," she answered, but there was mock respect in her voice.

I put her age at nineteen, but she looked younger in the jeans and denim jacket she wore. Our dress code is fairly strict, but working in the mail room she would have been cut some slack because of the physical nature of her duties. She reached down to pick up the envelope and her jacket opened, revealing a tight, white T-shirt, her small firm breasts, unencumbered by a bra, clearly outlined under the cotton. Her blonde hair was cut extremely short, and she wore no makeup.

Her whole appearance cried out Baby Butch, but I've seen straight teens dress the same way, so it was difficult to be sure. Perhaps it was just wishful thinking. Wishful thinking I shouldn't have been indulging in, not when I had a lover at home with whom I was about to celebrate an anniversary.

"What's your name?" I asked.

"Zoe," she answered lazily. "I just started today." She had looked me straight in the eye when she'd said her name, then shifted her gaze directly to my breasts.

So I hadn't been wrong, I thought. Even more reason not to keep her here any longer than necessary. "Well, welcome to the company, Zoe," I said hastily, "and please make sure that package goes out tonight."

"Yes, ma'am." The phrase was beginning to annoy me, so I was happy to see her leave and let me get back to work.

Preparing the last quarter report figures kept me occupied all afternoon, and I'd all but forgotten Zoe until the end of the day when she knocked on my office door and invited herself inside.

"Yes, Zoe?" I asked, not bothering to disguise my irritation with the interruption. I made a mental note to talk to Human Resources about teaching new employees proper office etiquette. "Is there something I can do for you?"

"No, ma'am. I just wondered if you needed me for anything else."

"No, thank you, Zoe. If I do, I'll call for you." The denim jacket was gone now, and before I could stop myself my eyes went to the naked breasts under her T-shirt.

Zoe caught me looking, and a small smile crossed her lips. "Are you sure there's nothing I can do for you, ma'am?"

The question would have been easier to answer if she hadn't been standing there brushing her fingers across her breasts as she asked it. I'd never seen a sexual move done so blatantly and yet so innocently. This mating dance had the expected effect. Soon my nipples were as hard as hers, but luckily mine were camouflaged by my blouse and the lace bra I wore under it. I was having more trouble concealing the other signs of excitement this little show brought out in me. My damp panties would remain my little secret, thank God, but I was sure Zoe could see the blush rising in my cheeks.

The moment Zoe saw my face she knew she had me. "That's what I thought," she said, answering herself, and in a moment she was across the room and in my lap, kissing me with wild abandon.

"Zoe, we can't," I protested, pushing her away. "Someone will see."

"It's safe," she informed me. "Your secretary's already left for the day."

I didn't take much convincing, especially once Zoe lifted up her T-shirt and displayed her breasts. I had them in my hands a moment later, reveling in her soft skin and her young, firm muscles.

While I stroked her breasts, Zoe opened my blouse and unhooked my bra, pulling it down and freeing my own, much larger breasts. We stood there, fondling each other, and then Zoe pushed me back down into my chair and lifted my skirt.

I didn't protest when she knelt in front of me, spread my legs, and lowered my panties down around my ankles. With the eagerness of youth, she attacked my pussy as if she'd never seen one before. What she lacked in technique she made up for in enthusiasm. She brushed my outer lips with her mouth, then sucked them in and out before slipping her tongue inside to find my swollen clit. It felt incredible. Karen is a wonderful lover, but having this cute young thing, almost a perfect stranger, eating me in my office was a total turn on for me.

I heard the sound of a zipper being undone, then felt the movement of Zoe's arm against my leg. She had unzipped her jeans and was fingering her pussy while she worked her mouth on mine. Soon she was moaning into my flesh, her voice vibrating inside me. "That's it, baby," I coaxed breathlessly, "just a little harder."

I came first, shuddering against my chair, but Zoe used her free hand to keep me joined with her. A minute later I felt Zoe's orgasm as she screamed it into me.

Suddenly the door opened and Karen strode into my office. "Hi, sweetheart. I hope you don't mind my dropping in, but I thought maybe we could go out to dinner." She stopped short when she saw us. Startled, Zoe stood up and turned around, her T-shirt still pulled up to her neck and her jeans down on her thighs. "What the hell!" Karen exclaimed.

"Karen, I can explain," I began. "It's not what it looks like." As if with my blouse open and my tits hanging out it could be anything but what it looked like. Especially with Zoe half-naked between my legs. Realizing I couldn't talk my way out of it, I looked into Karen's shocked, unbelieving eyes and admitted, "I'm sorry, Karen. I don't know what else to say."

I had expected yelling and screaming, maybe even tears, but suddenly Karen's expression changed. She smiled. "There's only one thing to say. Happy Anniversary, darling." At my bewildered look she nodded at Zoe and said, "I don't have to ask if you liked my present."

"Your present?" I asked, completely at a loss. "You mean you arranged this?"

"Of course. I'm not stupid, Joan. I could tell you were getting antsy, and that sooner or later there would be a little slip. I figured if it was going to happen anyway, I'd make sure I picked the when, the where, and especially the who."

"I don't believe this," I uttered, still not sure she was serious.

"Believe it," Zoe said, pulling down her T-shirt and zipping up her jeans. "I guess you were surprised, huh?"

"Surprised doesn't even begin to describe how I feel."

Karen came over and put her arm around Zoe. "And now that you've had your fun," she told me, "Zoe and I are going back to the apartment so I can have mine."

"You — and Zoe?" I gasped.

"Why not? After all, it's my anniversary, too. I think it's only fair I get as much pleasure out of the gift as you have, don't you?"

I watched, dumbstruck, as Zoe and my lover walked out the door. Then a second later Karen poked her head back in to add, "You're welcome to join us if you like."

I hastily arranged my clothes and headed for the door. I may have to rethink this monogamy thing. It could work out — with the right partner.

Laurel Fisher

Snooping

Momma always told me not to snoop. Nosy people find out things they'd rather not know. I didn't mean to, really. It was an accident. The computer system at work had crashed. Everyone went home at lunchtime except the poor woman stuck trying to fix it. When I got home, I tried to call a friend, thinking this would be a perfect day for a long, late lunch with a margarita or two, but the line was busy.

I changed and wandered out to the backyard to sunbathe instead, and a daydream washed over me: this would be one of the days my husband has time to come home for lunch.

My tall, strong, demanding husband. His view from the kitchen window would be my nearly naked bottom. He'd come out, kneel over me, fondle my ass. Tracing the outline of my bikini, his fingers would slip underneath to the wetness of my daydream.

He'd pull the fabric aside and tug me up to my knees, entering me abruptly, urgently . . . Suddenly I realized that the only heat I was feeling was from too much sun. I wandered back into the house, picked up the phone, and hit the redial button.

"Hello, can I help you?"

I hesitated a moment. Maybe a friend was answering the phone for her? Maybe she was in the bathroom? You can't get a wrong number with redial. Can you? "Um, yeah, is Lisa there?"

"Hold on." The phone thunked on the desk. "Hey, is Lisa around?" I could hear the voice in the background. "She's in the dungeon." The dungeon? What in the world was Lisa up to?

"You wanna tell her she's got a phone call?"

"You wanna get fired on your first day? Don't ever interrupt a session, airhead."

She picked the phone back up. "She's busy. Can I take a message?"

"Uh, I'm not even sure I have the right number. Lisa Sewall? 555-6284?"

A squeaky, inane giggle tickled my ear. "No way, hon. You aren't even close! It's Lisa Smith and 555-9447."

My heart was racing as I scribbled the number on the pad by the phone. I stared at it a moment in shock, not comprehending at all what had just happened, then tore off the top sheet and tucked it in my pocket. I nearly jumped out of my skin when my husband, Sean, spoke behind me. "You're home?"

"The system at work crashed. I've been outside."

"Who were you calling?"

"Lisa. It was busy." Oh hell, he must have heard me talking. "I mean she, um, wasn't home." He had a strange look on his face. I realized he must have made the call. But where? And why? Here I was standing in a string bikini right in front of him, and he was looking everywhere but at my body. The body he usually can't keep his grab-ass damn hands off of.

"Is something wrong?" I asked, uncertain.

"No," he grunted, a man-grunt, and walked away.

He fixed a sandwich. When he came back into the room, he apologized. Said he was having a crummy day. When he headed back to work, I did what any scared, suspicious wife would do: I snooped. There was a copy of the local *Nasty News* in a stack of magazines on his desk. It wasn't really hidden. When one of us goes to the liquor store we pick one up, just for laughs, to read the articles and giggle over the swingers' ads. Easy to do since we had each other. Or so I thought.

I flipped the pages. There it was, staring out at me in inch-high letters, the phone number I had accidentally dialed that afternoon. 555-9447*555-WHIP. It was for a fetish club. A dungeon. But why did he have to call them? I'd let him tie me up in a heartbeat.

The photo wobbled and swam in front of my eyes, and I was spreadeagled on the bed, wrists and ankles secure, blindfolded, gagged. My nipples tightened under his harsh fingers. I refocused and eyed the trio of luscious women in the grainy photo. Suddenly I couldn't breathe. Maybe it wasn't a what.

Maybe it was a who.

How important was this? Was it just a passing fancy, or could it destroy my marriage, take away my man, my life's mate? I thought we belonged together forever. He'd said he did too.

We were different from all the others. From all the statistics. What if it had all been some sappy illusion?

I always tackle a problem head on. Well, sort of. I tend to research it to death first. I suppose it's a way for me to take charge again, or maybe it just gives me a way to avoid the issue until the time comes for the inevitable confrontation. I needed to really know what he might be looking for. The public library probably wasn't going to be much help. Going through the paper again, I found a store that catered to leather people.

The clerk found me wistfully fondling a cat-o-nine tails (actually it was more like nineteen — I counted). He asked me if he could help, I took him at his word. Poor guy, I'm sure he didn't want to hear about my marital woes. I asked him outright what happened at those dungeon places. Kindly he pointed out to me that sexual contact wasn't allowed there, because that would be prostitution. That would be illegal. So being there wasn't actually cheating. If Sean had even been there. Then he told me that those clubs had mostly dominatrices. For submissive men.

Oh dear. My strong, take charge, utterly alpha husband? I could submit to him any day of the week, any hour of the day. But be his Mistress? It was becoming increasingly clear that I didn't know him as well as I thought. Hell, nine years and I didn't know him at all. I left with a book, a rented video, a handful of boot laces, a brass ring, a nice shiny pair of hand-cuffs, and trembling hands.

I barely had time to skim the book, but I could see that it was wonderful, incredibly informative about things I'd never dreamed people did to each other. Or themselves. I managed to thread the laces through the little brass ring and wrap a half lace into a handle during the movie, but it was tough to con-centrate. I kept finding myself kind of distracted. Okay, very distracted. Less than five minutes into the movie, when the Dominatrix made her big strong co-star lick her boots, I started to squirm. I watched in horrified arousal while she poured hot wax on his nipples and a few other interesting places. By the time she let him sniff her panties, I was drenched.

I practiced swinging the leather laces on the couch until I could control just where the strokes were landing. Not that I was actually gonna hit him with it. Just trail it sensuously over his body. Maybe a few gentle swats. Unless he was cheating. If he was cheating I was going to beat the crap out of him and throw him out on the street naked. I shook my head. I couldn't think about that now. I was going to handle this rationally. No teary accusations. I hoped.

I got the cattails going in a nice figure eight, running the strands through my free hand as I reversed directions. The feel of the leather sliding through my fingers was very stimulating.

And the snap! I quivered each time the strands smacked a surface.

The book said you should always try toys on yourself first.

Hesitantly, I swatted the tender skin of my inner arm. Youch! I tried it again, more gently. Then harder and harder, until I was looking in fascination at bright pink skin. The hall clock chimed. It was almost time. I stashed all my new toys and a pair of black heels under the couch. Tearing through my closet and underwear drawer, I settled on a lacy black bra and thong panties, the only things even close to sexy lingerie that I owned. If only I'd had enough money for that leather teddy with all the zippers. I heard the front door open and shimmied into a loose sundress that buttoned up the front.

Sean was home. A sudden dose of reality pierced my arousal. I'd almost convinced myself this was just a kinky seduction game. But it wasn't. My marriage might be in very serious trouble. What if I couldn't give him whatever he wanted from that place? Whoever he wanted? God, what if he'd already done something I could never forgive? I couldn't swallow when I saw the fresh red rose in my crystal bud vase. I felt like my heart was lodged in my throat. Sweet? Or guilty? I wondered.

He tried to kiss me, but I dodged his mouth. I blurted out a question. "Are you happy here? With me, I mean." So much for subtlety.

Sean looked surprised. "Aw, honey, you know I love you. And I'm sure if you would just hold still you could make me happy pretty quick," he added with a wicked grin.

I sighed inwardly and tried again. "Is there something new you want? Or maybe someone?" I asked outright. But he wouldn't give.

"Nope." His look was wary. Then lecherous. "Why, do you have a new fantasy to try out? How 'bout we go to dinner, and you can tell me all about it."

I shook my head and stomped out of the room. I'd never caught him in a lie before. Was it a little lie or a big lie?

Maybe he'd already been to the dungeon. Maybe lots of

times. My insides were trembling. When I regained enough self-control not to burst into angry tears, I came back. He was working out, bare-chested. Push-ups. He always followed the same routine, so chin-ups on the bar he'd rigged in the coat closet doorway would be next.

I had an idea. A very bad idea. But I did it anyway. I was hurt, I was scared and I was just plain pissed off. I reached under the sofa cushion for the handcuffs. I could almost see the printed words in front of me. "Never play when you are angry." Well, I wasn't playing. I wandered across the room with the cuffs behind my back. He gave me a thoughtful look.

"I'm almost done. Then let's go have dinner and talk."

I shrugged. "Sure." Damn right we were gonna talk. I waited until his back was turned and he had started his first set of chin-ups. He didn't even hear the metallic rattle over his grunts and growls. I stretched up, rubbing my body against his back as I flipped one loop around his wrist and the other around the bar. He let loose a lusty laugh and pressed against me, then realized exactly what I had done. He gave an experimental tug at the bar as I backed away. He turned and tried to grab me just as I got out of range of his long-limbed reach.

"What the hell do you think you're doing?" he demanded. "I'm not in the mood for a game."

The noise I made was most unladylike. "Not with me, anyway."

"You can tell me what the hell is going on any minute now." His voice was quieter, dangerously quiet. He was really not very happy about this. I could be in big trouble when I finally let him down. But it was too late to turn back now.

"I know about the dungeon."

He stared at me. I could almost see the wheels turning in his mind. How much did I know? "Damn. You heard me on the phone, didn't you?"

"Maybe I followed you there. Maybe I found a receipt."

"No!" His response was explosive. "You're bluffing! I *never* went there. I called them. Once. You can't believe I would go there without you."

"I *believe* you called them. I *believe* I gave you more than one chance to tell me about it. I *believe* you promised me you would tell me, up front, if you ever wanted anyone else!"

"I don't want anyone else. I didn't do anything."

"Not yet!"

"C'mon, I just called them. Let me loose."

"Nope."

"Whaddaya mean 'no'?"

"Just tell me what you wanted. Or who you wanted." I snapped open the paper. "Which mistress? The bleached blonde here? Or the dark-haired one with the big tits? Which fetish? Were you gonna have her dress you up like a woman? Or play horsey? Or what?"

"Damn it! I was just curious. I didn't do anything wrong!"

I took a deep, calming breath to keep from screaming at him. "I just want to know what you were thinking when you called. Whatever it is that you'd rather pay for than ask me to do for you."

He sighed and leaned his forehead against his captive arm. "I don't want to talk about this."

"I guess you don't want loose tonight," I tossed back. "Whose picture turned you on?"

"None of them!"

"Fine. If you really expect me to believe that, then tell me what you wanted. A mistress? A slave? Cross-dressing? Diapers? Pain? Humiliation?"

"A little pain, and a little humiliation, okay? Now let me down." He was blushing hard, but he looked me straight in the eye.

"But not from me."

"I wanted to rent the space, not rent a woman. For us. Read the damned ad again. They rent space by the hour."

"If that's true, why haven't you mentioned that particular yearning to me?"

"I didn't think you would enjoy humilating me," he answered wryly.

I unbuttoned my dress, slowly, and shrugged out of it. I turned around and bent over at the waist to pick it up and toss it out of the way. I felt the thong back of my black lace panties stretch into my crevice. "Maybe you just think I'm not tough enough, or sexy enough, to abuse you."

I could see a twitch of response in his jeans. "I never said that. I was embarrassed. I didn't know how to ask you to . . . to . . . " I cocked an eyebrow and waited. "I was embarrassed," he finished lamely.

"You hurt me. I thought you wanted someone else. Maybe you do."

"No," he said gently. "Never."

I chose to believe him. The fear and the anger flowed out of me. Most of the anger, anyway. Frankly, I needed to hold on to a little bit to carry this off. I stretched up against him to unlock the cuff that was looped around the chin-up bar. He closed his eyes and shook his arm a bit to get the blood flowing properly again. He reached for me, but I pushed his hand away.

"Do you want to finish this?" I demanded.

He studied my face. Shut his eyes for a second. "Yes."

I turned him around, clicked the dangling cuff around his free wrist. Yanking at the waistband of his jeans popped the buttons free. I shoved the jeans and his boxers down around his ankles.

"Your safe word is *blue*."

"My what?"

"My what, *ma'am*." I reprimanded him.

"My what, ma'am?" His tone was insolent, his grin wicked.

"Don't dis' me, or we stop right now. Your safe word. If you're nervous, use it. If you're scared," I taunted. "But not just because you don't like what I'm doing. This is my game, and you're here to please me."

"Yes, ma'am." His posture was straighter, his tone more subdued, but a touch of insolence was still there.

"I think you should be on your knees by now, slave." He turned to face me, his cock rising steadily. Kicking his ankles free of his jeans, he knelt at my feet. I stood before him, stance wide, hands on hips. He looked appreciatively up at my breasts, until I popped him lightly on top of his head. "Eyes down." His big blue eyes took the long route, checking me out all the way down, so I grabbed a fistful of thick brown hair and forced his head back.

"I don't think you're taking me seriously, lover," I sneered. "You fucked up. Bad. I gave you two chances, and you lied to me twice. You need to be punished." His eyes widened, then dropped.

"Yes, ma'am." When I was sure he'd finally gotten the message I let him go. Bending over the couch, I slid my feet into the black patent stilettos I had stashed underneath it. Hoping I looked high-class stripper instead of a kid playing dress up, I minced around the room lighting a few strategically placed candles and turning out the lights. His eyes followed me warily. In a slightly strangled voice he asked, "Ma'am? You're not going to . . . "

I contemplated his slowly wilting erection. "No, wussy boy. I'm not gonna use the wax on you. These are just for light. This time."

His erection returned, pointing to the ceiling. I stood, propped one foot up on the coffee table, and crooked my finger at him. He started to stand, but I shook my head. "Uh uh.

Stay on your knees." He waddled over to me on his knees, his cock bobbing and swaying. I struggled not to laugh at him.

"My shoes are dirty. Clean them." His expression was quizzical. "Oh darn. You're all tied up. I guess you have to use your tongue." I pointed at the shoe.

With the tip of his tongue he touched it, hesitantly. Within seconds he was lapping at it. Then he was worshiping it with broad, flat strokes. He covered every inch of the shiny blackness, paying special attention to the spike heel. He did such a beautiful job, I had to reward him. I turned around, bent over, and let him kiss my ass. He did that nicely, too.

I pushed him down over the coffee table, face pressed into the cold, polished wood and pulled out my last toy, the square black laces. Lightly I traced the line of his spine, from the base of his neck to the spasming pucker of his asshole. He didn't realize what was tickling him until I delivered the first light lash on his balls. His sharply indrawn breath and the quick move to get his restricted hands off his bare bottom encouraged me to go on. I took my first full swing at him. He gasped and flinched when it connected. I used light flicks to work out a steady rhythm, then settled in with a comfortable left cheek, right cheek that left him squirming and grunting, but not complaining.

When his light cream skin had turned a fiery pink I let up. I turned his head by his hair and asked if he was okay. "Do you want me to stop?"

"No, ma'am. Please, ma'am."

I laughed. "Are you begging?"

"Yes, ma'am. Please don't stop now."

I fondled his balls, gave his cock a long stroke with my hand. I found a long string of pre-come at the end of it. Getting as much of it as I could, I offered it to his mouth. He only hesitated for a second before he eagerly sucked his own fluid off my finger. "What do you say?" I demanded.

"Thank you, ma'am."

I rewarded him with a stinging shot at his shoulder. He recoiled slightly; he'd been expecting another slap on his ass.

I worked his shoulders for a while, left, right, left, right, until the skin color matched his bottom. I aimed another one down there, but this time he flinched too hard. The tender skin had finally had enough. I lightened my strokes considerably, fondling his balls again, and occasionally aiming a very light slap at the tightly wrinkled skin there. "Had enough?"

His answer took a little longer this time. "Yes, ma'am."

"Straighten up then. And turn around." I rested one foot on the coffee table again. This time I presented the crotch of my panties to his face. "Lick me." He settled back on his heels and tentatively reached out with his tongue, wondering what I would allow. Light licks up the sides, then the center swollen button. He tugged at the slick, silky fabric with his teeth, but I popped him on the head.

"No teeth." I ordered.

He went back to work with his tongue. He wiggled it under the elastic, moaned when he tasted my arousal. Ahh, his tongue felt sweet on my bare skin. Too sweet. I had to make him stop. "No. No skin. You can only taste me through my panties."

He whimpered. Then he lapped at the silky fabric with a vengeance. His flat tongue massaged and rubbed, then the tip teased and tormented until I couldn't take anymore. I pulled away with a shudder. My foot hit the floor and I turned my back to him. I straddled him backwards, wiggling my ass in his face. Dropping slowly to my knees, I pulled my panties to the side and guided him into me. Entry was slick and easy. I'd been needing him for hours. I eased onto the very tip of his rock hard cock. He thrust forward, forcing me onto all fours. I pulled off.

"Hold still," I demanded. "I'm fucking you. You are not fucking me. If you want to be inside me, don't move a single muscle. You're nothing but a dildo to me," I lied. He groaned, but held perfectly still.

I backed onto him again. I moved back and forth on the end of his cock, not allowing full penetration, with a slow, steady rhythm. When I heard his breath quicken I pulled free again.

I tucked his erection down between my thighs, and rode the smooth velvety hardness with my swollen clit. "Please, ma'am," he whimpered. "Please, please, please," like a mantra.

Then I guided him inside me once again, clear to the hilt this time, in one smooth motion.

I rested there for a long moment, not moving, just filled with him. My fingers circled my clit in an involuntary motion. I simply couldn't wait anymore. The swift contractions of a powerful orgasm took me by surprise, robbing me of the last shred of control I had left. I rocked back and forth with long strokes. His back arched as he did his best to meet me. Groaning with desperate need, he thrust his hips as far forward as they could go. I could feel the jerk of his cock, trying to strain upwards, demanding release. I clenched my muscles tightly, milking him for all I was worth.

"Oh, God." His words forced themselves through his tightly clenched jaw. "Ohh. My. Gawwwd." He pushed into me, short quick lunges, all he could manage in his awkward position. When he was finished, in danger of toppling over and taking us both down, I pulled free, collapsing on the floor. When I could move again, I crawled over to the couch and leaned against it. I pulled my panties back into place to catch the flow of spent lust. Sean moved clumsily toward me and lay his head on my breast. "I love you," he murmured.

"I know," I whispered, fumbling for the key to his handcuffs. "I just forgot for a minute."

Maria Mendoza

Mourning the Peasant

To Wes, for all the belief

You read the eulogy out loud as if you are a cheerleader on heroin. It feels good to get the words out to the congregation and yet, your soul is somewhere else, perhaps dreaming. The words come out of your mouth clearly but you cannot feel your tongue move. You cannot feel your body in that long, black dress and matching heels. You cannot feel the stream of sweat that trickles down your right inner thigh. But, in any case, your words are nice and they are causing everybody at your father's funeral Mass to cry.

And your arms —
We will miss holding them.
And your smile —
We will miss receiving it.
And your heart —
We will miss feeling it.

Before the last stanza of your eulogy, you want to cry and you search the congregation for a safe face. You see the face of your father's long-time lover and friend. Laia. She does not smile at you or encourage you to get rid of the sob in your throat; rather, she gives you a wide-eyed blank expression of openness and possibility. You understand. You let your tears flow but you keep your voice coherent. You keep your voice alive by imagining your father patting your back lovingly while you read at the podium. You imagine the smell of his skin and cologne, the smell of soft leather mixed with Grey Flannel. The scent strengthens you and carries you through the Mass and the graveside burial, as you shed your gentle tears.

After the burial, Laia, the Vinnifieds and you have a solemn tea on the patio of Laia's house. Everybody looks both tragic and perfect: all dressed in black and struck with downward eyes and mostly closed lips. Laia's maids scurry about diligently, making sure that everyone has enough cucumber sandwiches, popovers and various teas. Many kiss you as you sit, cross-legged, sipping mindlessly at your cup of Oolong. You either respond to them too vividly — flailing your arms around dramatically — or too passively — sitting still and pretending they had not kissed you at all. Throughout the tea, Laia either stays at your side or watches you from a close distance. She holds your hand, wipes your tears, helps you to freshen your makeup in the kitchen bathroom and wards off relatives who give you too many encouraging words. Laia is like a peregrine falcon, stalking moving prey that mindlessly scurry about in an open field. She is like a lioness, proudly raising her head above the pack to view the savannah she owns while keeping safe watch on you, her beloved cub.

Dressed in a black, flowing pantsuit and a Vivienne Westwood headpiece with an attached half-veil, Laia is a striking sentinel for your mourning soul. She is tall, nearly six feet, and very strong (lots of volleyball with your father on Galveston Beach and countless hours biking at Memorial Park). Her appearance is not so much beautiful as it is dignified. Now, her narrow eyes watch you as you nod your head at some cousin or aunt.

You catch her stare, you smile at her and wave with your

small fingers. She sets her tea down and blows you a kiss through her veil. Your soul stirs and you do not know why. You simply smile and return to the umpteenth conversation about what your father was like and your raw confessions over what you miss most about him. Basically, you tell relatives what they want to hear: how God will watch over your father, how the time was right and how he would reconcile things with your mother in heaven. Yes, you tell them the words they want to hear, family mourning talk.

You can barely speak without tripping over small sobs here and there but you simply look at Laia and this is so sufficient that you do not have to imagine your father's scent again. Once, when putting down your fifth cup of tea, you scan the faces on the patio. All are Vinnified faces. Nobody from your late mother's family. You have not seen a member of the Lopez family since your father divorced your mother when you were seven, except at your mother's funeral, five years later. Not one Lopez had informed you or your father about her death: You learned of it from your father's casual reading of the obituaries in the Sunday paper. It was an awful way to find out. You were twelve, just discovering your newly tender nipples and necessity for training bras. You had not even formed your theories or outlooks on death. All you knew was that it could not happen to anybody in the family.

The Lopezes hated your father not because he was an evil man, a lecher or even a swindler. It was because he divorced your mother on the grounds of spousal abuse. The Lopezes accused your father of insanity and called you a spawn of insanity for having defended your father both in court and to their faces. The Lopezes insisted that he was overreacting and that it was not possible for a woman to abuse a man, that it was not in a woman's nature to hurt or destroy anything or anyone. But you had seen that it was.

Now you do not think, "I have lost my mother and my father," but rather, "I have lost my father and his first marriage partner." You create safe distance between your mother and you. You build the high, stone wall. You tear your flesh away from her womb and think of your existence as having been fashioned by the grace of nature, despite the fact that, during your teenage years, your father pleaded with you to forgive your mother.

You help Laia and the maids clean up after the tea. Laia takes her headpiece off and twists her hair into a loose bun. Your makeup is tired from the tears and the vain powdering. In silence, you collect the tiny porcelain cups and saucers. Now and then, you eat a few untouched finger pastries left on tiny plates. Laia hums to herself as she wipes off tables and sweeps off debris, using a damp washcloth. Mahler's "Tragic" plays from the intercom above the patio. Today has been a sad day for you but you clean up as if you were getting your chores done before an outing with your father. You clean up with forced alacrity and precision, your fingers moving quickly, your stride relaxed and sure. But at the end of the patio clean-up, you go to the kitchen. Your eyes fall heavy on its floor tiles. You outline the pale, paisley shapes with your eyes and you feel disgusted.

Laia places her hands on your shoulders and presses her lips to your forehead.

"It's late, do you want me to run a bath?"

Still looking at the floor, you answer in a small voice.

"Yes, make it hot."

"Music?"

"Yes."

"Incense?"

"Please."

She gives you another kiss — this time, near your mouth, and walks away. You watch her body slice through the air calmly.

"Laia."

She turns around, headpiece in her hands.

"Um-hmm?"

"Thanks for being great today."

"I didn't do anything you didn't," she says gently. She turns away from you and resumes her walk down the long corridor, its walls flanked with mini ionic columns.

You take your shoes off in the kitchen and wiggle your blistered toes. The tiles are cool underneath your feet, but you decide to venture onto carpet, into the television room. Sighing, you pick up the remote control on the black leather couch and point it at the television. You press the button with your thumb as you pose yourself in front of the screen like a stiff effigy. Images. All you see are images: montages of kissing, fucking, home shopping channels, Hollywood films, cartoons, cooking shows and Congressional hearings. You stop abruptly on Channel 32. *The Firebird*, a classic ballet, is painted in front of your eyes.

Your father loved dance as much as you do, and you remember the many ballets the two of you attended together. You remember him coming to all of your performances, from when you were Clara in *The Nutcracker*, all the way to your first contemporary ballet with your university's dance department. *The Firebird* now makes you feel useless. You wonder who will watch your performances and who will buy drinks for the whole company after every performance at the nearby campus bar.

He helped bandage your toes before every *pointe* class. When you were sixteen, he refused to let you cut your hair short, for fear that it would make you less eligible for casting in principal roles. He was raving mad when he saw boxes of Ex-Lax fall from your bag as you climbed into the car after class one evening. He knew exactly what many dancers did to keep themselves thin. For five hours that man griped you out mercilessly and you sat there, your belly hungry and raw, your body 15 pounds underweight, your gaunt cheeks sucked in from crying. He didn't know whether to hit you or hug you as you sat there in perhaps what was one of the most pathetic states of your life. He finally squatted in front of you and looked into your pink face.

"I'm getting a nutritionist for you and a counselor and you are not going to pull this bulimic shit behind my back."

You had burst into tears, throwing your little arms around his neck. You felt his body soften as he, too, wept, his arms around your shaking body.

You force yourself to cease this memory process. You lay down on the floor, in front of the 52-inch television, and continue to watch *The Firebird*, starring Maria Tallchief as the principal. Dance seems so far away from you right now. You can't even think about rehearsal and costume fittings. You can't think of calling Lyle, a boy from the department whom you started to date only one week before your father's sudden death from meningitis. You close your eyes and moan lightly, drifting into an evening nap.

You dream.

Your father is barefoot, wearing the costume of a peasant. An orchestra plays beneath him. A saggy cap lies atop his smoothed-back, chocolate-colored hair and he has a ridiculous grin on his face. You are dressed like a tulip. Daintily, you approach your father *en pointe*, your arms reaching out to him. Your body is fragile, yet strong. Your footwork is careful and precise.

Your father prepares to run to you but before he can take off, a large, white ribbon shoots down and pierces his costume, ripping his pants. It wraps itself around your father's manhood, which becomes erect.

You scream.

You wake up crying and as you rub your eyes, look up to the ceiling. Laia stands over you, her arms crossed. She is in a terry cloth robe, her hair wet and long around her shoulders.

"Was it a bad one?"

You nod and sit up, still rubbing your eyes like a small child. She bends down and rubs your upper back. The black gabardine fabric of your dress itches against your skin.

"Go take your bath," she says.

"Thanks."

You let her hug you from behind, then you rise, turn off the television — cutting off the end of *The Firebird* — and wobble to the bathroom.

The dress falls from your body easily. You rip off the garter belt and tear away the black stockings. The front hook of your bra has left a pink indentation between your breasts. You unsnap it and ease your arms out of the silken straps. You stand in your panties, in front of the wall, its expanse covered with large, square mirrors that are all connected to each other. Behind you is the large square bathtub, its top carved into the shape of a shell.

You sigh at your small breasts, take off your panties and walk backward into the tub, all the while watching the triangular curve of your pubic hair and the slight sway of your breasts in the mirror. You step into the mountain of bubbles carefully, your eyes closing, your nostrils filled with the scent of jasmine incense, your ears caressed by François Couperain operettas. The water is hot and forgiving.

Laia and you are curled into opposite sides of the huge leather couch in the television room. You sip from cups filled with warm milk. It is night. You are both exhausted. You pick at a plate of leftover finger pastries on the coffee table.

"You're going to be wide awake tonight if you eat that many," Laia chides.

"No, I'll be fine," you say, as you shove the fifth pastry into your mouth.

"Does the department know that you won't be coming in next week?"

You nod, finishing off the sixth pastry. One more to go.

"Is this going to change the casting for *Apollo*?"

"I never wanted to be a muse anyway."

Silence. You know she is staring at you with sad eyes but you dare not look at her. You stare into your empty cup.

"More warm milk?"

"Please."

She stands up, takes your cup and breezes away into the kitchen. You stare at the television screen and hallucinate momentarily, seeing Maria Tallchief make her way across the stage of corps dancers. Laia comes back humming and gives you a newly warmed mug of milk. You murmur thanks and gulp it down twice as quickly as the first cup. It tastes like childhood and this makes you almost share with Laia a story about your father's excellent homemade cocoa that he usually made during Christmastime. You decide against it. You stand up quickly, make your way to the immaculate kitchen, and place your mug in the sink, along with the plate that is decorated by one uneaten strawberry-filled triangle.

You and Laia ascend the staircase together, hand-in-hand.

"It was a good service. You read well at the Mass."

"I was scared."

"I know, but you pulled it off. He would have been proud of you. Well, I should take that back. He was there, I'm sure. He was definitely proud of you."

"Thanks."

She pauses and squeezes your hand.

"Honey, I wish I had had the privilege to give birth to you."

You stop at the top of the stairs. A maid whizzes by carrying a bundle of towels. You let go of Laia's hand and look at her. Her face is so tired, yet strong.

"You know, I was really scared reading up there," you say. "I didn't think that any of them knew what the hell I was talking about. It made me angry that they were all crying. I didn't think they were stupid but I don't think they were crying for the right reasons. I think Uncle Jack and Aunt Marty cried because the funeral had cost so much. I think the other relatives cried because they were worried about Dad's company going to shit. I don't know but these are my opinions. I'm sorry."

"No, it's okay. Anger's healthy. I think they really loved your father. I had my own conclusions — I know that they weren't comfortable with me. They weren't comfortable that I had guardianship of you above your own blood relatives. I'm not even a family member."

"But everyone respects you."

"No, everyone is scared of me, honey. There's the difference. They see me as a replacement of your mother, a substitution. To them, I'm part human, part bitch. That's okay, though. I've gotten over it through the years and I know that they under-stand what I had with your father and what I have with you."

She grabs your hand again and continues.

"He was a good person. I love him so much. He didn't deserve this and we can certainly say that we didn't need to go through this pain. But these things happen and I think that there were some genuine mourners in our family today. Even those who we felt were ignorant in their mourning were really genuine in their way of handling pain, especially your Aunt Marty. I really don't think the funeral's price tag was the cause of her tears."

You shrug and bury your body into hers. She wraps her arms around you. Though she is nine years older than you — thirty-one — you feel that her body is much like yours. A year after you met her, you stopped hating her. You became comfortable with hugging and kissing her, feeling her safe body encouraging yours. Now, at the age of twenty-two, you feel as if you were fourteen again, safe within the confines of her chest. Now, you can feel a new sob developing in your throat. You can't bear another exhausting wave of tears but this is difficult because you can smell the lingering scent of your father on her — a hint of Grey Flannel. You squint your eyes and dry the beginnings of tears on her robe, coughing, pretending to clear your throat.

When you break from her embrace, you see that she is the one crying. You see that she has let her guard down for the day. Her tears are quiet and they fall from her eyes in steady showers. The overhead light of the hallway ceiling casts small shadows under her nose and eyelashes. Even when she cries, she looks unbreakable.

You kiss her cheek.

"You know, Laia, I don't think that you would have wanted to give birth to me."

"Why?"

"I weighed eleven pounds!"

You both laugh and you wipe away her tears with your fingers. She holds your hands upon her cheeks. She kisses the insides of your palms and returns your hands to your sides. Your body shakes.

"Goodnight, lovely." She gives you another hug. This time, it is quicker. She turns away, twisting her hair high above her head and placing it over her left shoulder. Her body swims in light and darkness as she floats between the beams of the tiny, overhead lights. You walk the opposite direction and turn right into a connecting hallway.

"Night." Your voice is small but you are sure it gets to her before you hear the huge double doors to her bedroom close firmly.

The sheets are cool and heavy on your naked body. Your new bedroom is vast and filled with darkness. You light a small candle on your night table and say a small prayer. You blow out the candle and thump your head into the king-size pillow. You close your eyes. Shortly thereafter, your telephone rings. You pick it up and force a half-friendly "Hello." It is Lyle. He wants to know how you are and expresses how much he wishes he could have come to the funeral. You tell him it is late. He tells you that you never go to bed before midnight.

"Please, Lyle. I need to sleep. It's been a hard day for me. We'll talk tomorrow."

It is as if he does not hear you, for he asks if you are coming to rehearsals next week and reminds you about costume fittings next Wednesday. You tell him, once again, that you need to sleep. You accidentally call him a bastard. You apologize. He says that he understands and will call you tomorrow. You thank him, hang up and return to your slumber.

Again you are awakened by nightmares of your father's body, this time being slowly dismembered. You feel yourself falling, but before you hit bottom, you wake up. Dried tears and fresh tears have painted your face. It is hard for you to breathe. You sit up, feeling the taste of stale milk in your mouth. You wobble upright and feel for your robe at the foot of your round bed.

You make your way to Laia's room. The hallway seems larger now and the lights are dimmer. The velvety carpet underneath your feet feels as if it will give way at any time. You open the doors to Laia's room and close them behind you. She is awake. She looks at you from behind Salman Rushdie's *The Moor's Last Sigh*. The grand halogen lamps at either side of her headboard boast a dim setting. She takes off her glasses, puts down her book and gives you a strange stare. She is engulfed in the huge, black mosquito net that forms a canopy over her bed, which is round like yours, but much larger. The black satin sheets make Laia look as if she were floating in a sea of crude oil. She is naked.

"What's wrong?"

You do not answer. You simply burst into tears and make your way into the familiar bed that you used to sleep in during your father's business trips when you were younger. The bed accepts your shaking body. You do not look at her eyes but merely move to her lap, which is covered, waist down, by a single sheet. She says nothing but plays with your sweaty hair and massages your forehead.

You mumble something about the nightmares. Laia listens with no interruptions or questions. When you finish, she turns your body around so that you are looking at her face bent over yours. Grabbing a Kleenex from her nightstand, she wipes your face.

"I'm really going to miss him, Laia." You cry, ruining her clean-up job.

She takes the wet Kleenex and throws it onto the floor. She encourages you to climb underneath the covers with her. She turns on a small, white machine on her night table. A soft sound of waves pours from it.

"Do you like that sound?"

"Yes," you reply, wiping snot from your nose.

She hands you a fresh, pink Kleenex and you both lay on your sides, knees bent, in fetal position. Your faces are close to each other and you can see that, in one of her hands, a new Kleenex is curled within her fingers.

Carefully, you begin to talk of your father. The conversation lasts two hours while the ocean plays obediently from the white box. You do not cry, nor does she. While Laia speaks, you notice the opening and closing of her pink mouth and the flash of her eyelids as she now and then turns to look at the circular top of the mosquito net. Halfway through the conversation, you notice her breasts push from the top of the black sheet. She does not notice, nor does this bother you.

There is talk of his love for your dancing. There is talk of his love for Laia's knowledge of foreign affairs and Lebanese cooking. There is talk of his screening all the men you have dated. There is talk of his helping Laia get over her tragic cocaine spree. Talk of how his former marriage partner abused him and, to a great extent, you. Talk of his excellent taste in clothing. Talk of his ridiculous fondness for golf.

After the conversation, you lay closer to each other, noses together. You cough, covering your mouth, and ask her a difficult question.

"Do you miss the way he touches you?"

A vast silence falls over her body. You can see it caress her face, arms, breasts and legs. She gives you a stare that is not angry but stunned. She answers with forced coolness.

"Of course I miss the way he touches me. And you? I can ask you if you miss his hugs?"

"Yes, they were big hugs. They were safe ones. I liked the way he would always open the car door for me when he dropped me off for school when I was little."

You pause, then say, "Laia, if I ask you for something, will you get mad?"

"Ask me, honey."

The words seem inane. They do not make sense in your head and yet they want to come out — like a baby that has to leave its mother's womb. You go over the question in your head, searching Laia's eyes for the courage to deliver it with your mouth. But she cannot give you her strength now, for she lies silently, awaiting your query.

"Show me," you finally whisper.

"What?"

"Show me."

"Show you . . . ?"

You whisper even lower.

"Will you show me the way he touched you? That's my question. God, I just want to know."

She laughs. She laughs loudly, turning onto her back and kicking her legs underneath the blanket so that you get glimpses of her naked body through the flapping sheet. This absolutely devastates you, her laughing, and you turn away from her. You do not have the strength to stand up and run to your own bed. You do not have the strength to scream, "Stop." So, you resort to the only action your body can bear. You let the infinite storehouse of tears flow from your eyes.

Laia's jig ceases. This makes you cry more. You are afraid of what she will say or do. You are afraid that she will offer to call up your old psychiatrist from the divorce era. You are afraid that she will give you a kiss on your shoulder and dismiss this as an act of post-traumatic syndrome.

Then you feel her arms around your waist, folding over your robe's tie. Your body shakes crazily and you want her to make you forget about the next day, or even the next minute of your life. She buries her head into the back of your neck, using her nose to lift your hair away.

"Alectra."

Your back arches and her hands move to the inside of your robe. She kisses the back of your neck softly, in small spurts. Your breasts face the knowledge of her hands — fingers pinching gently at your nipples. Her naked thigh moves carefully between your bent legs until you can feel the strength of her quadricep beneath your sex — the purple silk of your robe is the only barrier.

The smell of her behind you is consuming. She moves like a lioness or a python around your body, her fingers and tongue performing foreplay as if you were a delicately strung harp. Her breathing is careful and she does not move quickly. Her slowness creates a fire in your belly and you turn your body to her, facing her eyes which are drunk with ecstasy.

"Show me," you breathe, "show me how he kissed you."

Laia kisses your forehead, moving to your eyelids, cheeks, jawline, the corners of your lips. Yes, of course. This is exactly how your father would approach a kiss when making love to a woman. You tease each other with your lips. It is clear that Laia has control of everything that is taking place. You do not try to usurp her but simply reflect to Laia her own strength.

She closes her lips over yours. Your limbs fumble for her legs as her tongue bathes the insides of your mouth. You drink from her as if she were giving you an elixir for all the pains, all the mishaps in your life. Her kiss is both masculine and feminine, both overwhelming and yielding. You cry in her kiss and she pulls back momentarily, wiping your new tears, but she knows that more will follow. She returns to kissing you and your mouth receives this reunion wholly, as if one second of absence were an eternity of separation from that kiss.

Laia feels your hunger and she feeds it. But you, too, feel her mourning, her longing. Though you had asked her to show you her father's art of lovemaking, it now feels as if she and she only were on you — body upon body. You thought that you wouldn't feel as much loss if you knew the sensual side of your father, the part of him you never witnessed—but you feel more loss now, more distant from him than ever. You slap away the emptiness inside you, throwing your arms around Laia.

Bumping your nose with her elbow, she rolls herself on top of you, sitting up. Carefully, she undoes your robe and lets it fall at your sides, unfolding your body as if it were shedding a silk exoskeleton. You say nothing.

You reach up with one hand, cupping the side of her face. As in the hallway, she dips her mouth into the palm of your hand. She licks the fullness of your whole hand, licking each finger with such fervor that it feels like your hand will catch on fire.

She guides your well-licked hand to her breasts. Your fingers pass over them as if you were playing a piano made of fragile keys. She moans lightly, lifting her chin to the ceiling. You break free from her guiding hand. With both hands, you explore her torso, her ribs, the flatness of her belly. Her every muscle is softly defined. Your fingers dig into the contours of these muscles. Laia smiles down at you, approvingly.

Your hands then dance to the top of her pubic hair. Such soft downy hair! You stop and look at her eyes again. They are wet and open. She nods. You let your fingers flow beneath her mound. She tilts her hips up and toward you. You find the sweet mound, placing your two index fingers on it. She tells you not to be too quick. You nod, massaging it slowly. She wails as if she were a forever ringing bell. Her scent is strong and clean, a mixture of honey, musk and flowers. She leans back on her elbows, giving up her sex to you like a willing sacrifice.

The more you rub her mound, the harder she moans. She does this beautifully, from deep within her belly. Slowly, her hips move up and down, teasing your face and your fingers. She looks down the length of her body, into your eyes with a gaze that says nothing but is full of possibility. Your fingers wash her inner lips and you bend your head into your chest, blowing forward into her dark, moist sliver. She gasps, grabs your wrist with one of her strong hands. You both shed tears in this pleasure.

She turns herself over, so that the front of her hips is on your face and her own face, its flushed breath and mouth, are over your sex, which by now is rich with wetness and yearning. Her knees are at the sides of your face. You take caution in this position, breathing lightly on each other's inner thighs and knees. You run the tip of your tongue over the expanse of her soft down. You inhale her deeply. You are each a mass of starvation and mourning.

What happens next is not a product of mutual pain but of celebration — a joyous screaming with the body when none took place at the Mass. A shout for love, when it would have been inappropriate to do so at the tea, in front of somber family faces. A crying from the deepest parts of Laia and you, when the discreet dabbing of tears was not sufficient for either one of you today.

With heavy sobs, you approach each other as if you were women who had been denied the gift of touch, as if you had once been bound, hand and foot, and then beaten for your openness to the possibility of touch. Now all the tenderness and grace in that room spill over your body and hers.

You plunge your tongue into her moist flower. Her head arches up to the heavens and you feel this and plunge again. Through your tears, you search her chasm like a doe that thirsts for water so badly, that she will pierce the barren earth with her raw tongue for any drop of moisture.

Laia returns your affection, eating fully from your sex, madly burying her hair and face between your legs. This is a cleansing. This is a dance of comfort, closure and truth.

Arms, legs, faces, breasts and bellies take up the expanse of the bed. You consume her fully, as if you had no choice, as if taking of her with your mouth were more vital than air or food. She consumes you as if she were not human, but made purely of desire, a bound sack filled with arms, lips and legs, all aching to burst from her pores.

You find each other's peaks and this brings you both to a more urgent rhythm. She introduces her fingers to join her tongue's lovemaking. You gasp for precious air and suckle her with your mouth, driving deeper into her musky cavern.

"Alectra! Keep it like this," her voice pleads.

You obey, grabbing her ass and pushing her sweet heaviness into your face, shutting out all outside air and the dim light of the halogen lamps. She responds by lightly biting your swollen nodule, which sends preliminary waves of joy throughout your lower body.

You wrap your legs over her, your knees crossing above her head. She does the same, giving your wet head leverage with the backs of her full calves. Heavy sobs, moans, gasps and screams. The mosquito net nearly gets pulled off by the random movements of your bodies.

Suddenly, Laia's hips writhe upward and then crash down fiercely on your face. She is sobbing endlessly, grinding her sex deep into your mouth. You welcome her spasms by thrusting your tongue even harder inside her, your pink, deft muscle moving back and forth quickly. She screams your name, not even tending to your sex, and this alone — the simple bellow of your birth name — makes you come shortly after her.

Your back arches, as does hers — two cats in heat, two cats enraptured by instinct. The waves rush through you like a fiery liquid, more potent and more rhythmic than the recorded waves from the small white box. You swallow her honey. It is heavy and numbs your mouth; its sweetness is unbearable. You taste her pain and sacrifice. You taste all of her, in copious amounts.

She dismounts you and laps the rivers of fire between your legs like a grateful kitten. Her hair is stuck to her face in strategic pieces. Her eyes are closed, the lashes fluttering quickly. Finally, she opens her eyes and throws you an amorous glance and cleans off your swollen vulva with gentle strokes. Her tongue is pleasing and warm. You throw your arms over your head and breathe deeply. The smell of sex. The smell of two placated women. You smile reverently and speak.

"You're like a mother lion."

"Oh no," she warns coyly, bringing herself up to your face. "This was not an incestuous pity fuck, Alectra."

You open your eyes. She has pressed her face into the nook of your underarm. You hold her. It feels weird to have her poised below you.

"I know this wasn't incestuous. I've never thought of you like a mother. You've always been something more to me than that."

She kisses your chin and you continue.

"I said you were like a lioness because that's how you move: You're cunning and sexy and definite."

Laia thanks you and throws her leg over your belly. She is exhausted.

"God, I miss him so much," she says, near sobbing.

"It's okay. Laia, you're gonna be fine." You kiss the top of her head, smelling the strong wave of your own sex.

You both lay there, speechless, for an uncertain amount of time. A soft, gray light filters through the windows by the bed. Dawn. In silence, you feel her body relax, giving in to sleep. She snores slightly, her face still pressed up against your right breast. You hold her close to you and refuse the barrage of questions that try to make their way into your mind. You do not need to answer them. They mean nothing now. Your body . . . it feels cleansed and broken. A new vessel. The top of the mosquito net looks down at you. Its long netting forms a loose cage around your bodies. A womb. A black, translucent womb. You move slightly, sensing the wetness all around you. Laia wakes up, asks if you are okay. You tell her to go back to sleep and she gives in to slumber once again. You love her so much.

Soon, your eyes close and you, too, are slave to sleep. You hold onto Laia loosely and in your unconsciousness, the movie screen starts again. A tunnel. A short, dark tunnel that smells of gardenias and honey. Harmless bees zoom to and fro in this tunnel. You stand at one end, which is illuminated with a blue light. You look to the other end. Your body feels weightless. A cello plays loudly. Two figures at the other end, the opening also illuminated. One looks like your father because you recognize the peasant clothing, especially the hat. At his side is a woman dressed in an empire-waist dress and a large headpiece, on it, an attached veil that goes over her face. Under the veil, the woman also wears a black mask over her eyes. Her lips are painted white, matching her dress.

Your father waves at you slowly, the bees dancing around him. He blows you a kiss with both hands. He turns around to walk into the brightness behind him. You want him to look back but he does not. The sounds of the cello fade as he disappears, and the woman walks toward you slowly, removing her mask.

Joan Leslie Taylor

The Rose Velvet Chaise

It all began with the old-fashioned chaise longue, left behind in the rental cottage by a vacating tenant. The first time she saw it with its ornately carved dark wood and its worn velvet upholstery, Frieda felt compelled to recline on it and stretch out her long limbs. She had only stopped in to check on the cottage, to see what needed to be done before a new tenant moved in. But from the moment she sat down and ran her fingers along the silken old wood, and sank into the firm but comforting upholstery, something inside her opened wide, and it felt as if she'd just taken her first real breath in a long, long time. The scent of an unfamiliar perfume rose from the chaise; a hint of floral, with undertones of a Southern summer.

She found herself remembering the June day fifteen years ago when she'd first set eyes on her husband Blake at a Bolivian guitar concert. When her gaze fell upon him several rows below her and in the next tier to the right she'd felt an alteration in her body. Suddenly her skin had seemed so permeable she was sure she heard the strains of the guitar through her pores. And when something made him glance up at her, there was that feeling of opening wide within. She could scarcely bear the intensity of his dark eyes upon her, but neither could she look away. It was as if he were touching her. The feeling was definitely sexual. She felt his eyes, not just on her skin, but deep inside her. Her face felt hot and her vagina convulsed. A voice in her head told her to get control of herself, pull away from those eyes, and not leave herself open to the intrusions of a stranger, but she'd been drawn to this handsome man with dark eyes and prominent eyebrows, sun-golden skin, and a way of moving his hands that made her see them on her skin, moving up her bare legs.

Blake had courted her insistently. He was so romantic that Frieda fell quickly in love with him. Never had she known such a sensuous lover. He didn't just fuck her and roll over like all too many of the pretty boys she'd known. He took delight in her body, caressing her with his fingers and tasting her with his tongue, whispering endearments in her ear. They made love everywhere: in beds, in cars, on couches, and hidden in the sand dunes with the sound of the ocean pounding in their ears. Their passion had carried them to the wedding and beyond. Blake was as attentive as a young husband as he'd been during their courtship. He brought her flowers; they dined with candles and soft music. And they made love.

As the years went by, though, something changed. Frieda could not name what had been lost, but she was often overcome with a longing that filled her with sadness and confusion. She had a wonderful husband — smart, successful, good-looking — so why was she longing?

Lying back on the velvet chaise, she looked around the small room. There was something comforting about being here. An enormous sigh fell through her like water. Weeks and months and years of tension fell from her. She was at home.

There would be no more tenants in the little cottage. It was now hers. Her heart beat rapidly. Still on the chaise, she looked around the empty room watching the dust motes in the morning sunlight streaming through the dirty panes of French doors that led to the deck nestled under tall trees.

"A little paint . . . " she mused. "Maybe a small rug."

Frieda was a mystery writer. She had four titles to her credit, each a tightly written whodunit, cleverly constructed and satisfying to her small but growing coterie of fans. Blake, a brilliant consultant who flew all over the country straightening out computer glitches and designing whiz-bang systems, had set up one room in their spacious contemporary home for Frieda to write. Because she could not stay put at the enormous teak desk with its cunning compartments for pens and paper clips, he bought her a laptop computer. She roamed restlessly from room to room, for awhile perching uncomfortably on one end of the L-shaped leather couch in the living room with its soaring beamed ceiling and a wall of glass facing out on more view than Frieda could bear to see while she wrote, then moving to the glass and stainless steel table in the breakfast room, and later outside to what seemed like acres of redwood deck surrounding the house. It was a testament to her talent and skill as a writer that roving about the house like this Frieda was actually able to turn out a book a year. Blake kept adding technological marvels to her office, but Frieda could write no more than a paragraph within its confines.

Blake had also devoted his ingenuity to their bedroom. From a concealed panel on his side of the bed, he could control the lighting, change the piped-in music, roll back a screen above the bed to reveal a massive mirror arranged to reflect the action on the bed, or even set the whole bed or a selection of sex toys vibrating. He had assembled a world-class collection of erotic videos which he and Frieda viewed on the wide-screen television with speakers so realistic and precise that Frieda often imagined that the actors — panting and groaning, sucking and licking, thrusting and sliding — were right there in their king-sized bed with its black satin sheets.

Frieda and Blake had sex nearly every night when Blake was

not off in some distant city tweaking someone's computer. Blake was ardent and had the staying power of a much younger man. Frieda was more than willing. They pursued passion in every possible position, in every mood, and every way.

While Blake lay back and watched an erotic video, Frieda would caress his entire body, the fragrant massage oil letting her fingers, hands, and arms glide across his well-muscled flesh. He worked out using the latest high-tech equipment so he had not gone to fat, and was, if anything, more beautiful with each passing year. She liked moving her hands on his body: his firm chest, his broad back rippling with muscles, and his long muscular legs leading to his beautiful genitals, waiting like jewels for her fingers. Frieda wished she could caress Blake's cock and balls with the same leisurely care as she did the rest of his body, but every night at her first touch, his cock sprang into life and the massage was over. He'd slip two fingers into her moist and ready pussy, and before long they would both be at fever pitch, the sounds of the actors on the screen background music to their own groans of pleasure.

Yes, Frieda knew, Blake was still a good lover. He always made sure that she came, and he knew just how to bring her to the peak of arousal and then with the slightest movement to orgasm. Yet after Blake had turned off the video, dimmed the lights, silenced the music, and lay beside her fast asleep, Frieda would feel a distant longing for something she could not name. Many nights she left the king-sized bed and wandered the big house, roaming from room to room just like she did during the daytime, with a restless gnawing hunger.

That very day she first came to the cottage, she swept the worn hardwood floors and brought her laptop computer across the courtyard that separated the main house from the small rental. The moment she sat down upon the velvet chaise and began typing she knew that a change had occurred. Her feminist sleuth, Amber Queen, always so clever and efficient at ferreting out crooks and murderers and spotting clues the high-priced private-eyes overlooked, began behaving in ways unheard of in the four previous volumes. She showed up at the crime scene in a low-cut dress of flowing gauze in a rosy hue. What had become of her tailored suits in earth tones, much like the ones that Frieda wore? Amber smiled warmly at the police sergeant as she removed her sunglasses with the rose-colored frames that matched her dress. And she wore perfume with a hint of magnolias. By the end of the afternoon a tall dark stranger with brooding eyes had shown up. Frieda was breathless.

Later, preparing dinner in her own kitchen with its many labor-saving appliances, she looked out the window toward the little cottage and sighed. She could not wait to find out what Amber Queen might do next under her fingers on the keyboard. Or to feel that opening, that rush of excitement that came upon her whenever she settled upon the rose velvet chaise.

In the next few days she painted the walls of the cottage pale pink, the color of peonies she remembered from her grandmother's garden. She poked around antique shops until she found the perfect little rug, a small round table of the same dark wood as the chaise, and some lace curtains. She stopped at a boutique, not at all the kind of place she ever shopped, and bought a dress, all roses and peonies and camellias on the softest, sheerest cotton. Frieda had never worn anything with such a revealing neckline and so many flowers. As she handed the clerk her credit card, she added a pale pink shawl, so romantic and feminine she blushed.

She spent every day in the cottage, contentedly writing, following Amber Queen as she and the dark stranger solved the mystery of the cry in the boathouse. This was no longer just a mystery, but a romantic tale of seduction. The tall, dark stranger laid his hand upon Amber's arm, and then on her thigh. Frieda's heart pounded as Amber raised her lips to kiss the stranger. She was so aroused by the scene on her computer screen that she had to set the computer aside, lay back on the chaise, and give in to her rapidly accelerating arousal. Her body was hot, her skin reaching out, each pore longing to be touched. She ran her fingers down her neck and across her chest, wondering what it would be like to feel the fingers of a stranger upon her skin. The idea sent a wave of heat through her. Excited and frightened all at once, she unbuttoned the flowered dress and let her fingers find her breasts.

How soft and voluptuous her small bosom felt to her fingertips. Whose breasts were these anyway? Who was she, this woman undulating on the rose velvet chaise? Frieda's breath came in short pants as a wave of longing swept over her. Who was she longing for? *Close your eyes and see,* she whispered. The tall dark stranger appeared. He floated above her, his brooding eyes upon her, his sensuous lips reaching to kiss her, his fingers reaching to touch her. The scent of summer flowers filled the air.

Inspired, she reached for her computer and her fingers played on the keys as excitedly as they had on her breasts. It was a certain moonlit night — she saw it all — as Amber and the stranger forgot about clues and culprits and lay in each other's arms in the gazebo. Amber sighed. Frieda sighed. Amber moaned with desire, and Frieda's vagina contracted. Frieda watched the stranger's fingers move up Amber's leg, beneath her dress. . . . Whatever would her editor say? *The Cry in the Boathouse* was nothing like any of Frieda's previous books. Months ahead of schedule, Frieda mailed off the completed manuscript.

Blake, who read only technical books and periodicals, interspersed with an occasional science fiction title, was proud of his wife's writing career and gave her articles about the latest computerized tools used by police departments, so that her stories could be up-to-date and authentic.

"So now that you've finished your story you can take a break, right?" he asked her. "You could meet me in Rio," he added, running his hands down her buttocks and drawing her to him.

"Oh, I don't know," she stammered, thinking of the little cottage, but moving instinctively to Blake's hands. "I've got an idea for the next book. I must get it down before it slips away."

"I'm not leaving for another week. Please think about it," he said, his hands in her pants as he led her to the marvelous master suite with its automated love controls. "Is that perfume I smell?" he asked, burying his face in her hair and inhaling deeply. Frieda blushed as if she were with not Blake, but a stranger.

Day after day she worked away in the cottage, which continued to acquire furnishings and always had fresh flowers in an antique vase. She loved the old rocking chair she'd found at a garage sale. And the French drawings of nudes took her breath away, the subtlety of line calling up pleasure in her every time she looked up from her work and saw them. She lived with Blake, whom she loved dearly, in their wide beautiful house, but more and more the cottage was her home. Frieda had very casually mentioned to Blake that she was using it as a writing studio, which had surprised him, but he did not question her. He respected her work and did not intrude.

On the morning Blake left for Rio — an enormous computer network in snarls would require several weeks of his attentions — Frieda entered the cottage, already missing him. She could still smell him on her skin, and the memory of their early morning lovemaking sent a thrill, shot from her throat right down to her pussy still slippery with Blake's come. Every night that week he had begged her to come to Rio with him, but something in her would not let her leave the cottage.

In the glare of morning sunlight, she felt unbearably lonely, and she could not remember what had been so compelling in the little cottage. Amber's adventures suddenly seemed silly. What was the point of endless clues and dark strangers who came in the night and disappeared before dawn? She wanted Blake. But not Blake. She missed her husband of fourteen years, but, she realized, she missed him even when he was not flying off to Rio or Brussels, Miami or New Orleans.

Blake was so competent and so successful that their life, like their house, had become too big, too reliable, too elaborate. She missed the intimacy and excitement of when they had first come together.

Her hands trembled and her eyes clouded. Despite the warm sun, she shivered and wrapped herself in her pink shawl. Without turning on her computer, she curled up on the velvet chaise, a teacup in her hand and tears sliding down her cheeks. Longing rose in her. The soft folds of her flowered dress comforted her. Birds twittered in the trees outside. A slight breeze tickled her calves. She raised her skirt to let the breeze touch her thighs. It felt like Blake's fingers, but without massage oil. "I miss his fingers," she thought, "his fingers touching me, just to touch me, not part of a massage." A cry escaped her throat and she was suddenly weeping. "I want his hands on me without music, only wind and bird song!" she cried to the air between sobs. She slipped off her panties and let the wind tickle her longing yoni. "Oh, my dear sweet Blake," she whispered.

"Frieda?"

His voice at the door startled her. How could it be Blake here now in the cottage? But there he stood in the doorway, his white shirt open at the top, setting off his tanned face and revealing his strong neck. His dark eyes ran across her supine form draped upon the velvet chaise.

"Blake?"

He walked into the cottage and stood silently looking down at Frieda, her flowered dress in disarray about her waist, her cheeks wet with tears, and her pussy open to the wind. He did not say why he was not on his way to the airport. She did not ask. She reached one languid hand toward him. A sensuous half-smile on his lips, he held just the tips of her fingers in his two hands and looked into her eyes. She felt her whole being flow into her fingertips. He raised her hand to his lips. His mouth on her fingers brought a low moan from her throat. He moved his mouth along her arm, kissing each spot of skin as if he had never touched her before. Her skin bloomed under his warm breath as he moved his mouth toward her shoulder. Each kiss, each caress of his fingers on her skin sent tingles throughout her body. Each cell of her body wanted Blake's touch.

He opened her dress but did not remove it. Taking the fabric of the skirt in his hand, he let the cloth move through his fingers. He knelt beside the chaise and lay his face on her belly and reached under her, grasping her buttocks in his hands. He made no move to touch her moist vagina, as if his face on her stomach and his hands on her ass were more than any man could want. Frieda continued to moan softly, hungry for his touch. How had she lived so long without his mouth on her belly? She was overcome with the need to feel the length of him against her.

She put her arms around him and drew him to her. Deftly she opened the buttons on his white shirt and touched his fine chest, his dear stomach. She opened his belt, pulled down the zipper, and pulled him hard against her, belly to belly. Only the wind touched her pussy as they lay breathing together as one. Blake's mouth found hers and she eagerly opened her lips to him. His tongue filled her mouth, caressed her teeth, and reached toward her throat. She opened wider and wider, wanting to swallow him, dissolve all space between them. Her tongue moved eagerly across his teeth and met his tongue. Saliva ran on her face where tears had flowed before, before Blake had touched her.

His mouth moved down her neck to her breasts, her nipples erect and rising to meet his kisses. She arched her back and he slipped his arms under her, encircling her in his embrace. She buried her face in his chest, heard his heart pound loudly. This was Blake and not Blake, more than Blake.

Their bodies moved together, their breathing becoming faster, urgency building, their clothes dropping to the floor. She slipped out from under him, and he lay back upon the chaise while she touched his whole body with her hands and her eyes. Her fingers that had danced across the keyboard now wrote stories on the skin of the man she loved. He was her stranger and no stranger at all. She filled her hands with his marvelous cock and balls, brought her mouth to them, ran her tongue across each familiar and amazing centimeter of flesh along the length of his penis, felt the exquisite softness of the skin on his balls, rolled the mysterious inner jewels between her fingers. She knew Blake's penis almost better than parts of her own body, but there on the velvet chaise it tasted new and astonishing to her. It swelled in her mouth, pulsated against her tongue. She lifted her face and beheld this beautiful organ so wonderfully, perfectly suited to slide into her depths.

Without a word, Blake rose from the chaise and lifted her off her feet. He held her in his arms, gazing intently into her eyes, then lay her back upon the rose velvet chaise. Hungrily she drew him to her and let his penis slide into her like silk. Home,

Frieda thought. So perfectly home, his penis sliding in and out, stroking, caressing, remembering all the years of their loving. Her body moving, contracting and releasing, loving and reaching, together belly to belly, penis to vagina, cock to cunt, the breeze caressing their skin, the birds singing louder and louder matching the mounting crescendo of their bodies moving toward the peak of a new mountain.

I don't want this to ever end, she thought, willing their bodies to hold back from orgasm, tears springing into her eyes at the thought that too soon it would be over — but like a small craft nearing the edge of a waterfall, she was helpless to stop or slow the force rushing toward orgasm. Letting go of the last shreds of her customary care and control, like her heroine Amber, she surrendered. They had never in all their years together orgasmed at the same time, but there on the chaise in the little cottage with the lace curtains wafting in the breeze, an orgasm that had grown in them all the years of their marriage bloomed and burst into that little room with a cacophony of bird song outside.

They lay together silently, not moving, his penis now a quiet creature in her pussy overflowing with his come. She held him tenderly to her, loving the unmoving weight of him upon her, not wanting him to rise and leave. The loneliness of the morning cast its shadow on her.

"Come to Rio with me," he whispered in her ear, visions of lush tropical vegetation, the wild colors of parrots, and the scent of deep-hued jungle flowers in his voice.

"Oh, yes," she said, smiling, her fingers stroking his back and the first lines of a Brazilian mystery forming in her mind.

Nancy Ferreyra

After Amelia

Amelia's perfectly round mouth tugged at my nipple. Being passed around to so many strangers had stressed her out and she was suckling hard to calm herself, squishing her nose into the soft flesh of my breast and bumping her little fists against me. I stroked her head, smoothing wisps of brown hair. "Oh honey, it's okay. You're gonna go home with your Uncle Diego and Aunt Isabel soon." My brother and sister-in-law had agreed to take Amelia overnight so Miranda and I could spend some time together. We had booked a room here in this swanky hotel, planning to get "reacquainted."

I looked out over the patio railing at a glorious view of the San Francisco Bay, trying to imagine what the night would be like. After all these months, how would we begin? Before Amelia, I'd been able to seduce Miranda with a sultry stare and an intentionally exposed breast or shoulder. Her eyes would lock into mine and a flush would smarten her cheeks. I took great pride in my ability to penetrate my lover's reserved sexual nature and coax her into having sex almost anywhere. One of my most impressive coups was when I enticed her onto the balcony of a highrise where we were attending a community fundraiser. Once I had sparked her passion, she would not stop until we were both satiated.

But the baby had changed our lives so dramatically that

those lustful encounters were only dim memories. It seemed that neither of us had the energy or interest at the same time. It made me cringe to imagine us turning into an old married couple who only had scheduled sex on Friday nights or Sunday mornings.

I was responsible for initiating lovemaking tonight — Miranda had made it clear that she wasn't willing to risk being rejected again. But for the first time, I was unsure how to interest her. Now that my breasts were exposed six or seven times a day, the sight of them didn't have the same effect: When Amelia nursed, Miranda looked on with loving tenderness, nothing else. Twice, after the baby had dozed off while nursing, I'd caught Miranda eyeing my breasts where Amelia's puckered lips lingered an inch from my nipple. I had pulled Amelia close, pressing her temple against my sternum, Miranda's favorite place. Both times, Miranda had stared for a long minute with a look I couldn't identify before turning away from us. What was she feeling? Envy? Longing? Miranda used to nestle between my breasts after lovemaking, while I petted her head. Was she afraid that Amelia had taken her place? Or did she feel left out, thinking that Amelia and I shared a closeness that she wasn't a part of? Introducing this new person into our lives had shaken things up more than I had anticipated.

I wanted to talk about it, but didn't know how. When things were difficult between us, Miranda always brought them up. I tried to resolve things by *doing* something, not talking about it. One evening when Diego and Isabel had taken Amelia, over cartons of pad Thai and yellow curry vegetables I waited for Miranda to broach the topic, but she didn't. When we cuddled on the couch to watch a movie, I pulled Miranda close, cradling her head to my chest to show her that she hadn't lost her place. She sighed and let me hold her for a while before she raised her head to kiss me on the mouth. When I told her I still wasn't feeling sexual, she didn't hide her frustration. Untangling her limbs from mine, she perched on the edge of the couch and looked intently into my face, pulling her thoughts together. Then she told me that although we were still affectionate partners, she missed making love, connecting with me as a lover. I listened carefully, then tried to explain what was going on for me. But all I could say was that my body just didn't feel right, that I didn't want to be touched that way. She told me she accepted that, but she needed me to understand that she was closing down, that it was too hard to want something she couldn't have. She made it clear that the ball was now in my court.

I looked down into Amelia's grey-blue eyes, wide and staring straight into mine. I smiled and stroked her cheek. Releasing my nipple, she clucked her tongue against the roof of her mouth as she swallowed the last bit of milk. She caught her breath and let out a heartfelt sigh. Pressing my lips to her forehead, I was filled with her distinctive scent: a combination of talcum, breast milk and clothes softener.

"Are you finished?" I asked. "Or just taking a break?" I leaned her over my forearm and rubbed her back, trying to coax out a burp.

I buttoned my dress and turned to face the crowd, steadying Amelia's wobbly torso with one hand and pushing the joystick of my electric wheelchair with the other. I scanned the patio, searching for Miranda. Women in strapless gowns and men in linen suits stood in groups of threes and fours, sipping champagne and eating miniature *empañadas* and bite-sized bagels. I spotted Miranda, talking with Diego and Isabel. She was laughing, holding a tall full glass of champagne in her hand. Miranda didn't pay attention to clothes, whether or not they matched, or even if they fit that well. She only cared that

they were clean and that she wasn't missing anything important. Miranda's sister had let her opt out of wearing a
traditional bridesmaid's dress, so I'd picked out her black tailored slacks and a white sleeveless blouse. The afternoon heat
had forced her to finally shed her matching silk jacket, revealing her narrow, rounded shoulders and finely sculpted arms.

I watched Miranda, smiling as she talked to Diego and
Isabel. Nodding her head at something Diego said, she tucked
her golden hair behind her ear. A couple of inches shorter than
me, and lighter, Miranda was nonetheless pretty strong, able
to lower and lift me from most places. Before Miranda, I had
never been involved with a woman smaller than myself. Poor
planning on my part — to fall in love with one who could
barely lift me, never mind carry me for any long distance. And
while I'd gained twenty pounds, Miranda had lost weight since
Amelia's birth. Her lithe, toned body was the product of hours
spent at the pool and on the soccer field. I took a deep breath
and sighed.

How I missed her body. The feel of her smooth, warm skin
gliding over me, her lips and hands roving everywhere, but
always coming back to the same sweet places. Mostly I missed
her body under mine, her thighs wrapped around my hips, her
mouth grazing from one breast to the other while I pushed
into her deeply and slowly. When her fingers clutched the
small of my back, I would push faster, our hipbones bumping,
my cheek pressed against her forehead. When she came, she
would roll us onto our sides, pushing the dildo up into her one
last time, suckling intently on my breast.

Diego and Isabel walked into the hotel and Miranda turned,
flashing me her lazy grin. I remembered a morning about two
weeks ago: Miranda had been scampering around the house
getting ready for work. She had on her jeans and an undershirt, and was looking for a belt. I had showered and gone back

to bed and Amelia was napping. Miranda sat next to me on the edge of the bed, putting on her shoes and socks, and while we went over the day's schedule, I watched her backside: shoulders flexing as she pulled the laces tight on her shoes, the soft curve of her neck. I wrapped my arms around her hips, beckoning her to come back to bed with me.

"They're expecting me at work," she mumbled, glancing over her shoulder.

"Can't you go in the afternoon instead?" I asked.

"I need to come home in the afternoon and bathe Amelia."

We both knew Amelia's bath could wait until evening. Confused, I released her and leaned back against the pillow. She didn't look at me, but kept her flushed face down while she tucked in her shirt and buckled her belt.

When Miranda went into the other room to gather the rest of her stuff, I thought about my body. Of course she didn't want me. Not only had I gained weight since the baby, I was out of shape, the flesh hanging loosely from my arms, around my hips and thighs. My heavy breasts often leaked milk. Maybe that disgusted her. Before Miranda left, she poked her head in, hesitating for a few moments, then slipped her slender fingers from the door frame.

I hadn't really been ready for sex yet anyway. It had been several months since the birth, and I still hadn't gotten back all of my strength. What if I couldn't move the way I wanted to, touch her how I wanted to? What if I didn't respond the same way? I used to like Miranda to fondle and suck my breasts, but now the skin on my nipples was thick and tough; they weren't as sensitive. I didn't know how it would feel to have them touched when we made love.

At times I thought of Miranda while I fed Amelia. On the mornings when Miranda brought Amelia into the bed and curled up behind us, I would be filled with the same sensual

contentment I used to feel after making love with Miranda —
lying under the warm covers with Miranda's arm around my
waist, her soft breath on the back of my neck, and this tender,
perfect little creature feeding from my breast. I didn't know
how to put all of these experiences into words for Miranda. But
I wanted her to know, I wanted to tell her.

Miranda made her way through the crowd toward us, pausing at every third clique to chat briefly, before grinning at me
and moving purposefully in my direction until the next time
she was detained. This was a gathering of her family, and having introduced our daughter to everyone, she was completely
aglow. Her heart-shaped face shone, her grey eyes were bright.
The open joy on Miranda's face as she strode toward us
warmed my cheeks. I looked down at the top of the baby's
head and pretended to be fastening a button behind her neck.

"Hey, how's my angel?" Miranda knelt in front of Amelia
and me, smiling at each of us in turn. When Amelia caught
sight of Miranda's face, she flailed her plump arms, one hand
landing on Miranda's mouth.

"Diego and Isabel went to say goodbye to Laura and John,"
she said, her lips moving around Amelia's chubby fingers. She
took the baby in her arms and stood up. "Then they're gonna
take you home," she said to Amelia.

I looked up and saw Isabel leading Diego by the hand across
the patio. Diego reached for Amelia immediately. "Hey, little
Amelita. Are you ready to go home with your *tío* and *tía*?"

Sensing my desire to hold on to Amelia a bit longer, Diego
and Isabel gently convinced me it was time for them to go.
They assured Miranda and me that we could call if we wanted
to, but that Amelia would be fine.

Diego took a few steps toward me so Amelia's face was next
to mine. The deep baritone of his voice always put her to sleep.
I kissed her cheek. "Bye, bye, sweetie, we'll see you after your

morning nap, okay?" I whispered. Miranda kissed her on the top of her head, whispered tenderly and Amelia was gone. Watching Diego's back disappear, the skin on my chest felt bare. Without Amelia's body next to mine, I felt naked. Although we had spent several hours at a time apart from her, being away overnight felt different.

But it was time to fill the distance that had developed between Miranda and me, I reminded myself. I leaned my head on her shoulder.

Miranda took a deep breath. "How you doin', Trace?" she asked. "Need anything? More food? Something to drink?" She ran her hand down my spine, from the base of my neck to the small of my back. Goosebumps traveled down my arms.

"No thanks." I had eaten more than five of each *hors d'oeuvre* that had come my way. My appetite had tripled since Amelia was born. Miranda pulled up a chair and we sat at a table framed with black wrought iron, covered with a tempered glass top. "Are you having a good time?" she asked.

"Yeah," I said, my voice cracking a bit. I was nervous. I cleared my throat. "It's a nice reception. Beautiful day."

Leaning back, she looked up at the sky. "Isn't it, though?" She looked into my eyes. Her open gaze unnerved and mesmerized me at the same time. "Wow, our first night away from her. She's already four months old. Can you believe it?"

I shook my head and threaded my fingers through hers. "It's been a long time."

"It'll be nice," she said, swallowing some champagne. I leaned my knee against hers under the table and looked into her eyes, raising my eyebrows. We didn't notice Miranda's big bear of a father approaching until he tapped his hand on our table, a benevolent smile on his bearded face. "Hey, you two, we're heading inside for dinner."

Miranda tightened her grip on my hand, grinning up at him.

"Okay, Dad, we're on our way." She pushed her chair out and stood up. "Ready?"

"Actually, I have to use the restroom first," I said. "Can you come with me in case it's not accessible?"

"Sure," she said. Miranda led us through the patio, expertly judging the width of passages and either moving chairs or asking people to squeeze together in tighter clusters so I could pass. She glanced behind her every ten feet or so to be sure I hadn't gotten stuck behind. I followed her, wheelchair humming, through a dimly lit room with plush chairs and brocaded mirrors, into another room lined with toilet stalls. We stopped at the last one with a blue wheelchair sign on it. Miranda followed me into the long, wide stall, its green and white velvet walls completely enclosing us from floor to ceiling.

"You wanna go first?" I offered as she latched the door.

"Okay," she said, unbuttoning her pants. She sat down on the toilet.

"When you dumped our stuff in the room, did you notice if the bathroom was accessible?" Noticing the mirror on the back of the stall door, I adjusted the pads in my bra. Normally I'm small-breasted, but nursing Amelia had given me a bit of a bosom and I was taking advantage of it with a scoop neck dress that showed a little cleavage. Unfortunately, it also showed the pads I had stuffed in my bra to absorb the leaking breast milk.

Miranda tilted her head to the side, her long silver earring tickling her shoulder. "Yeah, it is." She shifted one hip and stuffed a wad of white toilet paper between her spread thighs. "The bed is huge. Looks like a king." She smiled sleepily as if she was lying against the plush pillows right now. Returning her smile, I glanced down at the few blond hairs peeking out from between her legs. She stood up and moved aside, buttoning her pants back up. When we traded places, my arm grazed the front of her silky blouse and I smelled her spicy cologne.

Miranda plopped down in my wheelchair, her eyes on me. "You look great in that dress," she said. "The green brings out your eyes. Did I tell you that?"

"I think you might have mentioned it," I murmured, lowering my eyes to the black and white tiles. After I finished, I flushed the toilet, reached for the grab bar and pushed myself up, my dress falling over my hips, my calves, the hemline tumbling around my ankles. Miranda was standing. Our eyes met.

"Sit back down," I said, my hand on her collarbone. I took a step toward her and she pulled me onto her lap. Sliding my arm around her shoulder, I looked into her clear grey eyes. A few lines creased the edges. "Hey," she said, a grin tugging at the corner of her mouth. She blinked slowly.

"Hi." I tucked a lock of her silky hair behind her ear with my fingertip and leaned my cheek against her temple. When I felt her hand on my hip, I closed my eyes and pressed my lips against hers, soft and sweet. Miranda tilted her head back and we kissed, our mouths tentative, the taste of champagne still on her tongue. Then she ran her lips over my neck, under my ear, and returned to my mouth, darting her tongue between my teeth. I put her palm over my breast to calm my pounding heart. Her fingers went to the top button of my dress and unfastened it, her kisses becoming sloppier, her mouth opening wider.

Miranda slid the top of my dress over my shoulders. She buried her face between my breasts, then planted wet kisses from my sternum, up my throat to my ear. "Hmm, Tracy, I've missed you."

Familiar stirrings gripped my belly, my thighs. "I know," I whispered. "I know."

I craved the feel of her skin. The buttons of her blouse were flat and the openings slippery, so I needed both hands to undo them. She watched my fingers, her chest heaving as I got down to the last two buttons. I tugged on the ribbed, cotton fabric of her undershirt.

"Take it off," I breathed. Clumsily she pulled it over her head. I slipped my hand across her round, firm breasts, catching her nipples between my fingers. Her skin was warm, like mine, from the afternoon heat. She unfastened my bra and stared at my breasts, my nipples just inches from her lips. I breathed deeply, each breath moving them closer to her mouth. Miranda pressed her lips to my throat and slipped the straps of my bra over my shoulders. I wanted to lie on top of her, curl my body around hers so tightly that I wouldn't know where I began and she ended. I opened my legs. My crotch was wet.

Miranda pulled away. "God, Tracy, what are we doing?" she whispered. "Let's check into our room."

But I didn't want to stop. The moment felt too fragile. When Miranda got up out of the wheelchair, I slipped my damp underpants down past my thighs and let them fall to the floor along with my dress. Miranda's fingers halted on the top button of her blouse, a blush coloring her cheeks. Sitting down, I took her hands and pulled her toward me. "I want you to touch me," I said.

She leaned over to kiss my mouth, then my shoulders, pushing me back against the chair. I cradled the crown of her head as she licked a wet trail around the curve of first one breast, then the other, then to my belly, her open mouth exploring every inch. She got down on her knees, her hands on my hips, my closed thighs before her lips. Her fingers kneaded my flesh, trying to spread my thighs apart. Wetness streamed across my middle ribs; my breasts were leaking. I tried to separate my knees, scooting my butt to the edge of the seat.

"This isn't working," I said. "I feel like I'm gonna fall."

"What do you want to do?"

"Let's move to the floor."

She planted a kiss on top of my pubic bone before getting to her feet. I backed the wheelchair away from the toilet and turned the power off, got to my feet and leaned on the velvet-covered wall, while she kicked off her shoes and pants.

"Help me down," I whispered. Miranda pressed her hips against mine and kissed me until my legs felt like rubber. I turned, pressing my back against her sleek skin, and she circled her arms around my middle, grasping her hands in front of me. I bent my legs as she slowly lowered me to the floor. The tile was shockingly cold against my bare skin. I raised my knees and spread my thighs.

Miranda looked me over; she noticed that my breasts were dripping. "You're . . ." she said. She looked from my breasts to my face, then at my breasts again.

"I'm leaking," I said. "It's okay. You can touch me."

"Are you sure? Do you need to pump?"

"No, I'm not full. I'm just . . . excited." I watched her face as she digested this information.

She blinked slowly, her hand playing with a lock of my hair. Then she nodded slightly and cupped my cheek in her hand. We kissed, sweetly at first, our breasts swaying, nipples lightly grazing one another's. Then my kisses became more insistent, pulling her tongue into my mouth, showing her what I wanted her to do to me. Miranda pulled me closer, and traced a smooth path around my thigh, resting her hand just inches from my throbbing cunt.

The floor was hard and cold against the bones in my back, but Miranda's body was warm, her skin hot against my belly, my chest. I ran my fingers lightly over her shoulders, down her spine to the small of her back, while her wet lips covered my throat, my chest. She looked into my face, her eyes dark with desire, before covering my mouth with hers. Wrapping my legs around her hips, I caressed the back of her knee with my foot.

From this position I couldn't really move, or raise my head to see anything. "I want to be on top," I mumbled. She rolled onto her back, sliding her body under mine, cursing when her shoulder hit the back tire of the wheelchair.

Pleased with the new position, I raised my hips above hers, spreading my thighs wide. I ran my fingers through strands of her golden, silky hair, spread out against a black square tile. She cupped my hips in her hands, then squeezed my thighs before reaching between my legs. When I felt her light touch on my bush, I sucked in a quick breath, and pulled her nipple into my mouth. She arched her back, pushing her breasts further into my greedy mouth, while she petted me, first with the back of her hand, then the pads of her fingers. I felt wet and wide, my cunt throbbing, wanting to feel her inside me. "Can I go inside?" she breathed. "Is it okay?"

"Uh huh," I whispered. "I want you to." We moaned in unison when she plunged her fingers into me. I rocked my hips in rhythm with her thrusting fingers. "Is it okay? Am I hurting you?" Her voice was thick and gravelly, her tone distracted.

"No." The fit of her hand in my cunt felt as gloriously thick as usual. "Do I feel the same?" I whispered.

"Yeah," she replied, her voice low. "You feel great." She fucked me slow and strong, her fingers making a clicking sound in my wet cunt. I lifted my body above hers and crawled forward, my knees and palms knocking against the flat tiles. She slid down the rest of the way, the moist skin on her back squeaking against the tile. I felt self-conscious about my stomach, so big and loose since the baby, and looked down to see if it was hanging as low as I imagined. I got a clear view of the top of Miranda's head, her chin turned up as her teeth nipped at my thighs, my belly. She slipped her fingers out of me and took my thighs in her hands.

"Come here," she muttered into my belly. I closed my eyes

and lowered my cunt to her mouth. She pulled back my lips and kissed my throbbing clit. Long, slow, deliberate kisses. Then she glided her tongue inside me, then out, traveling to the tip of my clit. My breath came out in puffs as I rocked my hips against her mouth, heat spreading from deep inside my gut. The palms of my hands were sore and my elbows ached from holding my weight. I was afraid they were going to give out. On the black tile below my chest I saw two little spots of watery milk gathering as it dribbled out of my swaying breasts. As Miranda covered my clit with her whole mouth, her tongue flicking hard and fast against me, I dropped to my elbows, panting and humping wildly against her face. I groaned with each hot flash as it rolled over me. Miranda ran her tongue over me a few more times, then raised her head to kiss my spasming belly. When she slid her body out from under me, I laid my cheek on the floor, my ass still in the air, the puddle of thin, sweet milk sticky against my chest.

Slowly I rolled onto my side, my hip falling against the wall with a thud, then sliding to the floor. Miranda lay down beside me, her cheeks bright pink, little beads of sweat on her forehead. I pressed my lips against hers, tasting the tang of my juices. "Still taste the same," I mused, burying my face in her neck.

"Hmm," she murmured, her voice low and hoarse in my ear. I lay still while she stroked the back of my head. Heat rose from her body; her heart was pounding wildly. She flung her leg over my hip and kissed me, pressing her warm, wet bush against my thigh. Reaching behind her, I traced a path following the line of her cheek.

I cupped my palm around her cunt and stroked her, my fingers getting tangled in her wet, matted hair. Spreading her lips, I squeezed her slippery clit while she planted hot, random kisses on my chin, throat, collarbone. I wanted to fuck her badly, put my hand inside her and make her pant and moan, but I wanted her to be ready, so I held on, waiting for a cue. Finally she pushed her ass away from my leg, toward my hand, and I dipped my fingers into her. Fucking her with only three fingers at first, I pushed them in and out slowly. In the mirror on the back of the stall door, I watched us: her thigh draped over my hip, my forearm pressed into her crack, my fingers hidden inside her.

When she pushed her hips back against my hand I knew she wanted more. Slipping around to her front, I thrust my hand inside her, pushing in all five fingers up to my knuckles. Curling my fingertips around the curve of her cunt, I pulled my hand out some, keeping my fingers inside her. I fucked her this way, pushing my hand in a little further each time until my palm was all the way inside her, almost up to my wrist. She rolled onto her back, pulling me with her, rocking her hips toward mine. I used my bent knee to thrust my hand inside her.

"Oh, Miranda," I whispered, my cheek against her temple. "I've missed you so much." She nuzzled one breast then the other, her mouth still avoiding my erect, throbbing nipples. "Let me take you," I urged. I followed the rhythm of her contracting cunt, thrusting when I felt the pull, so that I could be inside her even further. Clutching my ass tightly, she groaned as she came. Her lips grabbed my nipple, and I moaned, moving my chest toward her face. She twisted her middle, tossing us onto our sides, orgasms rolling over her like waves. With each one, she groaned, suckling noisily on my breast.

Miranda released my nipple and nestled her face between my breasts. I slipped my hand out and wrapped my arm around her shoulder, pressing my lips to the top of her sweaty head.

After a while, she kissed me, the sweet milk still on her lips. I smiled.

She shook her head slowly. "It felt so weird to touch your breasts," she said. "I wanted to, and I didn't want to."

"I thought so," I said.

"How did it feel?"

"It felt good."

"Yeah? It didn't feel wrong? Like I was trying to take Amelia's place?"

"No," I said. "You're my lover, my partner." I didn't think lying on the floor of a public bathroom was the place to reveal to her my sensual feelings about our daughter. We could talk more later. "Hey, we better get back to the reception," I said. "I'll bet they're finished with dinner."

Miranda sat up. "The toasts! I'm supposed to do one of those after dinner!" She looked around for her blouse.

We dressed quickly, checking each other to be sure our clothes were buttoned correctly. When I put my bra back on, I asked Miranda to get clean nursing pads out of my bag. She knelt before me and slipped them into my bra with the same tenderness as when she changed Amelia's diaper. But then her fingers lingered, and she pressed her parted lips against mine. I reminded her that today was her sister's big day and buckled her belt. We left the bathroom, a shy grin on both our faces. Our lives were going to be different for sure since Amelia had joined us — but not *too* different.

Kate Dominic

The Album

Kris and I keep a special photo album, one that's just the two of us together. No family, no friends, no professional accomplishments. Just us. Even the wedding pictures in there are strictly personal — me eating the cake from his fingers, him taking my garter off with his teeth, the two of us sleeping naked in each other's arms early the next morning. He actually got up and set the timer for that picture, cuddling back up against me just as the flash went off.

Over the years, we've made a habit of including everyday photos along with the special ones. It's our journal, although the album itself isn't particularly fancy — a plain leather binder with acid-free pages. Whole months can go by without our taking it down off the shelf. Other times, we keep it open on the dresser while we're deciding what to add next. But like any good book, it opens to some pages automatically.

The picture of us at the biker bar is one of my favorites. "Melissa and Her Pet," the caption reads. Just two leather dykes, dressed to kill in black and silver, sitting at a table with the end of a leash barely visible in my hand. It was our fifth anniversary, and the waitress took the picture. Kris' drag was perfect. Not that it doesn't seem strange to call cowhide and chains drag. But he was dressed to kill. The shot doesn't capture the smoky, sweaty ambiance of the bar.

Not quite. But we'd met in a bar, and somehow that made the picture perfect.

We met in one of those dives down on Sunset Boulevard. Kris was fronting a gay punk band from D.C. that was opening for one of the local big names. I walked in the door with my actor friends. As my eyes adjusted to the darkness and my ears numbed to the assault from the speakers, I looked up into the glare of the stage lights — at the most gorgeous human being I'd ever seen. He was obviously a guy. He was dancing in his jockey shorts, and no fake parts ever moved the way his did when he thrust his hips forward. He wasn't hard, just hung.

His chest was very muscular, despite his slender build. I could see his nipple rings move beneath the glitter of his sleeveless Judy Garland T-shirt as he danced. It was his face that really drew me in, though. Kris was truly beautiful, in the classic artistic sense. Soft hazel eyes accented with a minimum of the black kohl outlining obligatory for a punk singer, vibrantly full lips, and delicate bones framed by a cloud of straight blonde hair that just brushed the edges of his shoulders. A thickly studded leather slave collar covered his Adam's apple, and as he pranced around in his shiny combat boots, belting out one indecent song after another, his wicked smile sparkled in his eyes. I blushed when he bent over from the waist, knees locked straight and feet spread wider than his shoulders, and wiggled his ass up against the bassist. The other guy actually moved his guitar to one side so Kris could rub against his crotch. It was obscene and sexy, and I was in lust with Kris from the moment he stood up, vigorously rubbed his crotch, then looked at the audience in mock surprise as the front of his sweaty white jockeys swelled. Damn, that man is an exhibitionist!

Ed, one of the guys in our crowd, sputtered every time he looked at Kris. Now Ed is straight, straight, straight. But he kept shaking his head and saying, "I'm so glad I'm married! If that guy were in a dress, I'd chase his ass until I caught it! Damn, he's beautiful!" Then he'd shake his head and take another long swig of beer.

Cynthia, his wife and my former roommate, just cuffed him on the shoulder and laughed. It takes a lot to faze Cyn. After three beers she took Ed's car keys, then we left the rest of our friends and went upstairs to sit down and watch the show. Cyn was thoroughly enjoying Ed's dilemma. She had her hand in his lap under the table but I could see her arm moving, and she had a really evil grin on her face. Every once in a while, Ed would close his eyes and groan, and Cyn would lean over and tongue his ear while she poured another drink down his throat. She kept telling him he was going to have sweet dreams that night. I figured he probably would if she kept that up.

They were so engrossed with each other I knew they wouldn't miss me if I found some action on my own, so I pretty much kept my eyes glued to the stage, and to Kris, for the rest of the set. Just watching him gave me a major case of the hots, which is frustrating as all hell when you know the guy is gay.

I almost didn't recognize him when I bumped into him, literally, a couple of hours later. The headlining band was setting up and I didn't see Kris come up in back of me to lean against the balcony rail. I heard Ed groan, and when I looked at my buddy, his eyes were somewhere over my shoulder. Cyn just laughed, put her hand over his eyes and pulled him down against her breasts.

"Drunk," she grinned up at the space in back of me.

I heard this really clear tenor laugh behind me. I turned around, bumping into a very solid thigh, and there was Kris. He looked different with clothes on. Same T-shirt, but pink spandex pants and a wide black leather belt. He'd shed most of the makeup, but damn, he was still gorgeous. It took me a second to get over my initial shock at seeing him up close. Then I managed to clear my throat and compliment him on his band's set.

"Cute song about the ice cube blow jobs," I smiled.

"You heard us?" he asked excitedly. Kris is one of those people whose whole face comes alive when he talks. "There weren't that many people here when we played. I was afraid that'd affect the CD sales, but they're really moving."

Cyn nodded him towards the chair where Ed's feet were resting; Ed was passed out, so Kris carefully pushed his feet onto the floor and sat down. The headlining act was starting, so Kris pulled his chair right up next to me and leaned over so we could talk, or at least try to, between songs. It was too loud to really hear, though. When it became obvious he was reading my lips, I raised my eyebrows at him and he just gave me this big grin and pulled back the edge of his hair. He'd put in earplugs. I grinned back and discreetly lifted my hair so he could see I had, too. I think Cyn must have thought we were nuts with how hard we started laughing. It was right then that one of his band's publicity guys snapped a picture of us. It was supposed to have been a pic of Kris enjoying the rest of the show, but the photo didn't fit quite with the band's image, so the guy gave Kris the picture. It's the first one in our album. Kris called it "Fate."

After the show, he asked me out for coffee. We helped Cyn drag Ed to the car and waved them off. Then we walked down a couple of blocks to a little diner and split a piece of pecan pie. Three cups of coffee later, Kris shocked the hell out of me. He was telling me about how the band had started when he stopped in mid-sentence. He leaned over and he kissed me, full on the lips. All I could do was stare at him, stunned.

Kris is straight.

I suppose I should qualify that a bit. Kris is at least as straight as I am. Neither one of us could claim to be a Kinsey 0.

We're both young and horny and we work in entertainment. But our same-sex flings had usually been one-nighters. Anyway, we spent the weekend together, getting to know each other. Yes, biblically as much as anything else. Like I said, we were young and horny, and there's a whole lot of chemistry between us.

On Monday he flew back to D.C., and we started a long-distance romance. His band toured up and down the East Coast, and I landed a series of walk-ons as well as a few commercials, enough to pay the bills. Especially my phone bills, which by Fall were getting pretty impressive, even at night rates.

The band came back out a couple of times over the next eight months. By then, Kris and I were getting serious. That April we discovered that neither one of us had been sleeping with anyone else since we'd met. It's quite a shock to find out you've fallen in love with someone without even realizing it. That night he asked me to marry him. How old-fashioned, huh? And I said yes.

That summer the band moved out to L.A., and in August, a year after we met, Kris and I got married. Ed and Cyn stood up for us.

I have to admit, I'd never realized how much I'd like being married. We're both vegetarians and we can both cook, which probably kept us from starving that first year. But I really think I could have lived on the sex alone. We'd both tested negative, so I went on the pill, and we went crazy with a general frenzy of uninhibited fucking. We discovered we both loved missionary, and we spent hours with his hair and sweat falling down onto my face as he glided into me. There were times we went at it until we were so sore that the only thing that could soothe us was the thick, slippery cream of our orgasms.

We're also supportive of each other's careers. Having two performers in the same family can be a real downfall for a lot of couples. We stuck it out, and during our second year we both started working more regularly, which helped a lot financially. But we also started spending less time in bed together, and more time sleeping when we were there. The sex was still good — comforting and fulfilling, and to this day, just thinking of Kris lying in bed with a hard-on is enough to make me wet. But some of the excitement was gone, along with the frequency, and every once in a while I missed the frantic edge we used to have.

I hadn't realized that Kris was missing it too. It took us a while to figure out that communication is something you have to work at in a marriage. But I remember to the minute when we started talking about our sex life. It was just after our second anniversary, the day Kris called up out of the blue to ask me to lunch. I'd taken a temp job as an administrative assistant at a recording studio so we'd have some extra money for vacation, and he'd been working down the street that morning. At noon, the receptionist called to say Kris was waiting for me in the lobby, and I walked up front to meet him.

I'd gone all the way into the room before I realized the person standing in front of me was my husband. Then, it was a good thing I was too stunned to move, because otherwise I probably would have fallen over from the shock. If I hadn't seen him with scarves tied around his neck so many times before on stage, I'd never have recognized him. Or should I say "her." Kris was wearing a demure Laura Ashley floral print sundress, matching espadrilles, and a stylishly floppy straw hat with a large pink ribbon that complemented the scarf tied loosely around his neck. His, or rather her, hair was impeccably styled, a froth of carefree waves through which she brushed her carefully manicured nails. In short, she was beautiful. And as she winked seductively, each and every one of those lechers I was working with gave her an appreciative once-over as they walked out the door to lunch.

Before I could collect myself enough to say anything, Kris swooped over and embraced me like a long-lost friend, carefully bussing my cheek so as not to mess up her makeup as she whispered in my ear, "Your girlfriend has the hots for you, babe. Play your part. I've got us a hotel room a couple of blocks away."

Linking her arm in mine, Kris turned us towards the door. "Thanks, Jenna honey. You're such a doll."

"Glad to help, Krissie." As usual, the vacuous young lady gracing the receptionist's desk giggled as she spoke. "I think it's so neat when roommates stay in touch. Imagine, after three whole years, you only have one day in town."

Krissie hugged her breast to my arm. "You sure you don't mind covering for Melissa for a couple of hours? We have so much to catch up on."

"Oh, no problem," Jenna replied. "Everybody will be tied up at that finance meeting the rest of the afternoon anyway. Just have her back by 4:00 and they'll never know she was missing."

Jenna twittered, then blushed with pleasure as Krissie handed her a disposable "tourist" camera to take a couple of quick pictures of the two "roommates" together.

As we walked out into the sunlight, Krissie didn't give me much chance to talk. She linked her arm in mine, pressed her bosom against me, and kept up a running, steamy commentary about how nice it was to be back in L.A. where "grrrls" didn't have to worry about having their afternoons interrupted. Most of what she was saying was lost in the whir of the noon traffic, so I just let her lead me down the sidewalk, the light scent of her perfume tickling my nose. Ten minutes later, she swept me into a reasonably nice hotel room where there was a bucket of Chardonnay chilling on the nightstand, the covers were turned back on a queen-sized bed, and the sun streamed in through the gauze privacy curtains of a fifth-story picture window.

I'd gotten over my initial shock, so I turned to my erstwhile roommate and said, "To what do I owe the honor of your visit, Krissie?"

Kris came up to me and gently drew the tip of his finger over my cheek and down the side of my face. "We're getting too complacent, Liss," he said quietly. His fingers were soft and silky as he stroked further along the edge of my neck, making me shiver. "We're too good for that." The finger dropped lower, tracing the outline of my breast, then rubbing slow circles over the nipple. "I want to see the sparkle back in your eyes when I touch you." I could feel my skin reach for him and he smiled as the tip hardened under his touch.

"Now I'm your girlfriend, Krissie, your former roommate who's back in town just for one day, and I want a slow afternoon of the kind of girl-to-girl sex you used to have." As Krissie spoke, she started softly milking my breasts with her enamel-tipped fingers. "I want to get lipstick on your nipples and lick your clit, maybe even make you come all over my face the way you do when I press your G-spot just right with a nice, thick dildo. I brought a couple with me, you know.

"When I'm done I'm going to give you my pussy to play with, Liss. Maybe if I'm really lucky, you'll suck my girly clit. You've never seemed to mind that it's bigger than most grrrls'." She sucked softly on my lower lip as I finally smiled. "What do you say, love?"

I could feel Krissie's "clit" pressing against my leg, and all of a sudden, even though I knew it was Kris, I mean I really knew that, the whole time we were there, suddenly he was Krissie. I was kissing another woman in a way I hadn't for a long, long time, and I wanted her. I mean, my pussy was sopping wet and I wanted grrrl sex like you wouldn't believe.

"Krissie," I moaned, just her name, and I melted into her arms. Then we were kissing, the soft, wet, tasting kisses that usually only two women can share. I took her hat off and buried my face in her neck so that her perfume made even her sweat seem feminine. Salty and sexy and so very, very sweet.

Every giggle was part of the foreplay. Krissie stripped me naked, then stood me in front of the mirror so I could watch her playing with my body. She left pink circles of lipstick around my areolas when she suckled me, her soft hands playing my pussy with her carefully manicured fingertips.

When I tried to touch her in return, she shook her head and touched her sticky fingers to my lips. "This first one's for you, sweetheart," she murmured, shivering slightly as I licked. "Just let me make you feel good."

So I did. I lay down on the bed with my legs spread and Krissie got between them. The soft cotton of her dress brushed against my naked thigh as she nuzzled my breasts, licking and sucking and teasing. When my skin was so sensitized I could hardly stand it anymore, she kissed her way down my belly. Then she settled herself between my legs, took my hips in her hands and lifted me to her lips. It was Kris' strength, yet now somehow feminine as she slowly kissed my labia like she was making love to my mouth. First the outer lips, then the inner ones. And when she reached my clit, she played it like it was my tongue. With infinite patience, she stroked and sucked and nibbled like we were kissing. My whole body relaxed, and slowly, tenderly, Krissie's wonderful, loving mouth drew a climax from deep in the pit of my belly. She laughed, her tongue working constantly as I thrashed beneath her, screaming out my pleasure. When I finally collapsed onto the bed, she lapped the cream of my orgasm off me with her suddenly sandpapery tongue.

When I recovered enough to move, Krissie finally let me undress her. I drew away each piece of her clothing slowly, revealing my lover's body bit by bit. Except for a small triangle above her crotch, she'd shaved her whole body. Everywhere, her skin smelled and tasted of silky, soft peaches.

Krissie insisted I leave her underwear on, though she finally acquiesced to my taking her bra off when I told her how much I wanted to suck on her nipple rings. I reassured her that several of my female lovers had been small-breasted, so she didn't need to be self-conscious. Then I took her nipples, first one, then the other, into my mouth and worked them until she was moaning.

Though she insisted on keeping her panties on, and her garter belt and stockings, I untied the ribbons that held the slit crotch of her panties closed, then worked my lips over her thoroughly engorged and extremely large clit. It didn't take long at all for Krissie to come. She shook in my arms as I sucked her with the same tender intensity she'd given to me.

When she'd recovered, Krissie got out a couple of curved dildos, and we lay side-by-side and brought each other to "G-spot" orgasms that left the sheets soaked. Sated, we curled up and napped, and when I awoke, Krissie was finger-fucking me, not quite fisting me, but almost. I was so hungry for her that I came all over her hand. Again.

At home that night, we started talking, and well, we learned to talk about sex. Not just idle talk, but real communication. We talked about our fantasies, both the things we wanted to do and the things that were best left in our heads. And we've kept on talking — and doing — ever since. We're performers, and, I admit, we're sort of exhibitionists. And we like variety. So we've acted out a lot of our fantasies. We've been girlfriends and boyfriends. We've traded genders. We've done bondage and S/M in exotic scenarios. But it's always been just the two of us. When we're brutally honest with each other, we need and want the security of monogamy. We want to be all the people the other one needs sexually. Luckily, we're good enough thespians that we've been able to pull it off. So far, at least.

I'd be lying if I said it was all easy. Mostly it has been; but the most difficult time for us was pretty much the year we both turned 30. Some people call it the seven-year-itch. All I know is that Kris suddenly got so hungry for man-sex that for the first time, we were afraid for our relationship.

On the night he came home shaken because he'd almost picked up some guy after a show, I figured I only had one card left to play. Now I'm not a man and I've never wanted to be, although I've played one — successfully — on stage. Usually it's Kris who does the drag. But all I could think of was the day Krissie came to visit me at work. She'd been there for me. So I cut my hair really short, changed my clothes, and threw myself into a new character like I was playing for my life.

That's how we ended up in a gay leather bar near Modesto late one night about a week later, me with a slave collar on and Kris in a particularly nasty mood. We'd ridden into town on Ed's Harley, and after a quick stop to get a hotel room, we headed out for the evening. You can see the look on Kris' face in the picture the woman at the front desk took of us as we left on the bike. He was feeling mean and toppish and he was treating me the way he would some trick he'd picked up in an alley.

We were both wearing leather pants and jackets and our old but well-shined black boots, the ones we wear when we're doing heavy S/M. This time, though, beneath the jacket Kris was bare-chested except for a leather and nickel harness that gleamed like his nipple rings, and he had a diamond stud in his left ear. His hair was clubbed back with a leather bootlace and he hadn't been near a razor for three days, so his face seemed dirty as well as unshaven. Like I said, Kris looked mean, and I looked pissed. It's an unusual picture for us. Normally, we're smiling. But not that time. I'd become my husband's untrained little slave boy and was wearing the other earring in my right ear, just above where the leash clamped to the D-ring in my collar.

It was late when we got to the bar. Most everybody else there was at least half-drunk. As part of our characters, we looked pretty wasted too, although Kris had only been sipping at his bourbon and I'd just spilled some beer on my T-shirt to get the smell. I didn't want to get the shirt too wet, because although I'd bound my breasts, they'd still be noticeable if my nipples got too hard.

We were at a table in a dark corner, and I was starting to get more than a little annoyed at how often Kris was yanking on my leash. The room was crowded, and except for the occasional tug, he was ignoring me, trading crude comments with a group of guys around the table. I was getting even more uncomfortable from the rather sizeable butt plug he'd shoved up my ass when we first got to the hotel. He'd said he wanted his boy ready for him, and by midnight the "boy" was real convinced that the plug had stretched his anal muscles wide enough for a truck to drive through. The leather pants held the plug in tightly, and I was horny from squirming against it. Especially after the vibration of the bike ride.

Suddenly, Kris reached up and grabbed a handful of my hair, at least as much as he could of it, and shoved my face down hard against the wet, beer-covered table.

"What the fuck?!" I snapped, barely remembering to keep my voice low.

He yanked viciously on my hair. It didn't really hurt, it was more for show, but it startled me and I yelped. He'd never treated me like that before. He leaned over and growled in my ear, "You need some training, boy. I want your ass, and I want it now!"

I couldn't believe what I was hearing. I felt his hand on my hip, then the slow slide of the zipper moving down the back of my leather pants. I panicked. Shit, we were in a gay leather bar way to hell and gone in the middle of nowhere, and those guys would have killed us if they'd found out I was a chick. I was struggling against Kris when suddenly, I felt a strange pair of hands grab my forearms and slam me down against the table.

"Stop fightin', boy!" the voice snapped. "Your daddy wants your ass, he gets it!"

"Bullshit!" I yelled back, my voice higher than it should have been, but no one seemed to notice.

I jumped and gasped as Kris slapped me hard across the ass. Then the cool air kissed my crack and asshole as the zipper came down the rest of the way, and, mortified, I froze as Kris yanked the butt plug out of my ass. I mean, right there in front of all those people he pulled that plug out and dumped it in his drink! The other guy was laughing so hard the table was shaking, and his friends crowded around to make sure no one would disturb us.

Then I heard the quick tear of a condom wrapper, and the next thing I knew, Kris was bending over me, his weight pressing me hard into the edge of the table, and his thick, hot cock slid up my ass. Right there in the bar, with a good dozen people watching us, he was fucking me over a dirty, wet table.

Now Kris knows how much I like having sex in public, when we act like we're alone but we really know people are watching us. But this was way beyond anything I'd bargained for. Fortunately, my ass was so loose that he slid right in. The others may have thought it was a rough fuck, but he used that butt plug specifically because it was just the right size to get me ready for his cock. And he'd stuffed half a tube of lube up me when he'd put the plug in, so I was slick inside. I still struggled, though. The other guy was holding me down and I was just mad enough that it felt good to fight, especially since by then I was pretty sure the other guy was strong enough to keep me from getting away.

It was odd. I'd never had any rape fantasies. I sure as hell never wanted to be raped in reality. But suddenly, being held helpless while Kris pounded into me brought out a wildness I'd never felt before. I was scared to death those guys would discover I was a chick, and yet all I could think about was how hot it was for Kris to be fucking me in front of all those people. I climaxed from the anal stimulation alone. It was rough and fast, and when Kris was done he just pulled out, stuffed the icy plug back up my ass, and zipped my pants closed again.

I was still gasping when the other guy let go of me and Kris dragged my head up off the table, kissing me so hard his teeth drew blood. I could taste the copper on my lips as he said, "Your ass is mine again, boy, as soon as we get back to the hotel. Now move it!"

The people standing around were still laughing as Kris tossed a twenty on the table for a round of beer. Then he dragged me out the door, threw me on the bike, and took me back to the our room.

It was the most violent night we've ever spent together, and it turned me on incredibly: I knew, at a very fundamental level, that all I had to do was say "stop" and he would.

But I didn't say it. I stayed in character. I argued with him and mouthed off, telling him I'd never submit to him. I wasn't the least bit surprised when he stuffed my shirt in my mouth, threw me over the end of the bed, and whipped my bare ass with his belt until I was screaming. I knew I'd have bruises. It hurt like hell, and he was swinging the belt full out, with the buckle wrapped around his fist and the strap burning into my ass cheeks. But I wouldn't say "stop." I'd never played the part of an untrained biker boy before, of Kris' boy, and I wanted to do it. When he fucked me again, this time without a rubber, he put me on all fours doggy style so he was banging against my sore ass with each stroke, then he reached around and pulled on my clit, "jacking off my little slave boy cock," he called it. And he waited to come until he felt my orgasm shudder through my body.

I cried myself to sleep on his shoulder. My ass hurt, but that wasn't why I was crying. It was just so intense. So raw and violent. We'd brought out parts of ourselves we'd never let each other see before. When I brushed my hand across Kris' cheek, I felt tears running down into his hair. We clung to each other with the strength of those who have fought a war together and won, but now had to live with the knowledge of the demons that lived inside us.

The next morning, our actual anniversary, I fucked Kris with a strap-on. I woke up to find him spooned in front of me, pressing his ass back against me in his sleep. I cuddled against him for a while, listening to the soft purr of his snoring. Then I carefully disentangled myself, slipped out of bed, and got out the harness. I hadn't told him I'd brought it. I just put it on, along with my leather jacket and a motorcycle cap, and splashed on some of the male cologne I'd been wearing on the trip. Then I climbed back into bed, pulled Kris' top leg up towards his chest, and started playing with his asshole.

It didn't take long before he was moaning in his sleep. He was relaxed and loose as I stretched him, stuffing lube up his butt. He didn't wake up until the head of the dildo slipped into him, but then he woke up fast.

"What the fuck?" he grumbled, trying to lower his leg. He stopped only when he felt my fingernails digging into his thigh.

"I'm fucking you, boy," I said, low and mean. I slid my hand over his hip, slapping him sharply when he jumped as I slid further into him. "You're my little pussy boy this morning."

"Dammit, Lissa! How big is that thing? It's splitting me in two!" Kris can be grumpy in the morning, and he was tense as a bowstring. But my butt was still sore from the night before, so even though I stopped moving, I was in no mood to back out.

"Shut up and hold still," I growled. It was hard keeping my voice that low, but I felt I needed to stay in character. "If you fight, it's going to hurt. And I don't want to hurt you. But I am going to fuck you. I'm going to fuck your tight little ass until you shoot all over the bed. So relax, boy." On the word "relax," I pushed in a tiny bit further, hearing him hiss.

Finally, I felt his hips give and he moaned into the pillow. Then his shoulders twitched as his whole body untightened and he shook his head, laughing softly, "Whatever you say, sir. But may I please roll over and stick my ass in the air so I'm at the right angle to take your hard, hot cock? Sir?"

"Okay, boy," I said gruffly, trying to keep from smiling as I slapped his ass again. I let go of his leg, but I didn't pull out. I made him roll over with me in him, and I didn't back up when he lifted his pelvis to put a pillow underneath, just listened to him grunt as the fake dick slid in a little bit further. To tell you the truth, I didn't want him to see how big that latex cock was. If he'd had any idea what I was fucking him with, he would have pitched a fit.

When he was in position, I made him rest his head on his folded arms. "You can drop down and rub your cock against the pillow if you want, but you can't touch it," I said. Then I straddled his legs and pressed a little bit further into him.

I pressed further, and further, leaning onto his back as I moved forward. Sometimes I'd pull back and fuck in and out a few times, to keep him really loose. And on each stroke I'd go in a little bit further. But I still hadn't bottomed out.

That dildo was huge. It was ten inches long and two inches around, and I slid it damn near all the way up his ass.

"Jeez, Lissa. I can feel that thing almost to my throat," he whispered, grinding his hips against me. Then he got real still, and I suddenly realized he was looking in the mirror by the side of the bed.

"You want to watch your ass getting fucked, boy?" I asked quietly, knowing he was going to watch one way or the other. So I slowly and deliberately started backing out of him, not all the way, just until only the head was in him. I could see his eyes getting wider as he watched the monster pull out, then his whole body stiffened as I slowly started pressing back in again.

"Jesus, Lissa! That's too big! Really, I mean it! Stop!" He gasped and tightened hard beneath me.

I froze. He'd said stop and I did, in mid-stroke. But I didn't pull out. Instead, I rested my weight fully onto my legs and massaged his shoulders. "Relax, boy," I said, calmly, still staying in character and hoping he'd be able to drop back into the scene. "It's not too big. You've already had it in you.

"Come on, boy. You want to be fucked. You need to be fucked." I traced my fingers up his spine and smiled as I felt him shudder. "Relax and let me give you what you need. You know I'll stop if you really can't take it."

For the longest time he just lay there, looking at the dildo in the mirror. Tension gradually drained out of his shoulders. I dragged my hand down his back and caressed his lower butt cheeks, where his thighs met his lower curves.

"Give me your ass, boy. You know how much I want it. And I'll make you feel real good." I carefully massaged the tautly stretched skin surrounding the dildo, gently relaxing and stretching him. "Tell me you want it, boy. Tell me so I can fuck you. So I can press your hot come right up out of your ass."

A very long minute later, Kris relaxed underneath me. Then he looked back over his shoulder and laughed shakily. "Okay, sir. But will you kiss me, so I'm not so afraid?"

"Of course I will, boy." I bent over, opening my mouth, and gave him my tongue to suck on. Then I slowly started pressing into him again. He moaned softly as I slid further down. When my weight was resting full on him and I was deep in his ass, he whispered, "Please, sir. Please fuck your boy." I gave him one more deep, passionate kiss, then I leaned back up, grabbed his hips, and started fucking him hard — long, sure, deliberate strokes. He whimpered and twitched beneath me. Then, on one stroke, I moved just a bit differently, pushing down towards the front of his belly just a bit more, and suddenly he arched up and gasped like he couldn't get enough air into his lungs. I froze.

"That hurt, boy?" I asked, holding myself motionless.

"No, sir!" He gasped. "Please, sir. Please," His whole body was shuddering like he was suddenly very cold or scared. Then with a long, low moan, he dropped his head back on his arms and whispered. "Please, sir. Do it again."

Yeah, I grinned. I arched into him, a long, slow glide that made him moan with pleasure, then I pulled back. And when I slid in again, Kris let out a high, keening cry and his whole body shook as I pressed down hard into him. I didn't think he'd ever stop coming as that hard latex dick pressed comeloads of his semen right straight out of his prostate. The vibration of his body was almost enough to make me come. And still he kept shuddering.

When his body collapsed onto his arms, I pulled out. I took off the harness, lay down on the bed and ordered him onto all fours over me. His arms and legs were still shivering as I took his soft, sticky cock in my mouth and let it rest there, tonguing it gently while I slid my fingers in and out of his loose, well-fucked asshole. Then I told him to suck my hard man cock until I came.

"Yes, sir," he whispered, groaning against my hands as he took my comparatively very tiny cock into his mouth. But he sucked and played it for all he was worth, like a good little slave boy. It took me about two heartbeats to come all over his face, and without being told, he dutifully licked the cream from my pussy. When he finally turned around and collapsed into my arms, we both started laughing. We laughed until tears streamed down our faces.

"Damn, Lissa." he choked, shaking his head as he pulled the dildo from the harness and looked at it. "What the hell ever made you think you could get that up my ass?"

I shrugged. "You said you needed to be man-fucked, and this was as 'manly' as I could get!"

Then we were both laughing again. Before we left the hotel, we had the manager take another picture of us on the bike. The album captions say, "Before, and After." And we didn't make a journal entry to go with that trip. We're the only ones who need to know the details. Beyond that, the looks on our faces say it all.

This last picture, "Ten Years," is the one the concierge took of us as we were leaving for the opera in San Francisco last weekend. We decided to reverse genders that night, so Kris wore a glittering strapless gold lamé ball gown with a *faux* fur stole and the most realistic looking costume pearls I've ever seen. He was stunning. I wore a black tux and, as the picture shows, I've finally mastered makeup to show just a hint of a five o'clock shadow.

The performance was wonderful. We didn't even try to talk, just sat there quietly holding hands while the music flowed over us. When we got back to the room, I fucked him with the strap-on while I fingered his enormous clit until he shot all over the bed. And he gave my little clitty cock the most wonderful blow job, licking and sucking in all the right places while he wiggled a finger up my ass. I came like gang-busters.

But this morning, this precise morning, it's been exactly one decade since we first promised ourselves to each other. So we celebrated like any other long-time married couple. We had breakfast at home in our own bed. We took a long, slow sexy shower together. And then Kris climbed on top of me, plain old missionary position, his biceps flexing over me as he took his weight on his arms while he glided in and out, in and out, with all the timing we've learned so well over the years. When I couldn't hold back any more, when I cried out as my orgasm washed over me, I felt the deep, swelling thrust as Kris surged into me, his semen bathing my cervix — so deeply, profoundly satisfying. And so hot my body curled around him.

As I dozed off, I could feel myself smiling against his lips. This time, we didn't take a picture. But over the years I've learned to know Kris pretty well: I have no doubt I'll see a flash in my sleep some time before tomorrow morning.

Deborah Bishop

The Portrait

Lily remembered when she'd first wanted Adam to paint her. Not her portrait, as her parents had commissioned him to do, but *her*. Her body.

Her desire for him had evolved in layers along with her image in oils. For three weeks she'd watched him seduce the canvas with color — a stroke of purple, a touch of white, a vigorous rub of crimson — and she'd nearly gone out of her mind with the sensuality of his movements. She had witnessed this mostly from her seat across from him. But once, in the early stages of that first portrait, he'd allowed her to peek around his wide shoulders to watch him work. She'd wanted to seduce him then.

All she could think of was how his artistic brilliance simply didn't jibe with his Dallas Cowboy physique and steelworker's hands: great, clumsy-looking paws in raging conflict with the beauty they created. Now, twenty years later, she still felt that same pulsing awe — an intoxicating sense of surrealism — as she watched him work.

Lily plucked a grape from an antique table and sucked it, contemplating the back of the canvas. She savored a delicious moment of uncertainty. At forty, she was not as firm as she'd been the first time Adam had painted her portrait, but she didn't mind. What she lacked in youth, she made up for in other, more important ways. She was at the peak of womanhood. Strong, sensual, sage. She would do today what she had been too young and shy to do at twenty.

She watched Adam step back from the portrait and felt desire hum through her. Maturity served him well. He was more appealing than ever with flecks of silver at his temples and a sturdiness that magnified his masculinity.

"When will you be finished?" she asked, shrugging her coral straps low over her shoulders. Her nipples hardened against the satin lining of her dress, a prim Elizabeth Taylor remake straight out of *Giant*.

"Today." Adam's sultry eyes, intimate by now with every visible part of her, glanced at the outline of her swollen nipples as if he hadn't noticed. Always reserved. His unswerving gentility made her want him even more.

"So soon?"

"Hmmm, I have a new project to start tomorrow." Adam's voice rumbled in his chest, rich as crude oil.

The sound reminded Lily of stories she'd heard of petroleum thundering through her grandfather's early oil wells and exploding in massive orgasms of instant prosperity. But Adam didn't rumble to an orgasm. Instead, he frowned and pursed his lips. They looked sweeter than grapes.

"But don't you have to varnish it first?"

Adam smiled. "Yes, but that won't be for another six months."

"Right," Lily said, disappointed. She didn't want their sessions to end.

In six months, she'd be back in school working on the MBA she'd abandoned right after Adam had painted her first portrait. She eyed the hard lines of his body and found it hard to contain her longing.

"I need a break," she said with a feline stretch, and flexed her limbs with calculated grace. As she rose from the teal Victorian sofa, her chiffon wrap whispered to the floor behind her in a reflection of her thoughts.

Strip me, Adam. Fuck me.

Adam paused as if to listen and watched the ethereal fabric trail behind her in a coral heap. He cast her another shrouded glance as she approached, and resumed his work. She moved behind him and closed her eyes, savoring the melange of smells: turpentine, linseed oil and, underlying it all, the unmistakable scent of male arousal.

"Do you mind if I look?"

"Not at all. It's finished."

After a final stroke of his brush, he wiped magenta pigment from the bristles and stepped out of her line of vision. His perception of her was shocking. He had captured more than her likeness. Much more. She found it unsettling, exciting. As before, he'd seen through her, painted past her mundane exterior, and turned her inside out. Only this portrait was even more telling than the first. He'd transformed her into a creature beyond redemption: flame blue eyes, skin the color of white heat, hair as black as crude. She was plumper now, but still beautiful.

Did she really look like that? All that sex in one face? And yet, it looked exactly as she felt. Fuck-happy. Unfortunately, the portrait ended at her shoulders. He had passed over her cleavage, her carefully packed breasts, as if too polite to acknowledge them even on canvas, and worked his usual magic of blending his subject into the background. She would have given a great deal to see how he would handle a nude.

Trailing her fingers along the easel in a butterfly caress, she said, "It's wonderful."

He exhaled, his breath warm on her shoulder, his voice rough with something. Lust, perhaps. His burnt sienna eyes sparkled with mischief. "It helps to have a good subject."

"Just a *good* subject?"

He smiled. "Beautiful, then."

She returned the smile, satisfied. "Do I really look that . . . lewd?"

"Is that how you see it?"

"Yes, from the neck up." In a bold movement, she turned on him, letting her breasts rub against the coarse fabric of his shirt. "What happened to my chest, Adam? I look like I have one continuous tit."

He gazed at her breasts, heat flashing in his eyes, then lifted a critical eye to his work.

"Paint my body," she said.

His eyes flickered over the canvas and she knew he was considering its limitations.

"Here," she said, licking her finger and running it between her breasts.

He shrugged. "You're the boss."

When he started to add a strategic stroke of magenta cleavage to the canvas, she caught his wrist. "No. Paint my *body*, not the canvas."

The corners of his mouth lifted in a slow grin. "Oh."

With a swish of fabric, Lily slipped the dress from her shoulders, freeing her heavy breasts, and cupped them provocatively in her hands. Adam's cock ballooned in his jeans. Christ, it was nice.

When she stroked him, he groaned and said, "Lily . . . I don't know if this is such a good idea. Someone might come in."

"Then tell me to stop." Trailing her hands over his belly, she ripped open the hole in his paint-stained T-shirt and sucked his nipple into a hard pebble. He closed his eyes and moaned. Encouraged, Lily rubbed her breasts against his bushy chest. Shards of heat shot from her nipples to her cunt. Surrender flickered in his eyes and he touched her breasts. Lily indulged him a moment before jiggling out of his reach. She wanted to take it slow, save the best for last.

He followed her and she rubbed the ridge beneath his jeans. He closed his eyes and sighed.

"Get your clean brushes," she said.

His eyes blinked open. "What?"

"I said, get your clean brushes. I hereby commission you to paint my body."

At that moment, Lily saw his reserve snap. He pulled her against him, kissing her hard and fierce, and fucking her with his tongue. She sucked it, pretending it was his cock, then pushed him away. Adam stepped back, eyes bright with lust, and removed fresh brushes from his desk. With trembling hands, he slipped them from their plastic cases. Thin ones, fat ones, soft and stiff. Red sable, ox hair and pig bristles. He tested each one against a finger, sable against callous. Lily sighed in anticipation.

She sidled back to the sofa where she wriggled out of her dress. Underneath, she wore only a black lace thong. Adam followed her like a man possessed and, when she bent over to step out of the thin strip of lace, he drew his largest brush over her buttocks and between her thighs. She kicked her clothes aside and spread her legs, arching her back to give him better access. She was like a cat in heat, lifting its rump and tail in invitation.

He teased her cunt, wet with arousal, then grabbed her hips and pressed his groin against her. His swollen crotch grazed her clit and she purred and paused to savor the rolling motion of his hips. Then she scooped up the gossamer shawl and turned away, drawing it around her.

When he reached for her, she massaged his bulge, damp with her juices, and gave a throaty laugh. "No, you don't. Not until you've fulfilled your commission."

"All right. But first I have to apply a bottom coat," he murmured, stroking her buttocks and lowering her to the sofa. He guided her onto her stomach and brushed her from head to toe with light feathery movements. Lily moaned, feeling as though she would explode before she could possess him. He skimmed her back, shoulders and legs with the bristles, concentrating on the sensitive skin behind her thighs and knees.

Adam eased her onto her back, eyes glued to the shifting mounds of her breasts, and ministered to the tender undersides of her arms. He chose a sable detail brush from his collection; featherlike bristles encircled her breasts just shy of her nipples and drifted down her belly and between her thighs, never quite touching her where she needed it most. Eyes closed, she felt him stretch over her and back again, and then felt something wet touch her skin. She opened her eyes to find him squeezing grape juice on her chest.

He dipped his brush in the liquid pooling between her breasts. "You have a beautiful mouth," he said, painting her lips. "Lush. Made for sucking . . . and being sucked."

With a reptilian thrust of her tongue, she captured the bristles. Adam kissed her, pulling on her lower lip. She opened her mouth to receive him and they playfully lapped at each other. Then he broke away, laving the juice between her breasts with his tongue, licking a trail of burning sensation from her belly to her groin. She moaned and opened her legs wider. He painted her there, then licked her furrow from vagina to clit.

"Adam," Lily whispered and sighed, resisting her approaching orgasm. She wanted to make it last. He lifted his head and replaced his tongue with a stiffer brush. Urgency built in her clitoris, inflamed by the masterly movements of his fingers.

Suddenly, it would no longer do. Suddenly, she needed to be touched by something warm and hot, flesh and blood. She tossed his brushes aside and pressed his pigment-stained hands to her breasts. Her nipples puckered beneath the rough skin of his palms. She lay back, ecstasy bubbling in her throat.

"Please," she whispered. "Touch me ... touch me every-where."

"But your commission ... " he said in a teasing reminder.

Snaking her hands over his buttocks, she pulled him to her and buried her face in his crotch, inhaling the smell of desire. "Fuck the commission," she mumbled against his zipper.

He laughed low and sexy.

She fastened her mouth on the hot ridge beneath his jeans, wetting the fabric with her tongue. He grew rock hard beneath her lips and teeth and, when he cupped her head and moved against her, Lily knew she wouldn't have long to wait.

He pulled away, eyes glazed with need, and pressed her down. "I'd rather fuck you than your commission. But I'm honor-bound to fulfill my assignment."

Lily unfurled on the sofa, feeling as luxuriant as a strip of ivory velvet, and opened her legs. "How about just *filling* your assignment," she murmured, "right up to your balls."

"You're almost too hot to handle," he said, pressing against her hand. "Almost."

"Prove it," she said.

With a new intensity in his eyes, he bent to suckle her breast. She moaned deep in her throat and angled the other one at him. Weaving her fingers through his dark hair, Lily drew him the rest of the way down and wrapped her legs around his hips, gyrating against his erection. When he pulled away, his fingers fumbling urgently with his zipper, she followed him up and brushed his hands aside. "Here, let me."

"Hurry," he said thickly.

A moment later, his erection sprang out of his jeans.

"Oh, baby," Lily moaned and slid to her knees.

She tongued the purple head with long lazy strokes and gen-erously lubricated him before attempting to take him in her mouth. He tasted clean and salty and sinful, musky and male. In spite of his girth, she devoured him with relative ease, pumping up and down his length as far as she could go. With concentrated effort, she relaxed her throat and consumed another inch.

"God, Lily!" Adam groaned and pressed her head down.

When he began to thrust, she pulled back and licked him clean. "Enough. I want to feel your hands on me." She rose and pressed them to her hips. "Touch me, Adam. Touch me all over."

Adam responded with unparalleled enthusiasm, touching her breasts and thighs and hips with calloused hands, sparking jets of heat in her cunt. His cock, bobbing hotly between them, was more temptation than she could stand.

"Fuck me now," she commanded and rubbed it between her thighs. It rustled against her curls.

"Do you need it, Lily?" Adam whispered against the corner of her mouth. "Say it. Tell me you need it."

"I need it, Adam," she whispered. "I need it now."

He groaned and drew her back down to the sofa. She straddled him and guided him into her. Her lips stretched taut around his girth, unsheathing her own clitoral erection. He entered her in degrees and she gasped at the sheer sweetness of it. He felt like smooth sunbaked stone.

At first, he held back, pushing her toward fulfillment in careful stages, gently priming her with deliberate thrusts. But her control didn't match his and she wanted more.

"Adam, stop torturing me," she said breathlessly, and rode him with staccato whimpers of encouragement.

In response, he gripped her thighs and pounded into her with hot precision, drilling away at her reserve until he coaxed her closer and closer to the surface. Lily felt the ascent of his balls beneath her pelvis as they crept up his shaft and were slowly absorbed into his groin.

It was too much. She exploded in a crashing orgasm, losing touch with everything except Adam and her throbbing cunt milking his cock. He bucked into her, flesh slapping flesh, with a vengeance she'd never forget. On his final thrust, he held her hips against him and bellowed out his pleasure.

"It's a gusher," Lily panted.

Adam chuckled weakly. Then, after a moment, he nudged her with his hips.

"Lily?"

She lifted her head, heavy with satisfaction. "Yes?"

"Do you really like the portrait?"

"Are you kidding? I love it. It's even better than the first one."

"Really?"

"Yeah." She lowered her head again.

"Lily?"

Grinning, she crossed her arms over his chest and rested her chin on them. "There's more?"

He paused a moment and nodded; words never came easy to Adam. Most of his communicating took place on canvas. He lifted a curl from her shoulder and hooked it around his finger. "I just wanted to say that . . . well . . . these past twenty years have been the best years of my life."

She gave him her most tender kiss. "Me, too. Happy anniversary, sweetheart."

Michelle Stevens

Lesbian Bed Death: A Case Study

Don't ask me how it happened. 'Cause if you ask me, I'll have to admit that I don't know. I'm a doctor; I'm supposed to know everything. Right? Four years of med school, three years of residency, all that time being taught, trained to notice the fine details. Listening closely to every breath, every heartbeat, studying every inch of skin for signs of malignancy. I'm a good doctor, attentive. I have a reputation for detecting the elusive symptoms that other doctors miss. And yet, somehow, I didn't see it coming.

I wish I could blame it on subtlety. I wish I could tell you that the clues were obtuse. But the truth is, *I* was the one who was obtuse. I paid little attention to what initially presented as a mild discomfort; left untreated, it quickly grew. General irritability gave way to severe mood swings, marked by anger and depression. By the time I finally realized there was a problem, it was too late, the effects too acute. Untreatable. Incurable. Terminal.

Diagnosis: Lesbian Bed Death.

Like any patient with a fatal disease, I found the prognosis difficult to accept. The first stage is denial. I had plenty of that! For months, Amy would ask me over and over again why we'd stopped having sex.

"What're you talking about?" I'd ask. "We *do so* have sex."

"No, not for a really long time," she said.

"What about that night, you know, in the car?"

"That was four months ago."

"Oh."

Denial was soon followed by anger. Stage Two. Amy wouldn't leave me alone. I knew she was right. And it pissed me off.

"We have to talk about it."

"I don't want to talk about it."

"Well, then, what do you expect will happen? I can't just stop having sex! It's been seven months now. What do you expect me to do? We have to start working on it."

"I don't want to work on it. I don't want to talk about it. Talking just makes me more self-conscious. God, Amy, why can't you just let it be?"

It wasn't until she moved out that I hit Stage Three: bargaining.

"Oh, honey, please please please don't leave me."

"Well, what do you expect me to do?" she asked in measured tones over the line. I was standing at a pay phone in the emergency room during a thirty-six-hour shift. My scrubs were still wet with blood.

"I don't know. Just move back in. Amy, please."

"What's the point?"

"What's the point? You *know* the point. I love you."

"But Kate, we haven't had sex in over nine months."

"Oh, sex, sex, sex! Is that all it's about for you?"

"Obviously not," she chuckled sarcastically, "or I would have left nine months ago."

Then my beeper started going off. Shit.

"Look, Ames, we've been together for *six years*. I mean, there must be some way we can work this out."

"You didn't seem too interested in working it out when you thought I'd stick around forever."

"C'mon, Ames, please."

"Well, what do you have in mind?" she asked, after a deafening pause.

"Marriage counseling, Dr. Ruth books, anything you want."

Then, after a long sigh, "Fine."

She moved back in, and we started counseling. The therapist wondered how we'd met.

"It was our senior year at NYU," I said. "It was the first week of Fall classes, and I had put off buying my books — a dangerous thing to do at a school with 20,000 students. Anyway, the school store was packed. I think every kid at the university was wrestling over the last three copies of *The Norton Anthology*. I was actually doing okay, had every book I needed except for one, the *Gray's Anatomy Coloring Book*. But just as I got to the shelf, I saw this beautiful black-haired girl grabbing the last one."

"She asked me if I was taking her physiology class," Amy added. "And that pissed me off. I asked her why she just *assumed* I was taking some stupid science class. Was it just because I'm Asian?"

"I told her no, it was because she was holding a stupid science book."

"Then I was embarassed," Ames said. "I told her I needed the book for my nude sculpting class."

"Then I told *her* she better hand it over, because being a doctor was clearly more important than being an artist."

"To which I replied that I would *never* give a book to someone so arrogant."

"Then she started walking away. So I followed her and asked her if she would share."

"Oh, I shared all right!"

"Yeah, her phone number," I laughed.

Therapy seemed to be going okay. We talked about that first year, when things were hot and heavy. Amy told her how we did it in the dorm room, in the cafeteria, in the library stacks. Then I told her about med school at Stanford. How we moved to Palo Alto and Amy had to work two crappy jobs to keep us solvent.

"Uh-huh," said the therapist. "And did that ruin the sex?"

"No," Amy said. "The sex got ruined when we moved to L.A., and Kate started her residency."

"I see," said the therapist. "Tell me more about that."

And so Amy did. She talked about my thirty-six hour shifts, her weekends all alone and how we get beeped out of bed. She said that even when I'm home, I'm not really *there*.

"And how do you feel about this, Kate?" the therapist asked.

"Uh, I don't know," I said. "It's kind of all true, but Amy knew this would happen when she decided to marry a doctor."

"Yeah," Amy snarled. "Well, I just didn't think it would be this bad. And besides, being a doctor is no reason not to want *sex*."

"It's not that I don't *want* to," I shouted. "There's just no fucking *time*!"

"You have to *make* time," Amy hissed, in her most self-righteous tone.

And so I did make time. Don't ask me how. But one night, despite the patients, the nurses, the attending physicians, I managed to sneak home early and turn the beeper off. Amy seemed pleased that at least I was trying. We took off our clothes, and we got into bed. We kissed for a while, and I played with her breasts. But when I tried to go inside her, she yelled.

"Ouch!" She wasn't even wet.

"Maybe I should do you," she said.

But I wasn't wet either. That's when we hit Stage Four: Depression.

The therapist said we should start slower. After all, it had been a long time. So we tried a few things — cherry-flavored love oil, dirty videos, Twister — but nothing worked. The magic was gone.

Which brings me to today — our last visit to the shrink, because we told her that we're finally ready to accept it. Stage Five. The relationship is dead. We both know it, and we're calling it quits.

It's good, I guess, how it worked out. The lease was up anyway. And now I can get through my residency without all this bullshit.

The thing is, if this is for the best, then why do I feel so lousy? I mean, when Ames and I broke up, I thought it would be a relief. No more of her constantly nagging me to call her, to come home early, to snuggle with her under the sheets. No more of her skin, or the way she smelled, or the way she would wake me up with coffee when she knew I had an early shift. Jesus Christ, I'm a fucking idiot!

The front door opens. It's Amy. She got some boxes from the Ralph's store down the street. She doesn't even look at me when she walks in. Just heads to the bedroom to pack. I want to talk to her now. I want to go in the bedroom and tell her I think it's a mistake.

But it's too late. And what would I say, anyway? That we ought to go to therapy? Been there. Done that. Besides, it's not just up to me. *She* was the one who started this in the first place. Remember? All that crap about sex, sex, sex.

I grab my own box and head to the bedroom. Amy or no Amy, I'm ready to pack. But when I get in there, she's nowhere to be seen. Not in the closet, not in the bathroom. Where the hell did she go?

Then I notice a little lump under the quilt. The one her mom gave us for our fifth anniversary.

"Ames?" I ask with a raised eyebrow.

"What?" A muffled grunt.

"What're you doing under there?"

"Just leave me alone," she screams.

I know that scream. It's a lot like the one I heard when I told her, five years ago, that I was moving to Palo Alto. Before I asked her to come along.

"Ames?" I venture over to the bed, put one hand on the quilt. "Are you crying?"

"No! Yes."

I pull down the covers to reveal my wife's tear-drenched head. "What's going on?"

"Nothing. Leave me alone."

"What're you crying for?"

"What do you think?"

"I think you look like a big, old, soppy head."

She laughs a little, and I grab for the tissues on the nightstand. They're not there, must already be packed. I crawl into the bed and offer her my shirt sleeve.

"You better not blow your nose on it," I say. She laughs a little again. "Now, what's going on?" She cries some more. I lie my head on her head.

After a while, it's quieter. "I just can't believe this is happening," she says. "I mean, I thought we'd always be together. That's what we said. What went wrong?"

"We stopped having sex."

"Is that all?" she laughs. "Is that why? Seems like a stupid reason after six years of marriage."

"You won't settle for a marriage without sex. Remember?

You need a relationship that makes you feel alive."

"But now that we're breaking up, I feel dead inside."

"I know, baby. I know."

I use my shirt sleeve to gently wipe her eyes. Man, I forgot how black they are. So black you can't even see the pupils. Amazing, the way they reflect the light. When we first got together, I used to stare at them all the time. And her dark skin. Such a contrast to my pale white. I pick up her hand, hold it next to mine.

"Hey, remember, Ames? When we were in college? Remember how we used to just stare at your arm next to mine?"

She smiles, giggles, "I'd never seen such a white white girl! Or such a perfectly straight nose!"

"And *I'd* never seen such big lips!"

"All the better to kiss you with," she teases me with her old line.

Those black eyes are staring right at me now. And before I even know what's happening, they've pulled me in. I'm kissing her. Very lightly. I want to feel the soft, soft mouth. My fingers, by rote, are already stroking the thick, warm hair.

I'm gone now. Lost to her. To it. To us. Everything I do now will be automatic. Ritualized. It will slip on comfortably, like a pair of well-worn jeans.

I will lie on top of her, so she can feel my weight. My hip will press against her stomach. My breasts will lightly brush her breasts. I will pick up her hands, lace my fingers in hers.

I will get a little more forceful then. I will pin her arms down with my own. Quickly, I will part her lips with my tongue because I know she likes to be taken by surprise. She will fight back for a moment — but only a moment. Then, I will feel her body relax. And I will know she has given in.

After that, it will all happen quickly. And slowly. Like there is no time. I will suck on her neck, her ears, the insides of her elbows. Gradually, my mouth will find its way to her chocolate nipples, warm and hard. I will suck on them hungrily, deliberately, as my hands gently cup her breasts. Then, as I suck harder, faster, as I flick my tongue back and forth in steady rhythm, her hips will press into my thigh.

I will let go of her arms then, letting my full weight fall onto her. My fingers will find their way to her face, her lips, then slide into her waiting mouth. My tongue will explore her stomach, her shoulders, the round contours of her breasts. As I bite into the dark, salty neck, she will surely moan. From the pleasure, from the pain, from the sheer intensity of feeling. She will try to pull away, turn her head, anything to stop, slow down, release the pressure. But I will not let go.

Instead, I will suck harder. I will sink my fingers deeper into her warm tongue. I will press my leg harder into her undulating crotch. Neck to mouths to fingers to hips, our bodies will move as one. Moving back and forth, tiny waves to bigger waves to violent waves, until that old, familiar sea finally washes over us.

Then, after a while, after the waves have stopped and the mouths have stopped and it is quiet, she will open her big, black eyes to look at me. She will part those big, soft lips to speak to me. And she will say . . .

"Katie?"

"Huh?!"

I'm startled back to our bed. The one waiting to be thrown in the moving truck. I look around at our nearly empty bedroom. Boxes stacked everywhere. Wow. I guess it's back to Stage Four: Depression.

"Whatcha thinkin'?" Amy asks. She's got a funny smile. One I've never seen before.

I shrug and start to climb out of the bed. I gotta get this over with. Fast.

But before I get very far, Amy's pulling on my shirt.

"Katie," she asks, that same funny smile on her face, "You wanna play doctor?" And then she does something she has *never* done before. *She* pushes *me* down on the bed and sits on top of me. Then, with the skill of a surgeon, she glides her hand through the waist of my jeans.

Prognosis: Very, very good.

Marcy Sheiner

The Adventure of Marriage

When I was younger I was what I guess you'd call a swinger. I went to sex parties, did threesomes with men and women, and slept with just about anything that moved. I tried bondage, dominance and water sports. I loved it all. So I hope I won't seem too old-fashioned when I say that what really turns me on now is the ups and downs of my relationship with my husband.

I met Danny in that wild anything-goes world, and we ended up as a fuddy-duddy monogamous couple in the suburbs. I am so in love with this man that the mere sound of his voice gets my pussy wet. When we got married eight years ago, I wondered if sex with just one person would get boring, but I have been amazed to find that we keep discovering new ways to excite and satisfy each other. Everything that happens in our lives and in our relationship seems to get expressed in the bedroom. We have periods of distance, and then the return to intimacy makes our lovemaking feel brand new. We fight and make up and then we fuck our brains out. We go out with friends and something happens to turn us on, and we rush home to merge our flesh.

It hasn't always been this way. Danny, always a great fuck with a terrific body and awesome staying powers, didn't know how to treat a woman outside of bed. He didn't realize that what went on during the day affected what would go on at night. In other words, he was unromantic, self-centered, and insensitive. A perfect example of this behavior came just five months after our wedding, on my twenty-eighth birthday.

When I was a kid I had so many bad, even traumatic, birthdays that now I like to do it up big. For me, getting laid is an essential ingredient to the celebration, as is getting presents, especially from my "significant other."

Well, it turned out that Danny had to be out of town on business for a few days before the big event — but he'd be returning on the evening of my birthday. I wasn't thrilled that he'd be gone during the day, but was looking forward to him coming home in time to fuck me. I spent the afternoon with a few friends, and at 6:30 picked up Danny at the airport.

It had been three long days since I'd seen him, and I could hardly wait to fall into his arms. But when he got off the plane he gave me a distracted peck on the lips and said, "I've been looking for a present for you in airports all day."

"In airports?" I said, stung. "You were going to buy me a present in an airport?"

I couldn't believe he hadn't found something for me before he'd left — and worse, that he was telling me in such an off-hand way. During the drive home I figured out that he realized he'd screwed up and felt guilty, but I didn't really give a shit about his feelings — I was too involved with my own. I hurt, and when I'm hurt, I seek revenge.

For the first time since I turned sixteen, I didn't get laid on my birthday — I told Danny that I didn't feel well. The next day I waited for him to give me a present, or a card, or surprise me with a fancy dinner. Nothing. Not the next day or the next or the next.

And so he didn't get to fuck me; every night for a week I coldly declined. Finally he asked me what was wrong. I told him I was pissed that he'd ignored my birthday. He apologized, but I told him it wasn't enough.

"You have to be punished." I slid out of bed and switched on the light. Slowly I lifted my white silk nightgown over my head. I cupped my size 40-D tits in my hands and held them up like an offering of ripe fruit.

"You like to suck on these babies?" I asked.

"You know I do," he moaned.

Gently I released my globes, then slid my hands down to my crotch. I parted my cunt lips. "And you also like to put your hard cock into this warm wet hole?"

I saw his cock rising underneath the blanket. "Damn right," he said happily, obviously thinking that this teasing was a prelude to lovemaking.

Slowly I turned around and stuck my butt out. Danny loves to bite and suck on my ass cheeks.

"And you *really* like to chew on these, don't you?"

He lunged forward, but I quickly evaded his grasp.

"Uh uh uh," I said, turning to face him and wiggling my finger as if he were a naughty little boy. "Only grownup men who know how to treat women get to touch."

I put my nightgown back on, switched off the light, climbed into bed, and turned my back on him. I sensed his hand moving around his dick to relieve himself.

"Don't you dare! If you have to do your dirty business go do it in the toilet."

I don't know if Danny jerked off or not, because I fell asleep. The next day he brought me a fancy birthday card.

"Big fucking deal," I said, tossing it into the garbage. That night I replayed my teasing routine, this time sticking my fingers into my cunt and holding them under his nose to give him an aromatic whiff of what he was missing.

The next day he brought me a box of candy; I fed it to the dog. That night when I stripped I stood above him with my legs apart so he could look up at my bush. He begged me to sit on his face, to let him touch my breasts. "Anything," he pleaded. I laughed and told him when he learned how to behave like a real man, he might be allowed access to my precious body.

"But I brought you a card and candy."

"Fuck you," I said, turning my back on him for the third night in a row.

The next day it was roses. "You're getting warm," I said, putting them in a vase. He came up behind me and pinched my ass. I slapped his hand. "I said warm, not hot."

He groaned as I fell to my knees, unzipped his fly, licked his dick until it was hard, then stood up and walked away, laughing.

The next day he brought me a pair of elaborate dangling earrings and a matching necklace. I took off all my clothes and put on the jewelry, feeling like an exotic princess, and danced for him, shimmying my body in front of his hungry eyes before climbing into bed and turning my back on his hard-on.

"Aw, Chrissy," he begged. "What more do I have to do? How much more money do I have to spend?"

"It's not about money, Danny. It's about you loving me enough to want to show me you do. It was my birthday. I wanted to know that you were really glad I was born." I started to cry. "You hurt me, Danny. You hurt me real bad."

He reached out and took me in his muscular arms. I snuggled closer and rubbed myself against his hairy body. It felt so good after such a long time apart. I cried as he hugged me and stroked my hair. When he turned me onto my back and tenderly kissed me all over — on my breasts, my belly, my thighs, I finally softened completely. When he came to my cunt he ran his tongue up and down the inner lips, pushing deep inside me, lapping up my juices like a grateful puppy. My hurt melted in a surge of arousal.

His tongue spoke eloquently in a language I understood better than words. It told me that he cherished me, was sorry he'd hurt me, and would never do it again. His hands reached up to caress my tits, and he kneaded my nipples until they grew taut between his fingers. He blew hot air on my pussy, then took my clit into his mouth and sucked, making me cry out. I could have come then, but he released my clit and moved on top of me, sliding his long hard cock between my aching cunt lips. I gripped him with all the fervor that came from having gone without for so long, sucking his hard-on into me. We began our long familiar ride, spinning to greater heights of ecstasy, higher and higher, to the final explosive climax. Danny cried out as his cock began shooting into me, pumping like a piston and spurting hot come into my steaming cunt. I pressed closer to him and the muscles deep within me spasmed, squeezing every drop of fluid from his organ as I too came. Waves of satisfaction rippled through me, heightened by all the emotions between us.

We've come a long way since then. Last year, on my thirty-fifth birthday, Danny reserved a room in an elegant hotel where we spent two days drinking champagne, ordering shrimp cocktails from room service and, of course, fucking like lions in heat. He's learned to bring me flowers occasionally, tell me he loves me often, and make those little romantic gestures that let me know I am loved. Of course we still have our disagreements, and I can't say he's never hurt me since then — but our relationship, and our sex, gets better and better. In fact, I'd have to say that marriage is just about the most exciting sexual adventure I've ever taken.

Lisa Prosimo

Blue Moon over Paradise

Sam was tired. He stretched, rotated his shoulders, tried to work the ache out of his muscles. Just a little more work, then he'd stop. A few more bushes, that's all; then he'd call it quits. It had been a long day and he suddenly realized he was hungry.

He gathered the last of the dried brush and carried it to his truck, looked around at the work he had done and was satisfied. Sam liked the hard work, it made him brown and fit. He would buy himself a beer, have a steak for dinner at The Shady Pine, turn in early and be up slightly before dawn, get started before the heat took over. He looked at the dry brush, the dead trees that needed to be cut down. About a week's worth of work still to be done, two weeks in all. Not bad. Good money and a guest house thrown in, too.

As Sam pulled away from the property to head for town, he looked through his rear view mirror at the stately old cabin that stood among the trees. It seemed strange to call that monster house a cabin, but that's the way the townspeople had always referred to the McEnery place. When he was a boy he used to come out with his friends just to stare at the thing. That was in the days when the place had a caretaker, Mr. Jenkins, who stood on the porch and yelled at them to "get the hell off this property before I call the sheriff!" Except for an agent who checked on the house occasionally, the place hadn't truly been cared for in years. Now the owner wanted to come back, and the agent had hired Sam to clean up the brush and remove dead tree branches.

Sam was back home in Paradise, doing a job his father had done, one he swore he would never do, and in a place he had run from years before. Funny how people change, he thought. This place, this work, made him content. San Francisco, the city Sam had called home for over fifteen years, had somehow lost its allure. Without knowing why, he no longer looked forward to getting up in the morning and going to his job teaching at the university. Only gradually did he come to understand that he had stopped caring about political science, political correctness, and politics. He found his mind drifting back to Paradise, wondered what was going on in the woods where he used to hunt and fish as a boy, began to pine for the life he once thought he hated. It seemed so easy to slide back into that life after his father died and he had to come back to put his affairs in order. His regret was that he had waited too long. One morning, his father just didn't wake up, dead of a heart attack. As Sam filled boxes and cleaned things up, he knew he wanted to come home.

Gloria was shocked. They'd lived together for six years, she reminded him. Their lives were good; they had excellent jobs. Why would he want to change anything? She asked him if it was something she'd done. No, he assured her. Nothing. She asked if it had anything to do with her receiving tenure while he had not. No. He just wanted to go home, he said. To do what? she demanded. Clean out brush, take dead branches off trees? She laughed at him, said he couldn't be serious. He said he was dead serious.

"I don't want the life I have, Gloria. I want to do something different. I want to work outdoors, feel the sun on my face. And I hate to be told there's no honor in that sort of work. I know there is."

He watched the tears spring to her eyes and run down her cheeks. She had hurt him by laughing at him; now he had hurt her. "I won't go with you, Sam," she whispered. "I can't."

He had come back to Paradise alone, and for a time he felt hollow in the place where she had been. But he filled his days with work, and more work, grateful that people still remembered his name and were willing to employ him. One morning he woke up to find the void had filled in much the same way a wound grows new tissue. He was scarred, but the organism still served.

Sam might have stayed in town at the house that now belonged to him, but he chose instead to return to the McEnery place, to the little guest bungalow that had come with the job. He liked being in the woods, and close to his work. All he had to do after waking up was wash his face, put on his clothes and get on with it.

When Sam pulled onto the property after his trip into town, he saw a Lincoln, long and black, in the driveway. The downstairs windows of the main house were open, the curtains drawn back to let in the evening breeze. It was just slightly past dusk. He peered up into the sky. There would be a moon tonight, almost full, cool and bright. He went into the house, dropped onto the bed and fell asleep almost immediately.

Sam awoke to the howling of a coyote, forgetting for a moment where he was.

Light from the moon spilled across his skin, parched in the hot night, and he tossed for only a minute before admitting he could not fall back to sleep. He sat up, reached for his jeans, thought better of it, and went out onto the porch. There was no one to see him naked and he wanted his body to catch what little air that moved. He sat in the shadows, hidden under the canopy, watching the moon hang upon nothing as he breathed in the clean sweet air he hoped would act on him like a sedative. If he didn't get enough rest, he would be worthless come morning.

The bright circle of the moon stood against the big house and Sam noticed the French doors on the upstairs balcony were open. The room was black, but the light picked up the sway of the soft gauzy curtains, tinting them a pale blue. A figure emerged from inside, female, wrapped inside a white sheet dyed moon blue, too. She leaned over the railing and sighed, the sound making its way across the expanse to the little bungalow where Sam sat in the darkness. From the way she moved, he knew she was young, between twenty and thirty, he would guess. She stepped away from the railing, threw her head back and shook out her hair. She let go of the sheet and it fell to the floor. Sam moved forward just a bit, to get a better look. The woman stretched her arms out to her sides as far as they would go and sighed again. The moon's radiance tinged her body and Sam could make out the curve of her hips, the contour of her breasts as she moved slowly, like a cat gauging its surroundings. She sat down in an old rocking chair, the only piece of furniture on the balcony; propelled herself forward, then dropped back. Forward and back in a steady, almost hypnotic cadence. She rocked for a few minutes, her head back, her arms hanging loosely over each rest, her feet planted on the floor. The moonlight caressed her shoulders, her breasts, her belly. Slowly, she shifted her body, leaned into the far side of the chair, brought her arms over her head and slipped one leg over the armrest. She shifted again, moved her pelvis closer to the edge, stretched her leg as far as it would go. Her body draped the chair like a shawl as she continued to rock back and forth.

Sam moved toward the light, just short of the end of the black that shrouded him. He monitored his breath, sure that if he had heard her sigh, she would hear his breathing. A concentrated warmth caressed his groin. The porch groaned under his weight and he moved back a bit, just in case she might follow the sound. But she wasn't paying attention to the night. She brought one hand down to her face, placed her fingers in her mouth then drew them out. She altered her position another fraction, moved her hand over her vulva and slipped her fingers inside.

Sam heard her soft, quiet, "Ah . . . ," almost a gurgle, as she rocked into her fingers. The old chair squeaked in protest, but she pushed it relentlessly as her fingers moved faster and faster. The woman's body jerked upward, seemed to devour her hand, and she moaned; moved her head from side to side. She kept the steady rhythm going, became one with the chair, and as she rode herself to climax, she let out a loud cry, a sister sound to the coyote.

Sam felt the woman's release, saw her body relax into the old chair. He envied her, wanted part of her climax. He could have reached down, brought himself off, but the thought repelled him. He didn't want to share the act without her knowledge or consent; that had never been his style. He'd been trapped into watching her, compelled to see it through, and now he was suddenly ashamed, felt like a Peeping Tom. Quietly he retreated out of the shadows and went back into the house.

They walked toward him, the woman and the old man. The man's body bent slightly, his legs bowed, his hands, one on the woman's arm, the other holding a cane, twisted like the bark of a tree. Sam left off bundling the dead branches, straightened up, pulled his handkerchief out of his pocket and wiped the sweat from his brow. "Morning," he said.

The woman's face was passive. In sunlight she was beautiful: long black hair, clear brown eyes, flawless skin, full lips; a little past thirty, he decided. He took her in with one glance, careful not to let his eyes linger too long. If he had seen her any place but here, would he have known her as the woman who presented her orgasm to the moon? The man smiled in Sam's direction, but couldn't see him, he realized. Sam extended his hand, placed his fingers lightly over the man's. The man grasped Sam's hand and shook it. "I'm Justin McEnery. Leah tells me you've been working non-stop all morning. Says the place is starting to shape up," he said, his voice gravelly, but warm. "Just wanted to let you know I appreciate it."

"You're quite welcome, Mr. McEnery. And thank you, sir, for the work. My name is Sam Warner."

"You a local boy?" asked McEnery.

"Yes, sir."

"I'm a local, too. Been a long time." He sniffed the air. "Place still smells the same, though."

"Yes, I guess it does," said Sam.

While Sam and McEnery talked, the woman, Leah, hung back quietly, not once looking at Sam directly. She kept her eyes on McEnery when he spoke, but looked into the sun or past the trees whenever it was Sam's turn, and yet he knew instinctively that she was acutely aware of him; was sure she felt, as he did, a certain type of current pass in the space between them. Could the old man feel it too, Sam wondered? Blind men can see things sighted men can't.

"Well, we'll leave you to your work," McEnery said. He turned away from Sam and he and Leah started to walk back to the house. "Oh," he said, stopping suddenly. "Come dine with us tonight. Our housekeeper won't be here until the end of the month, but Leah is a wonderful cook. Take pot luck, Sam."

The old man's invitation astonished Sam, and he was even more surprised when he heard himself accept the bid.

Digging in his closet like an awkward teen, Sam considered what to wear to dinner at the McEnery's. Finally, he settled on a pair of jeans and a fresh white T-shirt. They were in the woods, for God's sake, what else should he wear? And what should he take over there? The four beers from his remaining six-pack? Hardly. His one and only bottle of wine, which he'd already opened? No. He settled on a bouquet of wildflowers for Miss McEnery's table.

Leah answered his knock, the same passive expression on her face. "Good evening," she said, and he noticed that in spite of the absence of a smile, her voice, full and rich, was welcoming. Sam handed her the flowers.

"They're beautiful," she said. "I'll put them in some water."

You're beautiful, Sam thought, as he followed Leah into the dining room.

The table was set informally, stoneware instead of porcelain, and he was glad. He and Leah sat across from each other, while McEnery sat at the head of the table. They made small talk during the meal, which was simple, but good, and he noticed that McEnery didn't eat very much. But he drank constantly, downing two glasses of wine to every half glass of his and Leah's. Each time his glass was empty he drummed his fingers against the stem and Leah replenished his wine. And as the old man spoke, his words crowded in on each other until they were just a series of vowels and consonants sticking like glue to his lips. Sam had to lean in to make out McEnery's sentences.

"LivedinSanFranciscotoolongSam.Gladtobebackhome."

"Yes, sir. So am I." Sam explained that he had lived in San Francisco, too.

Leah said very little, almost nothing to Sam, but she was very tender with the old man. At one point she served him a fork full of food and murmured in a little girl's voice, "Daddy, you need to eat more."

Sam wondered if Leah were McEnery's only child, if she had come back from another life in order to care for her father whose health was obviously on a downward spiral. There were a lot of questions he would have liked to ask, but these people were his employers.

"My dear . . . I think I'm tired."

"Yes, of course," said Leah. She looked at Sam. "Would you help me take Mr. McEnery to bed?"

Sam jumped up. "Certainly," he said.

They stood on either side of McEnery, guided him out of his chair and walked him to the bedroom at the back of the house. The old man was nearly asleep on his feet and Sam wondered how she could manage getting him to bed alone every night, since Sam was sure by the way McEnery had tapped his glass and she had filled it, that his heavy drinking was a ritual.

Sam took the old man's shoes off and helped Leah slip his shirt over his head, then he discreetly left the room. Leah soon came out and quietly closed the bedroom door. "Thank you, Sam."

"No problem," he said. They stood for a moment against the wall in the hallway, looking at each other. Sam felt that strange current flow between them again, same as it had that afternoon. He was awkward, his hands and feet suddenly big and clumsy.

"Well, I'll see you out," Leah said finally, and Sam realized he was being dismissed. At the front door, she said, "He wasn't always like this. It's just been the last couple of years. Before that he was so vital . . . He grew old overnight. The blindness is from diabetes."

"Diabetes?"

"Yes. I know what you're thinking. The drinking. I can't stop him."

She said the words defensively and Sam was startled. None

of this was his business. Why did she feel she had to explain anything to him? He opened his mouth to speak, but she had opened the door, stepped out, and he followed. "Good night, Sam," she said, and before he could say a word, she stepped back inside and closed the door.

Sam walked to the bungalow. He was full of food and wine and a vague feeling about what had actually taken place between Leah and himself. She had been neither rude nor friendly, simply perplexing.

That night, from his window, he watched the moonlight play against the open French doors, just as it had done the night before. But Leah didn't come out and after a while Sam left the window, sank down onto his bed and entered a dreamless sleep.

Leah came out of the house and walked down the driveway to the mailbox. Sam stood in the clearing not more than a hundred yards away and knew she had seen him. He almost waved to her, but stopped himself when he realized she had no intention of acknowledging his presence. She had served him dinner the night before, this morning he was not worthy of a greeting. She came up the drive clutching the mail in her hand, looking at the face of each envelope as she walked up the steps and back into the house. He resolved not to care that she had snubbed him, even as he was conscious of the desire that stirred him.

Toward the end of his work day, as he was cleaning up, Sam turned and there she was, standing before him with her arms folded across her breasts. "He wants you to come to dinner again," she said, a soft contempt in her voice.

Her manner puzzled him, brought up an anger he didn't understand. "He made you come out here to ask?"

"Yes."

Sam sneered at Leah and bowed in an exaggerated fashion. "Well, m'lady," he said. "Please convey my regrets to Mr. McEnery. Explain to him that I have another engagement." He turned away. Now it was his turn to act as if she didn't exist.

He attacked the brush and the leaves and branches furiously as he thought how glad he would be when this job was over, when he could get away from this exasperating woman and her dying, drunken father. He told himself that over and over, as he put his tools away, as he scrubbed the grime from his body, as he sat on the porch and drank his four remaining bottles of beer.

No food in his stomach, lightheaded from the beer, Sam wasn't sure what he heard coming from the big house. A crash, glass breaking? Then Leah's scream. He ran across the small meadow that separated the two structures and threw open the door.

The old man sat at the dining room table, same as he had the night before. Leah stood holding her hand before her. Sam noticed a broken glass on the table and a smashed wine bottle on the floor across from where she stood. Above the shattered bottle, wine, red as blood, stained the white wall.

"Sam. Please tell Leah I'm sorry." The old man had tears in his unseeing eyes. He looked up in Leah's direction. "I'm sorry, my dear. I would never hurt you. Sorry."

Sam picked up a napkin and wrapped Leah's bleeding hand. The cut wasn't bad, but her body trembled as if she were in shock. He settled her into the chair, then turned his attention to the old man.

"I didn't mean it, Sam. What did I do?"

"I don't know, sir," said Sam. "Let's worry about it tomorrow. Right now, we'll get you to bed."

The old man nodded, allowed Sam to lead him to his room.

Leah sat in the same spot where Sam had left her, still trembling as she stared at the white cloth that covered her hand. Sam gently pulled her out of the chair and slipped his arms around her, whispered against her hair, "It's all right."

After a few moments her body relaxed against him and she began to cry. "I can't. I can't do it anymore. I can't watch him . . . "

"Sh . . . sh," he crooned, his voice low, soothing.

Sam swept Leah up into his arms, surprised by how light she was. She rested her head against his shoulder as he carried her up the stairs. He knew which room was hers. Sam sat Leah down on the bed, went into the bathroom and gathered what he needed to dress her hand.

"It will heal in a few days," he said when he had finished. "Now you need to rest."

She hadn't said a word during the time it had taken him to care for her wound. Now she grabbed for his hand. "Don't," she said softly. "Please don't go."

Sam hesitated, then stood up. Leah reached out, her arms encircled his waist, she drew him to her, buried her cheek against his belly. Her touch inflamed his groin; the warmth spread over his legs and up to touch his nipples. He felt his knees grow weak, felt his penis harden against her face. She ran her cheek along his erection, traced with her chin its outline inside the denim. She looked up at him and Sam read the hunger in her eyes, and more. Longing, sorrow, loneliness. He reached down and ran his fingers lightly over the outline of her lips. Leah grabbed for Sam with her teeth, nibbled at the tips of his fingers, sucked. Sam's breath stuck inside his throat. He had never wanted a woman more than he wanted Leah.

She undid his belt while she watched his face. Sam closed his eyes, concentrated on the sound of leather slipping out of the buckle's grasp, the tinkle of metal on metal, the sound of his zipper opening. He felt keenly the soft flesh of her hands, one covered by a gauze bandage, as they stroked his hips slowly, pulled down his briefs and freed his cock. Leah reached beneath him with one hand, caressed his heavy sac, while with her other hand, guided him inside her lips. He moaned, felt her mouth on him, hot and wet as her tongue slipped over and around his shaft, licking lightly, but thoroughly, making him harder, pulling the skin on his balls taut. Sam was aware of the moonlight spilling into the room, the pitch of their breaths, the moist, light clicking of Leah's mouth as it slid over his cock, taking him in deeper and deeper. The room became a tiny world of sensation. Nothing outside existed. He moved inside her mouth, in and out slowly, and with each inward thrust she sucked him soundly, relaxed her lips as he withdrew, then sucked again, pulled, coaxed, called up his essence. And he felt it rising, almost there, almost there inside the perfect rhythm of lips and tongue, intense and absolute. He groaned, pressed forward, bounced on the balls of his feet as he surrendered his orgasm to her in a jolting burst of light.

Sam fell to his knees, his strength drained. He looked up at Leah sprawled across the bed, her eyes closed, her chest rising and falling. He pulled his clothes off and joined her. He caressed her cheek and she opened her eyes. "Sam," she said, reaching up to touch his face. He kissed her, a deep, probing kiss, exploring with his tongue her taste and his own. "I knew this would happen," she said. "That's why I didn't want you around."

"Are you sorry?"

She sighed. "No."

Leah's face filled with wonder, fascination, and him. She looked vulnerable and so incredibly beautiful his heart melted. He bent over her, scooped her into his arms in a gesture of protectiveness. This time the passion exploded in his heart and he made a conscious effort not to cry out his joy. He wanted to tell her that she had made him feel as no other woman had ever made him feel, but all he could say was, "Leah."

She pressed against him, her need pressing through the thin cotton of her dress, her skin hot, firing his skin. He laid her down, lifted the dress over her head, slipped it off her body and dropped it to the floor. She reached for his hands and moved them to her breasts. Her eyes closed and a sigh left her lips as Sam kneaded the firm flesh, made tiny whorls around her nipples with the tips of his fingers. Leah shuddered beneath him, whispered his name, grasped his hair in both her hands and brought his lips down on hers. She sucked his tongue, his lips, his chin; kissed him until he gasped for breath. Sam pulled his mouth from hers and rested his head against her breasts for a moment, then let his tongue roll slowly over each mound, flood the nipples before drawing them, one at a time, deeply into his mouth. She cupped her breasts, squeezed them together as he kept sucking her rock-hard nipples against his tongue. He buried his face inside her bosom, breathed in her warm scent, planted moist kisses in the valley between her breasts, licked and kissed his way down and over the soft slope of her belly; felt her smooth, silky legs under his hands. He placed his palm over her soft curls, slipped his finger into her wet cleft and pressed gently on the delicate folds at the mouth of her vagina. She arched into his hand as if a bolt of electricity had entered her body, and Sam felt the energy from that shock leap into his. He pulled her lips apart and met the mouth of her sex with his mouth. He savored her wetness, drew her juices against his lips. He sucked and licked, ran his tongue into the deep crevices and over her sensitive clitoris. Her body jerked up, rose to keep itself fastened to Sam's mouth. He was lost in the taste of her, the soft warm slickness of her. He wanted to go deeper, deeper, drown inside her womb. Leah clutched his shoulders, thrust into his face, abandoned herself to his ministrations. She cried out, and he could hear the tears in her voice, their force rising up from her cunt and into her throat; spilling over her lips. "Oh, Sam . . . Ahhhhhh . . . ," she groaned, and he felt the impact of her orgasm wash over his tongue in a baptism of their spirits.

Sam lay with his head against Leah's belly as she ran her fingers through his hair. The glow of the moon bathed their bodies like a gentle lagoon. He dipped his tongue into her navel and she sighed. "Let's never leave this bed, Sam," she said.

"Okay."

He thought about the old man asleep downstairs, and he was a little ashamed for being grateful that McEnery had been too drunk to have heard them. This was the first time he had ravaged a man's daughter while he was a guest in the man's home. Perhaps he should have been more ashamed, but he wasn't. He had Leah under him, the taste of her still in his mouth. He was smitten.

"I wanted you the minute I laid eyes on you, Sam."

"Me, too."

"Yes? That day in the garden?"

Should he tell her about the night before that day in the garden, when he'd seen her on the porch in the moonlight, say that he'd begun to want her then? No. He decided to keep that his secret for now.

"Yes. That day in the garden," he said.

She rolled out from under him, scurried into the crook of his arm, laid her hand upon his chest. "There's so much I should tell you, Sam, about the way things are . . . "

He gently covered her mouth with his hand. "Shush," he whispered. "Not tonight."

He had discovered in making love with her a different kind of appetite, a hunger that pervaded his being, a desire to possess her, not in a way that smacked of ownership, but a blending of her soul into his. His discovery did not come in a series of thoughts, but through an arrangement of emotion as he kissed her, touched her, moved inside her. He, over her, she, over him, his hands holding her torso steady as he thrust his cock up into her again and again. His penis deep within her, Leah shuddered over him, and he shared the impact of her orgasms, first one, than another. "Please. I don't want you to stop. Don't ever stop," she whispered. To hear her speak, to watch her face as she came thrilled him so, as if her orgasms leapt out of her body and into his. Sam cried out as the energy poured out of him to fill her, and still it was not enough. He wanted to melt further and further into her, blot out the bed, the room, even the moon, everything except the soft cries that spurred him on to reach her center, the place where he wished to mark her, stamp her his, the way a wolf marks its territory. Again, over her, his chest shaking and heaving, her arms around his back, drawing him close, fusing to him, her tears flowing free, warm against his skin, attentive to each other's desires, with an absence of self-consciousness or judgment. Sex and love, pure and beautiful and committed.

The tides cannot resist the moon, and like them, Sam could not resist the pull on his body, the drawing of his being toward the house where somewhere inside, Leah stood. Was she making breakfast for her father? Folding laundry? Thinking of him? Would she come out of the house if he willed her to?

Leah, Leah, like a buzzing in his head as he hacked the brush, freed twisted vines, and uncovered smothered walkways. "The mail man was here. Come out and get the mail. I want to run my face along your legs, your thighs; I want my tongue to taste your skin again." The sun stood high in the sky, the sweat trickled down Sam's body in rivulets, and he trembled with desire.

The door to the big house opened, Leah stepped out, her

arms wrapped around two jugs, one with tea bags floating around inside, the other filled with clear water and ice. She set the tea on the porch, came down the stairs and walked toward him, the ice tinkling against the glass jug like wind chimes on a breezy day.

"Hi. I brought you some water. Thought you might need to be refreshed."

"I do need to be refreshed," he said, drawing her to him. "Come inside the bungalow with me."

She laughed. "Sam, I can't. He just woke up a little while ago. I gave him his insulin and some breakfast, but I've got to watch him."

"I know," he said, but he was pulling on the skirt of her dress, walking backwards toward the bungalow. She followed, weakly protesting, laughing and shaking her head.

Behind the door he kissed her, took her tongue into his mouth like a starving man, held her to him so closely the sweat on his body stained her dress. She pulled away, looked up at him helplessly. "My knees are weak," she said. "My head is light. See what you do?" He kissed her again. "It's so good," she murmured against his mouth.

"What is? Which part?"

"All of it."

"What's the best? The kissing; the touching. Licking. Fucking."

"Yes, yes, yes, yes." She pulled away from him, looked deeply into his eyes. "Trust."

"What?"

"I trust you. There's nothing I wouldn't do for you, wouldn't want you to do to me."

"Wilder and wilder?"

"Yes," said Leah. "Wilder and wilder."

She pushed him up against the door, climbed on top of him;

he grabbed her, dug his fingers into the soft flesh of her ass, kissed her mouth as if he hadn't kissed it in a long, long time. Such a rich, juicy mouth. He opened the buttons at the top of her dress, peeled the cloth aside, and took her nipple between his lips. Leah wound her hands into his hair as his busy mouth worked. His strong arms lifted her high, turned her so that her back was to the door; and his head disappeared under her dress, to the sweetness of her cunt with its soft black curls over deep pink folds. He savored the smell of her; the taste of her, heard her moan above him. Heard her say, "Sam . . . I want you inside me."

He brought her down; they stood toe to toe, her breath coming in gasps against his chest. She looked up at him. "Sam . . . please . . . "

He turned her around and gently pinned her arms with his hands. "Bend over, Leah," he said. "Put your hands against the door."

She did what he said. He moved closer to her, threw her skirt over her back, bent to kiss the soft flesh of her ass. He brought his arm under her, slipped his finger inside her moist lips; she was hot and wet and he spread her juices along the crack of her ass. She moaned in anticipation, spread her feet wider apart, drew closer to him.

He rested his hands on her hips. "Do you trust me?" he whispered. She turned her head, nodded. With one hand he undid the zipper on his jeans, let them fall. He pulled on his aching cock, drew out the moisture at the tip and spread it over the head, then with his hand, guided his cock into her tiny hole. He pushed slowly and felt her tense around him. "I don't want to hurt you, Leah. I want only to give you pleasure. If you want me to stop, I will."

"No . . . I want this," she said.

"Relax," he said. "Take me in. You do it, move against me. I won't move at all until you want me to." She arched slightly, moving him further inside her. She moved again, then again, inching her way over him until she had all of him. "Good," he said. He brought his hand under her again, stroked her dripping lips and Leah began to moan, moved her hips back and forth against him.

"It's so good, Sam. Do it with me, move with me now."

"Like this?" he asked, pumping in and out of her slowly.

"Yes, like that. Don't stop."

His balls were so full, he wanted nothing more than to explode within her, but he held off, took her lead, kept pushing in a steady rhythm until she could take no more, cried out that she was going to come. Her muscles tightened around him as she began to spasm, and at that moment he drove two of his fingers deep inside her cunt. She shuddered, lost control, and in her excitement almost broke away. He quickly grabbed her hips, drew her back, slammed against her, meeting the end of her orgasm with the beginning of his.

She went limp under him and he withdrew. He turned her around and tenderly kissed her eyes, her ears, her lips, her neck; whispered his love to her.

"Sam, I've never done anything like that before."

"And?"

"It's quite amazing."

"That it is," he said.

Her eyes clouded over. "I wish I could stay here, make love with you all afternoon, but I've got to get back."

"I know. But tonight, when he's asleep . . . "

"Yes."

He held her face in both his hands, kissed her lightly on her smiling mouth. "Go on, go take care of your father. I'll see you later."

The smile on Leah's face dissolved, she stiffened and pulled

Sam's hands away from her face. "What is it?" he asked. "What's the matter?"

She searched his eyes. "My God, you don't know," she said.

"What?" He was suddenly afraid.

"Justin isn't my father. He's my husband."

Somehow he'd heard the words, understood them before they formed in her mouth. He's my husband. My husband. My.

His dimension had shifted. Paralysis ebbed around his body; Leah's, too, for neither of them moved. He forced himself to break their silence, an act of will.

"What have you done to me, Leah? What kind of game are you playing?"

She started to cry, and in a broken voice, "No game, Sam. No game."

"You fucked me, Leah, with your husband asleep in the bedroom right below us. Jesus Christ, you called him, 'Daddy!' I don't fuck other people's wives!"

Leah moved her hands over her ears. He lunged for her again, grabbed the sleeve of her dress and it came away from her shoulder with a cracking sound.

"Sam, please don't."

"Please don't," he repeated, lifted her and carried her to the sofa, flung her unceremoniously onto the cushions. "Now, you tell me," he said, his face close to hers, his voice terse. "Why me? Because I was here? Because I was available?"

How many dawnings had he experienced in his life, that time when the light goes on and everything is crystal clear? Here was another fountainhead of truth, one he had no stomach for. He had pronounced this woman his simply because he had wanted her, because they had made love flawlessly. Why had he believed that's all it would take to give him the right to her? He could picture her, his Leah, rounding her back over that twisted old man, bringing her hips to his with a deliberate sway, fucking him. The image sickened him. But why should it? He was the interloper here.

Leah sobbed into her hands. She looked like a child who has just been scolded for touching something she should not have. What did he look like? Did he look like a man guilty of touching something he should not have? All at once, he was tired. "Jesus, Leah," he said quietly. "I run a tree service, not a stud service."

Leah took her hands away from her face, wiped her eyes on the skirt of her dress. "It wasn't like that, Sam. I swear."

"He invited me to dinner, he sent you looking for me. He lined me up for you, isn't that true, Leah?"

For less than a moment, she hesitated. "Yes . . . but, you've got to listen. Please."

I should tell her to shut up, he thought. Tell her I don't want to hear what she has to say. I should throw my gear together, get the hell off McEnery's property. I have no claim to McEnery's property. But he sat watching her, wanting to hear, and fearing what she might say.

"I married him when I was nineteen. I've always called him 'Daddy;' it started as a little joke between us."

Sam felt his gut wrench. He turned his face away from her, but he couldn't block out her words.

"He was wonderful; we had a good life together. For a long time, he was a young man. Nearly thirty years older than I, but young in so many ways." The wistful sorrow in Leah's voice forced Sam to look at her again.

Fresh tears stained her cheek. "He hates being sick, says he wishes he had the courage to end his life, even begged me to help him. . . . " Leah rose from the sofa, went to stand before the window. The sun was high in the sky flooding the small room with a scorching light, yet she shivered, wrapped her arms around her middle, drew into herself. "I couldn't do that and he stopped asking." She turned to look at Sam. "And I couldn't do the other thing he begged me to do. It seemed as though everywhere we went, the ballet, the opera, out to dinner with friends — there was always someone — even in the pitch black of his blindness — someone he would pick to pair me to. A colleague of his, a business acquaintance, a waiter... It's the reason we came here. I'd hoped in the quiet of these woods he would forget, stop bringing it up, just let me be there for him, let me comfort him until he died in peace." She sat down, began to reach for Sam, but stopped. "You've got to understand something, Sam. It was good for us, for me. He wanted that for me, still. But I never ... until you."

Jealousy and guilt lay on Sam's stomach like a bad meal. It had been good for them, for her and the sick old man, when he wasn't sick and he wasn't old. She peered into his eyes. "I can't apologize for that," she said. "Did you think I came without a past, Sam? Does anyone? Do you?"

"No," Sam whispered.

"He's dying. I love him and I always will. But I love you, too. Is that wrong? Is it wrong for him to want a second chance for me? Is it wrong for me to take it? Tell me, Sam. If it's wrong, I'll walk away. You won't have to."

Sam's quiet breathing filled the room. Finally, he took a deep breath, looked through the window at the sunshine. "Have you ever noticed that sometimes there are two full moons in a month? A blue moon. It doesn't happen very often, but it does happen."

Leah's brow wrinkled in confusion. "What does a blue moon have to do with this, Sam?"

He smiled. "Nothing, really. It just came to me when you talked about second chances. I know about second chances, Leah. About starting over."

Sam stood up, gently drew Leah to her feet. "Do you still trust me?

"Yes, Sam. I trust you."

"Okay, then. Go take care of him."

Leah opened her mouth, but no words came. She nodded and left the bungalow and he watched as she walked to the big house, opened the door, and went inside.

Sam stood on the porch of the little house, picked up the gloves he had been wearing earlier, put them on and gathered his tools. That afternoon he would begin to clear away the dried brush atop the higher peaks.

Diva Marie

Simple Gifts

"How's my little girl this evening?" I inquired upon entering the room. He was positioned in the exact manner I had instructed him: all fours on the floor, face down into the pillow, ass sticking in the air behind him.

He raised his head slightly to answer somewhat breathily, "Fine, Mistress."

His voice only gets that seductive air when he's in lingerie, I thought to myself. The items I wore were of a more aggressive kind: a tight-fitting, black patent leather teddy with garters, shiny black stockings, thigh-high patent leather boots, and lace gloves.

My red hair fell partially around my face as I bent to fix one stocking, and I caught him peeking at me from the corner of his eye. "Enough." I said, slapping his upturned ass. "You will get a full view of me later."

"Yes, Mistress." He raised his head.

"Turn your head away from me. There you go. I can hear you without you raising your head." I lifted my booted foot, and placed it on his ass. "Tell me how you felt in the lingerie store today, when you knew the clerks were laughing at you."

"Embarrassed, Mistress. But I admit, I liked it, too."

I removed my foot. "I, for one, loved it. Of course, you do realize there will be more shopping trips like that one?"

"Yes, Mistress."

"You'll get used to them after awhile. Pretty soon, you won't think twice about picking up a girdle on the way home from work," I teased, and gently kicked at his behind.

I moved a wardrobe mirror from its place behind the bedroom door to the other side of the room, positioning it so he could see himself. "Look at that pretty picture. Do you like it?"

"Oh, yes, Mistress."

"Good. I want you to watch everything from this angle, in this mirror." I moved behind him and picked up my gift, the one he had crafted just for me, just for tonight. "It's well-made, slave. I might even reward you twice for making it." He didn't reply verbally this time, just shivered.

The harness was made of fine black leather, accented with silver studs and spikes. It fit perfectly around my waist and through my legs. I saw the alternating emotions in his eyes as he watched me pull it on, his fear and his arousal. *Which feeling feeds off which?* I wondered silently. "Have you ever in your life played with a woman in a strap-on harness?"

"No, Mistress, and definitely not one with such a big cock attached."

I nodded — this was a big one. Looking it over, I estimated at least eight inches in length, and two inches around. I knew he'd never taken as much in his life, and the thought of using it on a near virgin caused quite a flow in my crotch. "This is your last chance, slave. You can get out of this now, with no retribution from me. Are you ready?"

"Yes, Mistress, I'm ready."

Slowly I walked around to face him. Each step sounded menacing on the hardwood floor. "Look at it," I demanded, and pointed to my cock. He raised himself off the floor. "Worship it."

Without hesitation, he took it into his mouth, rocking his body back and forth while he moved his lips over the full length.

I grabbed his hair. "You like to suck my cock, I can tell. Take more of it." I shoved his head down onto the dildo, one, two, three times, then pulled it out. "You're good at giving head, too," I smirked.

"Thank you, Mistress," he grunted.

I walked back to a position behind him. "Watch the mirror," I hissed. "Don't close your eyes, and don't look away."

I knelt behind him while I spread lubricant over the shaft and head of my new cock. I lifted it up to his asshole, and pressed down on his lower back to move him into position. Very slowly, I inserted it.

It seemed to take forever, I wanted inside him so much, but I knew he couldn't take it any faster and still enjoy the experience. He gasped only once, when the head slipped inside him. I was proud of him for being so quiet, and for watching my cock's progress in the mirror without flinching.

Once inside, I reached around his abdomen and pulled him onto my lap as I leaned back onto my legs. He was sitting directly on top of my strapped-on cock; it was entirely inside of him. He groaned when I began to move him up and down, and each time I deliberately pulled the shaft out a little further with each stroke. Soon we had a rhythm established, and I knew he wouldn't be able to contain himself much longer.

"Pull your clit out from under those panties, girl. Stroke it while I pump your new cunt. You've got thirty seconds to come, or don't bother."

I was foolish to have given him such a long time. He came in what seemed like a microsecond, and once he started, it didn't feel as if his muscle spasms would stop. Finally he relaxed. "Lie down on the floor," I said, and I removed my cock.

While I detached the harness, I soothed his ass with a little more lubricant. Then I slid my body up next to his and situated myself in his arms.

"You can take care of my needs when we wake up in the morning," I whispered as I kissed his cheek. "Oh, and happy anniversary."

"Can you believe it's been four years already?" He smiled.

I couldn't. But I was already wondering what to get him next year.

Red Jordan Arobateau

Prince Valiant, Queen Serena & the Peepshow Palace

Serena. Of Mediterranean descent. Her face was wide and full, framed by dark curly hair. Her eyes wide with a greenish hue. Big face. Dark white skin dotted with black hair on her arms and legs. Stocky. A peasant body.

Valiant. A medium-sized butch. Sandy brown hair. Freckled face.

Valiant had not always led such a tame life as she had since this marriage. She'd once been the center of attention, a butch-around-town. But she'd met Serena when she was no longer a baby butch, already worn out from chasing after gals. She was quite ready to be settled and a loyal husband.

They were poor, landless, of the vagabond class. Physically Serena looked ambiguous; she usually wore ladies' pants or tight-fitting jeans upon which she'd stitched some fancy design — embroidered flowers, rainbows. She wore peasant blouses with frills and ladies' boots — though tough, shit-kicking boots — a femmy kerchief over her wild black hair, and a jacket to wrap herself in as a defense. One might think she looked like a strong amazon female and let it go at that — but when she was with Valiant, which she usually was, it was obvious what the two of them were: Queer.

They lived on the third floor — a walkup — of the Avondale Hotel. Dank. Worn carpet. Dusty walls of corridors and stairwells colored beige, no paint in years. A few faint veils of cobwebs showed it was not attended to very often. Theirs was a large room with a makeshift kitchen at one end, a tiny bathroom with sink, toilet and shower stall made of metal rusted into the floor. A kitchen table and chairs sat in the middle of the large room, with a bed set in a corner.

Valiant and Serena had worked for a few seasons for upper middle-class people, even some rich ones, as housecleaners, but they kept losing jobs — Valiant was convinced it was because they were gay. Now, with only a handful of gay guys left to work for, they earned only $150 a week. They'd purchased a broken down car four years back when the jobs had been plentiful. And they didn't live entirely in a depressing, starvation fashion — but not very well either. They were always living on the edge, with never enough money. They'd not paid rent in several places, moving from apartment to apartment, finally coming to rest in this furnished room with a bath and what passed for a kitchen. When Valiant thought about her happy childhood it all seemed to fit — like a penance of sorts — maybe she was finally being forced to share the misery of the majority of the world's people.

At least they had no dependents — not a cat or a dog or even a plant. Footloose and fancy free. And their relationship was full of hugs, love, tenderness and real sex. Serena was no occasional woman — she was a 24-hour, 365-days-a-year woman. She was Valiant's wife.

They'd been married seven years and shared a body language. One would start a sentence, forget what she was saying, so the other would finish the sentence for her. They enjoyed the same TV programs, the same food.

Nights Valiant took her burden of sex to Serena: clit held in her hand, pussy lips squeezed between two fingers, the dripping juices of her vagina. She sought out her lover and her hot loving, and they fucked each other's pussies. It was one of the high points in their relationship. They were not hand-holding lesbians, nor were they spinster sisters. They did nasty, wet, bodily-fluid-exchanging real sex.

Valiant was the more passionate, always inspired to take her wife, to investigate the scent, the heat and eroticism of a woman. Serena's stocky peasant build was sturdy enough to bear up under the full weight of her lover's butch body.

Though they were in love, Valiant still needed to soothe her depression and add zest to their sex life. She did it like this: She was a regular attendee of the Peep Show Palace.

Valiant and her friend Devon ducked and dodged traffic and pedestrians as they walked through the city streets, past multi-million dollar car dealerships, large corporate offices, huge modern skyscrapers, toward a row of grubby residential hotels which still survived in the shadow of the silver and gray towering giants. Homes for the mind-damaged; or for starving seniors; drag queens and kings; other creatures who didn't fit in anywhere else.

The two butches entered a building and descended into the netherworld of the sex industry. The dark interior. Ads for girlie videos, porn, flashing lights all colors of the spectrum, advertising GIRLS!

They turned into the lobby, hands stuffed inside their trousers, sweaty fingers clutching their carefully hoarded green one dollar bills. It was dark inside. Glitzy lights in a galaxy dotted along the ceiling. Music piped in from the center showroom flooded the Palace with the pounding insistence of a masturbatory jerkoff. Mindless men stumbled through the Palace, in and out of booths that showed fuck videos, all in a heightened state of sexual arousal. The place was full of them.

Once in awhile other female customers graced the place —
curious giggling Asian coeds with their boyfriends spilling over
from nearby Chinatown; lost tourists; dykes like Valiant. None
stayed very long. There were no other females today; they were
the lone adventurers in a sea of milling men waiting in front of
a row of doors, a neon sign over each one flashing "Occupied"
in red, or "Vacant," in gold.

They mingled in the dark with the men walking around
waiting for a booth, staring up at the signs over the doors waiting for a golden flashing "Vacant" to appear. Finally they got
two booths side by side.

Valiant stepped into the tiny coffin-tight cubicle. With a
whiz the machine ate up her dollars and the metal screen
slowly lifted. For a few furtive minutes of bliss she watched
pink and tan nude flesh. Women gyrated in front of her, their
legs spread, wearing disinterested looks.

The flesh pit pulled Valiant in, soothed her soul. She lost
herself in that comfortable dark hideaway, and experienced
the high-powered big-money environment. Some deep dark
animal lust, not simply of sexual gratification, but of conquest,
enabled a spiritual release by melding her erotic force with a
nude pink stranger behind glass.

Five dancers strut. Awesome. As a team — all that beauty, all
that power. Nude on high heels, hair coifed, some with pubic
hair shaved. Tits bouncing, pert nipples, backbones erect,
heads held high as if they'd trained in finishing school with a
plate on their heads. Smiles full of sparkling teeth. Four whites,
one tan-complected African-American. Bored straight ladies
undulating slowly, not wasting too much energy, pacing themselves, like race horses, for a full six-hour shift.

Valiant fed dollars, and then when the green stuff ran out,

quarters, into the slot to keep her window open and view the nude girls. She wound up spending all the money in her pocket, bankrupting the household budget for the week. Just to see inside the glass-walled cage of carpeted pink walls and mirrors the warm, naked bodies, the soft hot thighs, the pubic hair as the girls opened themselves up with their fingers; to see pink pussy lips and vulva humping up and down, riding the air.

The peep show dancers thrust their pelvises forward and back, butts jerking, humping in giant arcs, tan and pale skin; they sashayed nude on top of their tall high heels, making devouring arcs, humping air. Strutting on their high heels before mirrors sparkling bright as a drag queen's sequins.

Soon a slender young girl slid down the pole. Valiant got hot in her cubicle. Through the glass she and the girl shared a physical intimacy; the dancer worked her slim hips and tits tantalizingly, while Valiant got hot, blood racing to her clit. Erotic closeness of the dancer pumping, grinding her pussy in the direction of Valiant's face, inches away. Her pale white stomach downed with fine blonde body hair; moist pussy inches away, but separated by glass.

After viewing nude girls Valiant's soul would be at peace, a bridge having been built out of herself into another, leaving her body with a vague tingle of horniness which was not at all desperate, but pleasant, exciting, and expectant — knowing she would fulfill that lust at night with her accommodating wife, Serena.

Valiant's underpants were soggy. Yes, she would take her hot lust and her love embraces and kisses home to her wife that night — or maybe the next, if Serena was too tired, simply put Eros on hold, then summon it up once again, those erotic images, the heightened sexual energy from recent memory of the Peep Show.

From a cubicle around the side of the showroom a shutter slid down. A broke dyke stumbled out from the high tension erotica into the dark hall; hands jammed into the pockets of her sports coat, she looked like a little man walking hurriedly over the red carpeted lobby, and out.

"This drives me crazy," Devon said when they got outside. "Tits and ass. You're lucky you got Serena to go home to."

When Valiant came to bed in the wee small hours of that morning, Serena awakened. "What took you so long?" she murmured. "Do you want to make love?"

"Yes, my queen." She lifted Serena's nightgown, fumbled her pussy folds to find her joy spot.

"My prince," Serena cooed. "Prince Valiant." She lay back on the sheets.

Valiant knelt at the fragrant flower, probing the sweet fleshy folds. With her thumb she stroked Serena's curly wet pubic hair over her vulva, then bent to kiss her thighs. The tip of her tongue licked over her wife's thighs, then flicked, pink, into her pussy. With each forefinger of both hands she smoothed aside the pubic hair and parted the pussy folds. From Serena's viewpoint, Valiant appeared to have twin mustaches on either side of her nostrils as she went down on her. Valiant savored her lover's salty taste.

Once Valiant's mouth was pressed fully upon Serena's sex, her hands reached up and groped for her breasts. As she fondled her tits, squeezing the nipples between her forefingers and thumbs, suddenly she stopped. Her mind had gone blank. The bed stopped its motion.

"What are you doing?" Serena asked in an exasperated tone.

"I thought I was making love to you." Valiant paused in mid-lick, glancing up, her eyes round, questioning. The rest of her body lay like a lump under the covers.

"Well, it seems like you're just fumbling around. Your mind's not on what you're doing."

"Uh . . . I'm sorry," Valiant said sheepishly. In truth, she'd suddenly been struck with pangs of guilt for spending their money at the Peepshow Palace.

"Well, come on. I'm ready," said Serena, slightly pissed. She lay, thighs spread wide, extending her legs, one foot pointing to the right, one to the left, ending in twinkling red nail-polished toes. Her pale white butch squirmed on top of her. In the meeting of their pearl clits, the rub of their hooded cowls, in the hot pussy of her lover, thrusting with urgency, Valiant sighed, "Queen Serena."

"My Prince Valiant," Serena cooed.

Lying between Serena's sturdy thighs Valiant rode her fast as her muscular arms supported the weight of her torso and her white hips began grinding round and round. Their clits became firm and hot, moving together nestled in their mashed-to-gether vulvas, and Serena moaned, a low, guttural warning. Valiant ceased her movement, reached out and grabbed a pillow to put against her wife's face.

"We have to be quiet," she whispered.

"I don't have to!" Serena shouted, pushing the pillow away. "I can scream all I want."

But Valiant couldn't forget about what other tenants might say when she had to face them in the halls the next morning. Once before, during a passionate bout of Serena's sex-satisfied screams, someone had knocked on their door asking if everything was all right. And on another occasion, the manager had informed her to please keep their voices down in the future.

Still, Valiant kept up the passionate pounding of her lust.

"Ohhhhh! Ahhhhh!"

"Serena, please. People will hear," Valiant pleaded, her hips stopped in frozen mid-motion, the palms of her hands sweating.

"I don't care," Serena screamed, tossing her head from side to side. "I'm not ashamed."

Serena humped her hips, jostling for better clit contact, and the two resumed the rhythmic motion of their union. Fire. Fire between their legs. Melting fire. Melting liquid fire. And they were coming.

Serena's passion-rocked cries cut loose to fill the room and echo down the dusty halls of the Avondale Hotel. Faster, faster Valiant pumped, her white ass gleaming in the moonlight. She came with all the frustrations in her soul, pounding out along with her lust all the anxiety and repression she faced daily, all the effacing of her real self.

"Ah, fuck! Ah, fuck!" Even Valiant cried aloud now as her loins melted, a molten shock of orgasmic fire shot through her body and the muscles of her hips and legs and back and arms shuddered.

Sweat poured into the sheets. The dark wild-haired woman cut loose, her voice rising in a second orgasm of even greater intensity, shattering the night stillness, "Ah you butch, fuck me. Fuck me. Ah!"

Finally they collapsed and drifted into sleep. Moonlight shone through the glass.

Susanna J. Herbert

Three Note Harmony

Chocolate Chip Cookie Dough. Cherry Garcia. Macadamia Nut Brittle. Which to choose? Isn't it ironic that we're allowed 31 flavors of ice cream, yet only one flavor of sexuality?

Vanilla.

Man-to-woman, cock-to-cunt, sex-to-sleep.

Not that smooth, creamy vanilla isn't wonderful. But imagine how dull life would be without the occasional dollop of Fudge Ripple. As a girl, my experience with boys was about as exotic as a swirl of Tastee-Freeze. We would "court," we would grope, we would long for more, virginities firmly intact. Both dates and desserts were sweet snacks for an uninitiated palate. How fortunate that time has taught me the infinite joys of a lavish sexual feast.

Derek and Reg began playing together at seventeen. Guitar, that is. Only guitar. Derek left East London for Chicago when his father died and his mum ran off with a sailor from Liverpool. "Reg," short for Adam Reginald, was a Windy City native, raised on Pete Townshend and Willie Dixon. When they met sparks instantly flew. Brought together by an intense love of music, coupled with a passionate, tenacious drive to succeed, their relationship was equal parts Lennon/McCartney and Ali/Frazier.

Derek was tall, wiry and, in his own words, "an insufferable bastard." His thick, semi-sweet chocolate hair was never combed and his dark, scowling, scoundrel's eyes could bore through cast iron. No pretty boy; still, women were attracted to him like bees to clover. His somber sexiness stemmed from a lightning-quick wit, uncanny talent with a Stratocaster, and the world's sexiest ass.

Reg had the radiant face of a fallen angel; a mischievous meld of metallic blue eyes, silky blonde curls and a smile that could melt lead. He was Adam after the first bite of apple. His shoulders and biceps were hard and chiseled, his torso reminiscent of Athenian sculpture. He possessed an intellect as singular as his body. Derek would often complain, "One guy can't 'ave everything! If his cock is longer than two inches, there's no bloody God!" Divinity notwithstanding, Reg had a throbbing eight-inch penis that stayed up all night.

Fortunately, Reg wasn't obsessed with his looks — in fact, he was delighted when, during an argument over a new lyric, a hard right from Derek broke his perfect nose. Or maybe he was just thrilled that the uppercut he shot back knocked Derek on his ass. Did I mention they were best friends?

Derek likes to remind me that he and I connected first. I had graduated from Northwestern, a copywriter who struggled each night to create The Great American Novel. I lived in a tiny flat off Davis Street which, in the '80s, was still a deal. Derek was my part-time neighbor, since he was banging the girl next door. They fucked loudly, and I knew how he came before I knew who he was.

Finishing Chapter Nine would often take a back seat to enjoying the porn soundtrack that wafted through my walls: "Christ, love! Grab me cock! Yeah! Suck it!" Her squeals of ecstasy made me crazy with wonder. What the hell was he *doing* to her?

As they fucked, my hands spent less time on the keyboard than on my aroused body. As her moans grew louder my hands traveled, caressing each spot I'd want a lover to kiss, nibble or suck. I was completely swept into their erotic current.

I would softly stroke my outer lips, feeling the slippery, hot wetness ooze from within. My clit would emerge, hard and hungry, eager to be teased by my thumb. I used my fingers to mimic his cock, letting her moans orchestrate exactly when and how deeply to penetrate. As I probed deeper, I would thrash about, breathing in short, moist bursts. When I came, I'd try not to scream. I had lost my virginity to the vanilla boys, but none of them had fucked me with the fervor and relish of this nocturnal fantasy.

Arriving home late one night, I was drawn to the most hypnotic, soulful guitar I had ever heard. When I reached the third floor, a disheveled lump in worn black leather sat in front of my neighbor's door playing a Gibson, surrounded by shards of broken glass. Blood trickled from a gash over his eyebrow, but he seemed neither to notice nor care.

"You're cut!" I stammered.

"She chucked the mirror at me," he replied calmly. "Got any tea?"

Twenty minutes later, a bandaged Derek was sipping chamomile ("Bloody piss!") and we were engrossed in the first of endless discussions about life and love. Things were finished next door and I was the only one upset about it. He had merely lost a place to crash. I was losing an incredible source of interactive entertainment, years before the invention of CD-ROMs.

I didn't let Derek know about the wall-to-wall intimacy we had shared. Truth was, I couldn't believe this intelligent, complex and sensitive man was the Fuckmonster from Apartment 3. That night he slept on my couch, but never ventured into my bed. Instinct told us we were destined to be friends. That alone was pretty damned precious.

Derek slyly played matchmaker when he invited me to see their four-piece band at an underground club in New Town. I was blown away. Too pure for punk, too much mettle for metal, after six years of sweating blood, they were on the verge of greatness. Derek's lyrics were cut-glass poetry, and Reg ripped them out as if emerging from a frosty mountain stream into a wildflower-covered mine field. One look at Reg and I fell instantly in lust, unaware the combustion would later forge the love of my life. Afterwards, the three of us walked to the lake, sat on the rocks, and talked and laughed as if we'd known each other for years. Derek was clearly pleased.

It began in the back seat of Reg's beat-up '73 'vette, Derek at the wheel. As we rattled north on Lake Shore Drive, going far too fast, Reg's hand moved to my bare thigh and caressed the flesh between my skirt and stockings. Our first kiss was a swim in a soothing pool that seemed to go on for days. My hand was on his crotch (Did he put it there? Did I grab it?) and the size of his hard-on made me gasp. Reg loved to kiss as much as I did, and he augmented tender touches with quick, unexpected bites to my neck. The heat was overpowering. I couldn't let him go, yet I wasn't prepared to make love in the back seat of a moving vehicle, my new pal in the driver's seat. I didn't do such things. Or did I? Before I could decide, Derek called out, "Look 'ere, Reg, don't be a bastard to this one or I'll kick your ass. She's awright. She's got a brain — and killer tits!"

Derek dropped us off at their apartment, and left to meet his flavor-of-the-moment. Once inside, we quickly shed our disheveled clothing. We faced each other — so closely his breath tickled my skin — but didn't touch. We swayed, my nipples caressing his smooth, hard chest, his arms running down my back, his hands squeezing my ripe ass. We couldn't stop touching each other, exploring new and enticing terrain. He fed me his fingers, ten tiny cocks, connected by an equal number of minuscule cunts. Every nerve ending became sexual. We fell onto the bed and kissed and kissed as his cock throbbed against the outer lips of my pulsating cunt.

He adored my breasts with sweet kisses and soft sucking, squeezing each nipple between his forefinger and thumb. His tongue moved like a hummingbird's wing, down to my belly. Slowly spreading my legs, he lightly tickled my inner thighs as his lips explored my cunt. I rocked. I gasped. I may have died, traveled to Venus, or recited Yeats in a Celtic tongue. He brought me to the brink, again and again, knowing just when to stop and when to begin. The feeling was like running naked from a sauna into a fresh snow bank. My senses exploded in orgasm.

I was starving for his cock. Veins throbbed from every angle, crying to be licked and sucked. I swallowed the shaft and ran my tongue around his undulating balls. He threw his head back and yowled. I wanted to ride him to climax, but there was no stopping either one of us. As he called out my name, he came deep into my throat. Spent, we held each other. Heartbeat to heartbeat, he traced my face with his finger and said, "Derek was right. You are special."

I asked, too casually, "Does he always get you women?"

"Don't insult yourself. Or me," he said sharply.

"Let's rest." I said. "I want you inside of me. Maybe later."

"What do you mean, later?" He rolled on top of me, and we rocked in a dozen combinations until well past dawn.

Three years passed. Reg and I were in love. We all shared a place, although Derek — who chewed up and spat out women like sticks of gum — rarely slept at home. A record label had shown interest in some of the band's demos. I sold some fiction. It looked like we'd soon be able to afford to stock the fridge without stealing food from wherever they were playing. Things couldn't have been better, but Derek was suddenly behaving cold towards us in the club and distant whenever he actually came home. Repeated attempts to talk were met with stony silence. We tried logic, humor and threats to break through. Nothing. Finally, frustrated, Reg called him an unfeeling asshole. Derek shoved him, hard. Reg hit the table with such force, dishes smashed to the floor. Unhurt but stunned, he pushed Derek back toward the wall.

I'd seen them yell and roughhouse like schoolboys when arguing about their music, but never with this level of fury. I pulled them apart and Derek stormed down the hall, shouting, "Piss off, both of you. It's over."

When I got to his room, he was throwing clothes into his backpack.

"Derek, what the hell is going on? This is insane."

"Leave me alone."

"Goddammit! Why are you lashing out at us? We love you."

"Bullshit."

"What's 'bullshit'? You're my best friend."

"Not anymore. Don't want your friendship." Cut and dried.

That stung. We were *comrades* who'd been through everything together, good and bad. We'd painted each other's rooms, nursed each other's needs, ripped apart and praised each other's work. Hurt and furious, I snapped, "What have I ever done to deserve such fucking coldness from you?"

He spun around, silencing me with a piercing stare. "I'm in love with you."

I lost all composure. "We . . . can . . . work it out. . . . "

"No, we can't." He spoke quietly, without apology. "I'm in love with '*im*, too."

Absolute silence. My mind was spinning through a montage of memories we three had shared. There'd always been women on the periphery — women who Derek happily pushed away before they got too close. Still, I never would have guessed this. When I tried to speak, he cut me off.

"I didn't plan it, but that's how I feel. You're the only people I care about in the fucking world. And you've got each other. And I'm thrilled for you. But it kills me. So, I'm going." He was crying. Fearless Derek. I put my arms tightly around him and felt my own tears fall.

"Why didn't you tell us?"

"Are you insane? 'Oh, by the way, I know I've always been straight, but I fuck boys now, as well as girls, pretending they're you.' He'd never understand."

From the doorway, Reg broke the silence. "I understand."

Reg entered. Together we clumsily held each other. I wept like an idiot, afraid I'd come between their friendship, afraid ours was over. Slowly, silently, the energy shifted. Derek tenderly ran his hands through my hair, again and again. Reg kissed me, and licked the salt from my cheek. I closed my eyes and felt a new pair of lips brush mine: Derek's. Reg squeezed my shoulder, urging me to continue. I kissed my dearest friend. He was urgent, a bit rough but soothing — like raw velvet. His stubbled cheek gave me goosebumps. I felt lightheaded, as simultaneously Reg ran his tongue along my neck and behind my ear.

Together they undressed me, then removed their own clothes without any physical contact. For now, I was the conduit for their sexual energy. Nothing was said, unusual for the three of us. Not that things were silent. We'd touched upon a new language.

I cupped my hands and squeezed my full breasts together. Each man chose a nipple to explore. Now Derek was the gentle one. The hot, moist kisses from his soft lips offered a thrilling contrast to Reg's more insistent sucking. The dual sensation was so intense, my knees buckled. They slid their arms through mine, to keep me upright. Suddenly, we were face-to-face-to-face.

No one moved. No one dared breathe. Our eyes mirrored a mixture of excitement, tenderness, and sheer panic. Reg, who had never touched a man sexually, looked shaky. Derek was clearly fascinated, but didn't make a move. I took the lead, playfully gliding my lips to Reg, to Derek, to Reg and back again, each kiss subtly maneuvering their faces closer together. Then I stepped back. Reg gasped, not quite silently. Derek had never looked more vulnerable. Hands glued to their sides, they tentatively brushed their mouths across each other, a precarious nuzzle that longed to become a kiss. At last, their lips relaxed into a yielding embrace. It was a bit awkward, but genuine. Neither quite knew where or if to touch. Arms stirred, then froze. It was sweet. It was hot. And it grew hotter. Much hotter.

I had never been turned on by gay porn, but this was the most erotic dance I'd ever seen. They clutched at each other, simultaneously reaching for me. Transfixed, I felt two hearty erections nudge my thighs. Wild with emotion, I dropped to the floor and went for their cocks.

Derek's was smaller, but magnificently thick and uncut. Reg's shot straight out, swollen and glorious. I squeezed the torrid, turgid flesh, sucking one throbbing head, then both. The taste was sweet, then salty; scent of soap and sweat. Delicious. Above me, I watched them bite and kiss, listened to them moan.

I was soon on the bed with Derek's tongue at my clit. Reg looked on, methodically stroking himself. I purred in ecstasy, remembering the Fuckmonster from Apartment 3. I tried not to explode, but the way Reg watched us — along with Derek's singular skill — set me off. Reg kissed me as *he* wildly came. There were more tears, now of joy.

Derek hadn't climaxed. He was ecstatic, but I felt we had to go to the next level. Reg knew my thoughts and looked nervous — but hard. I got on my knees and rubbed my ass against my lover's crotch. From behind, Reg plunged slowly into my cunt. Derek slid beneath me, took his wondrous tongue and touched my clit. Licked and fucked. A bolt of electricity shot through me. Why had no one told me such sensations were possible?

As much as I didn't want Derek to move, I nudged him toward the hungry cock ravaging my pussy. Reg froze for an instant, then realized there was nothing to fear. Each time he pulled back, Derek sucked and nipped every emerging inch of hot flesh. Reg loved it. Derek's cocksucking skills were so dexterous, I was overcome with voyeuristic desire. I thrust my pelvis forward and, before Reg knew it, my cunt was replaced by his best friend's eager, talented mouth.

What a sight! Derek teased Reg as he had teased me, teaching me a thing or two about fellatio in the process. Inch by glorious throbbing inch Reg's cock disappeared into Derek's insatiable mouth. Reg was in another world, panting Derek's name and mine as his pelvis thrust deeper and deeper down his partner's throat. Derek's own cock was rock-hard by now.

I could no longer merely watch the boys at play. I pulled back Derek's foreskin and tried my damnedest to mimic what he was doing to Reg. Through the lust and sweat, Derek looked at me with a tenderness I had never seen in his face before, all the while sending my darling Adam Reginald into another stratosphere. Reg fiercely came, followed a millisecond later by a writhing Derek who, after swallowing Reg's come, rubbed his exploding cock across my body. Both men, competitors in everything, raced up and down my flesh, seeing who could lick the most come off my belly and breasts.

After that, it's difficult to recall exactly who did what to whom. At one point, I tried to get Reg to suck Derek. I remember being massaged by four hands and two cocks. Some time past sunrise, someone cried, "I love you."

Who said it? Who were they talking to? Who knows?

We all said it. We all meant it.

Shar Rednour

June's High Holy Day

June says that she has always relied on her imagination to make her gifts special — and let me tell you, what I get on my birthday is nothing like that homemade vase her mom got last Christmas.

Of course I had fantasies before meeting June, but as with so many people, they stayed in my head. Then came June, who thinks that Willy Wonka is real; she won't let me throw her stuffed animals on the floor for fear of hurting their feelings; and she values storybooks more than diamonds.

Sometimes the fantasies simply involve a special pair of eyeglasses or maybe a certain place or certain words, but many times our fantasies involve other people — characters — some with leading roles, others with only cameos — and, of course, a smattering of extras. The extras seem to be the ones who really make the fantasy — and sometimes they're the hardest to find.

I started seeing June almost eight years ago. It wasn't love at first sight but rather love at first *kiss* which came right after staring at each other for fifteen minutes or so. On one of our first dates — after fucking for ages, then eating in bed and drinking wine and all that — I was lying on my back on June's bed listening to Sade when June had one of her bursts of high energy and ran into her closet. She emerged wearing only her dad's Schlitz muscle shirt and a pair of gogo boots. She danced over my face before sitting on it for a few minutes, then disappeared into her closet again, this time reappearing in a *Cat on a Hot Tin Roof*-style slip and vintage high heels. She made me cream: one outfit and persona after another. We laugh about it now, but at the time I couldn't believe how fucking incredible she was and she couldn't believe it was turning me on so much.

None of her other lovers ever got it. Ever got June. Or Jeannie, Elizabeth, Sophia or Endora. Those are just the ones with names — there's also Slave, Bitch, Mommy, and Kitten. Lucky me — I've gotten them all and more. Since June's sexuality is inextricably intertwined with being an object of desire, my turn-on was her turn-on. After all, what's a show without an appreciative audience?

Other lovers had just laughed; they didn't get the boner she'd expected. So when I was thrilled, it was one more way we saw soulmates in each other. Sharing our fantasies and making up new ones became an intricate part of our sex life. What we can't act out we turn into stories. Begging her to "tell me a story" and jacking off as she filled my ears with what my dirty mind had only dared to dance with became my favorite position. She'd dress up as Ginger Grant seducing the professor on "Gilligan's Island," or become the big-breasted wife in a Russ Meyer flick — and she has the closet to do all this.

On date number four we listed all the sex make-believe we wanted to live out. Have we calmed down over the years? Well, we've been sick, unemployed, crazy, depressed, and bogged down with family dramas — so, no, we haven't gone to bed with nasty stories every night. But let's just say the surprises never stop.

For example, she just now sauntered in wearing only a red bra and a tiny, tiny apron.

"Honey, I'm writing." I don't sound very convincing. She's

trying to distract me by *faux* dusting my desk with a feather duster attached to a butt-plug that sits snug in her ass. Help me.

"I am so sorry I didn't get your room clean while you were out!" She wiggles her saucy ass, flips her wild, black hair to look over her shoulder.

"The other maids and I were having such a good time." She's pulling her breasts out of the miniscule bra and pinching her nipples. "Am I bothering you?"

"Sweetie, you know I gotta finish this story," *Fuck,* she's so hot. The anal thing always throws me over the edge.

She has her ass on the desk and is wiggling again. Mommy.

She turns around and her lips are two inches away, "Oh, big business man are you? You didn't put out the 'do not disturb' sign." She blinks big as if *innocennnnnnnnnnnxxxxx@@@######*

I'm back. Oh shit, I think I got lube on the computer keys. Where were we? Oh, yes, the fantasies. I could go on . . . . But first you need to know about June's High Holy Day — her birthday.

June believes in celebrating birthdays. She celebrates the person, the mom for giving birth, and the dad on his anniversary of a joyous day. For at least a month she celebrates in big and small ways. Her favorite saying is, "Get what you want" and she truly believes that we can all have almost any fantasy come true. Since knowing June, fairy tale birthdays have come to life — both mine and hers. Eight years of real life that's better than a fantasy; make-believe made no-big-deal in our cynical world. Adults forget how to play.

We're lying in bed. Today was her day off, but I worked like a dog. We are feeling sexual but I am not in much of an initiating mood. She taps her finger on my chest. "What do *you* want?" she asks.

"Tell me a story," I say. And she begins:

You've been told that there's a new gift waiting for you in the west wing. The tails of your velvet coat swing behind your tight thighs and ass. The soles of your fine leather riding boots strike the glimmering polished marble floor assuredly. You push open the doors and there she is. Long, dark, curly hair falling around her face, the sheer tunic the servants dressed her in revealing her curves, her dark nipples. There's a gold shackle around her ankle that keeps her on the jewel inlaid solid gold four-poster bed, along with the chains around her wrists. She lies on piles of silk. The servants have followed your commands to the letter. She has been bathed in flower waters, massaged with oil of olives, stroked in every crevice and cranny. It may be awful that she has been cap-tured and she may always prefer freedom but you know that she will be treated better here than anywhere in her peasant world. The servants have fed her berries of delirium, put smoke to her lips and prodded her pussy, sucked at her nipples, male and female putting their genitals to her mouth. To initiate her. As you circle the bed you see the blue and purple marks on her wrists from fighting. The oils have soaked through her tunic so that it clings to her, a second skin.

'Wake up, my sweet,' you say.

Her eyes digest you. And you, in your princely cockiness, know that she wants to hate you but you don't look like the monster she's heard about. Your skin is smooth and hairless over your hard jaw, your shirt and jacket are open enough to reveal a chest of smooth muscles and she looks to your crotch but there your shirt tail hides whatever she is looking for.

Her black eyes tighten on you and you swear that she is going to spit on you, you've seen that look before. Instead she says, 'Bring your cock to my mouth, you do have one? Bring it to me . . . . Master.' She licks her lips. Oh, if only you were that stupid! You slap her hard across the face then circle back away from the bed and say, 'Oh, you will choke on all of me but first let me treat you, yes, to some of the sweet honey our land produces.' Slaves hold jars of honey above her twisting legs and drizzle it over her thighs and into the hair of her cunt.

Two guards, each with a huge black monster dog, appear. 'Have the dogs clean her,' you say. And she screams.

The two well-trained canines jump onto the bed and thrust their noses between her legs. . . .

How can I explain the orgasm? I explode.

I know I should be finishing this story but a girl's gotta have some fun too. June and I are playing hooky. We've called in sick to work. Please don't tell anyone in San Francisco this — we'd be embarrassed if they knew we don't go strolling through the Castro — but we pretend we are tourists and go down to Ghirardelli Square at Fisherman's Wharf. We hold hands, moon over each other, blocking out the tourists' stares. We share shrimp cocktails, little bottles of wine, and a loaf of bread while sitting on the edge of a pier. We walk, talk, browse the street artists' wares and make out in doorways.

We leave barely in time to beat rush hour. People are just beginning the push out of doorways into streets, into people. I grab June's hand and we jump on a 68 bus which heads down the length of the Embarcadero. We slip into the last available seats. Soon people are hovering over us and every space is taken.

Her hand lies casually in my lap and she does that absent-mindedly-fingering-your-clothes thing. When she discovers the hole in the crotch of my pants she says "Honey, you never did patch these jeans."

"I tried. I gotta get a better patch."

Her middle finger slips through the hole and past my BVDs to my clit.

"Now, now," I admonish, putting my hand on her wrist.

She pushes her hand down and whispers into my ear, "*You are gonna make a scene and we don't want that, do we? Right now it just looks like my hand is resting in my girlfriend's lap —* no one is counting how many fingers are present."

I relax my hold on her wrist and feel her relax her hand again. "Good," she says, then raises her voice for the benefit of any eavesdroppers. "Oh, honey, look at that," pointing to nothing outside the window.

I smile and say, "Wow."

Delicately, just barely, she strokes down the hood of my clit, over and over. The tenderness of just the tip of her finger is such a tease. I grip the bar in front of me as if I were on a rollercoaster that is getting ready to take off. June leans over me, acting like she's looking out the window. Under her breath, into my ear she begins:

It's the street fair and we are snaking through the crowded streets. I have on a mini-dress and no panties. You have shaven my cunt bald and my pussy lips bulge hard with blood. I am so turned on that I almost come with each step. You tell me that you have a plan and that I will get relief soon. I moan; I am thinking that you are going to finally touch me and not just tease with your hand on my ass. You push me into a stinky booth full of barrels of empty beer cans and an old ice cream cart. I sit on the cart and pull you in between my legs so you'll kiss me. You do. You stroke my thighs and pull at my ass. We're moaning and kissing and grabbing at each other. Suddenly you flip me around and bend me over the ice cream cart. 'You want to be fucked?' you ask me. 'Huh, you need some dick up your cunt?'

*I gasp, 'Oh yes! Please, please fuck me.' My pussy is so
swollen I think I'm going to die.*
*You hold my elbows and push your pelvis into me. 'You need
some dick, huh?'*

My knuckles are turning white from gripping the bar. "I
don't know how much longer I can do this," I say.

June laughs and says, "Just laugh through it because you're
not getting out of it." She laughs, once again pointing to something out the window.

"I mean it," I say.

"So do I," she says, and moves her action on my clit up a
level, hitting my favorite rhythm.

She continues the story:

'You need some dick, huh?' you ask.
'Yea, Baby, please I really need your dick,' I answer.
'Did I say anything about mine?' you say and I gasp, startled.
*I start to turn my head and you grab me by the back of my
neck and push my head down. 'Don't turn around, Bitch, did
I say you could turn around?' Then I hear you say in a low
voice, 'Pull on up to the bumper, boys, she is wet and ready.
Don't touch my bitch though, you just get to sink your dick
into her.'*
'No!' I scream.
'Shut up, Bitch.'
*And then sliding up to my pussy is slippery, latex-covered
warmth. 'It's warm and soft, Daddy,' I say, 'not like your cold
rod.'*
*You tell the guy, 'Slam into her.' And he does. His big dick
splits my lips right open and he is scratching the itch I've had
so bad and even though I want a hard fucking I am afraid to
fuck him back for fear of angering you. I know I should just
hold still.*

*'Fuck her harder,' you growl, and he does. He fucks and fucks
and I scream and scream. You watch my asshole as his dick
goes in and out of my pussy. You see my asshole puckering,
begging for your cock . . . .*

"Oh, shit," I moan, interrupting June. I am going to come any
second. I release the bar in front of me to punch the wall of the
bus, then grab it again, "Fuck," I say, under my breath.

"Laugh," June says in a sing-song voice, her finger never
stopping.

The orgasm grips my cunt and clenches all my muscles, "Ha
ha, that's quite a knee slapper," I scream through gritted teeth,
as I come, trapped on an overflowing bus. "Oh, boy, June, what
a jokester!"

You know how your pussy just twitches and twitches with
aftercome? That's what mine is doing right now.

"What are you doing, June?"

She has plopped into my lap and is scrolling down, reading
what I have written so far.

*You've been told that there's a new gift waiting for you in the
west wing. The tails of your velvet coat swing behind your
tight thighs and ass.*

"These are all the times I told you dirty stories," she says,
squinting at the computer. "And this one too?"

*I am going to come any second. I release the bar in front of
me to punch the wall of the bus . . . .*

"Bobbi — that just happened!" she exclaims. "Are you telling
everything?"

"Honey, I'm trying to be realistic." I did wonder how far she was going to let me get, you know, broadcasting our sex life to anybody out there.

"And look," she points. *'Shut up, Bitch.'* It's just all these stories where I'm running a foul mouth and getting you off. At least tell some of the ones where we actually have sex and it's not just me talking dirty."

"Sugarplum," I say, scrolling up to very first paragraph, "what does this say?"

What I get on my birthday is nothing like that homemade vase her mom received last Christmas.

'What I get on my birthday,' see? I'm just leading up to it."

"Oh," she sighs, probably a little disappointed that she doesn't get to remind me of more of our stories. "Okay. Just checking on you. 'The Nanny' will be on in thirty minutes, the clock in here is wrong so look at the one on your computer." She kisses me, then gets up from my lap.

"I'm going to work. Tell Fran I said hi." She waves over her shoulder and is gone.

You need to know that I am mostly a top, but June knows that I can be a bottom if it's in the service of her pussy. Also know that she likes to confuse her participants, so that just when you think one thing is going to happen, some other twist or tease will surface.

So, it was eight years ago, my birthday. We had been together nine months but weren't living together yet. I awoke to a knock on my door. A young butch in a thrift-store tuxedo and a punky young femme in a flouncy mini-skirt and tap shoes greeted me with their version of "Happy Birthday." The femme threw herself into my arms and planted a big kiss on my mouth. As I stood there dumbfounded with purple lipstick all over my face, the butch slapped an envelope into my hand. Then they were gone. I tore open the envelope and read, *"Be clean, shaven, fed, packing your dick and feeling good by 5 p.m. You'll be fetched. PS: You'll have a mind-blowing time but you must trust me and most importantly trust that I know you.*

This trust was a big deal. I'm really not inclined to put myself in vulnerable positions; in fact I've only done so with June, and only in our most intimate moments. I tried to calm my worries by telling myself that she probably just had a bevy of babes for me to fuck.

I had lunch with my sister and spent the rest of the day getting ready. My emotions were all over the place. I felt nervous excitement at such a fancy date, annoyance that I hadn't seen her all day, horny anticipation solely from not having her in my arms for 48 hours, and trepidation — that whole birthday responsibility thing, thinking she is doing so much and what if I hate it? I don't want to do something I don't enjoy and have to pretend to be happy — I mean it is *my* birthday.

A friend picked me up, smiled, said, "don't worry," and drove us to an obscure Victorian in the hills overlooking the Castro. Once inside, I was left alone until June appeared from a dark corner wearing a robe.

"I love you." She kissed me. I pulled her hard into me and kissed her back, anticipation shoving me into her throat. I wanted to remind her who was boss. I grabbed her ass and slammed her into my pelvis.

Her fingernails went into my neck. "Yoowww! Time to slow down, Big Boy." She kissed me once more, sweetly, but pulled away before I could get crazy again. "Listen to me, I love you. You trust me?"

"I'm not good with surprises."

"This will be one of the most amazing nights of your life but you have to give me total control and know I will use it wisely. It's that or nothing. But don't just say it, you really have to trust me. So?" She pressed into me. Her smell made me swoon.

I took a deep breath. "Okay, you have total control." I pulled her to me tight again. "But remember, I'm trusting you."

"Last thing: nothing will happen tonight that I won't know about. Nothing will happen that isn't okay with me."

"What are you talking about — *I* don't know anything; I hope *you* know what's going on."

She shook her head, which meant I didn't understand. "Kiss me now, you won't be seeing June for awhile."

"What?" My heart fell; I wanted to spend my fucking birthday with her!

She pecked my lips. "Trust me. I said, you won't be seeing *June* for awhile."

I contemplated that clarification as June left me. Minutes passed and then a strong, English-accented voice bounced through the hallway. "Oh, another scummy slave." My friend Jeanie emerged from the shadows.

"Jeanie. What are you doing?"

"It's Salinka the slavemaster to you, you piece of slime. You types think you can just charm your way out of everything. Well, now you're really stuck. Follow me peacefully, or I'll bring in the heavies." She slapped a two-foot long leather paddle in her hands then turned back toward the darkness. Her auburn hair missiled out into short pigtails held by studded leather cock rings; they looked anything but childish. She wore a shiny new leather gladiator skirt and chest harness; thrown over them was a ratty army jacket left hanging open. She came across as some sci-fi post-war sadistic prison warden. I watched her high, round ass as I followed her. Soon I was stripped of everything but my dildo and harness and put into leather shorts and a spiked collar. I begged to keep my boots and Salinka allowed me to wear them.

"Hold out your wrists."

"No, Jeanie, come on, you're not supposed to do that, are you?"

She smiled sweetly, bent down to whisper in my ear as I sat on the floor. "Probably not, it's just for fun, come on, now, don't ruin the surprise." She winked.

I decided to stop worrying and go along for the ride. I held out my wrists.

Jeanie — that is, Salinka — clasped big, real shackles around my wrists. "Hey, Jeanie, these are pretty serious, I —" *Smack.* She hit me hard across the face.

"That was for calling me 'Jeanie,' you filthy worm." *Smack.*

"That was for being such a pathetic asshole that you thought you could talk your way out of the Queen's lair." Her accent had returned and I forgot who Jeanie was. I raged at this slave master for hitting me so boldly when I had done nothing to deserve her wrath.

"Don't ever question me. Get down." She kicked me between the shoulder blades, knocking me down to my elbows with my ass in the air.

"I know you don't like this, but you better take it on your ass or I'll break the teeth out of your handsome little mouth." She paddled me. I wouldn't give her the satisfaction of even a moan.

"I'm getting bored down here. Aren't we supposed to be doing something?" She hit harder.

"You're a smartass, aren't ya?" She kicked me in the shoulder, knocking me sideways, then pulled me by my hair to her pussy. "You want to be a good boy? If you're good then you can have a taste of Salinka. What the Queen doesn't know won't hurt her."

I was ready to go from pain to lust; just seeing her tits shake as she smacked me was driving me wild. I heard June's voice in my head: *"Nothing will happen that isn't okay with me."*

"Oh, please Mistress Salinka. I learned my lesson." I licked my lips.

She laughed. "Oh, don't grovel, my pet. Come here to Salinka's pussy." She shoved my face into her cunt. I wiggled my nose and tongue through her wiry, black hair until I felt the softness of her inner lips with my tongue. I nibbled, bit and licked like a little puppy. Salinka's firm grip on my head never faltered. I let her guide my mouth to the right position so she could fuck my face until she bucked and came in my mouth.

She pushed me back on my haunches. "Let's get you to the Queen before that bitch sends the hounds after me." Clink. She snapped a leash onto the collar.

I crawled on my hands and knees up a flight of stairs, around a winding, dark hallway to a large oak door. Sounds of laughter drifted into the hallway. Salinka kept me still, waiting. She bent down and sneered, "Why don't ya stick ya nose down there at the crack and see if ya can sniff her out, slave. Can ya sniff out the Queen?"

She pushed my head to the floor where a sliver of light, smells and sounds teased me. I *could* smell her and I could hear her full, hard laugh. I wanted to float like a magic carpet under the door and plant myself beneath the Queen's precious feet.

"Sniff, I said!" Salinka's harsh voice shattered my daydream. I scowled at her. She pushed my head down again, holding it there. "Sniff like the dog you are." I sniffed a little; when she relaxed her grip I jerked back and spat at her feet.

"You piece of shit!" *Smack.* It only half hit because I rolled out of her reach. She was grabbing at me when the door opened.

Suddenly I was staring at boots polished so high that I could see my reflection in them. I looked up into the face of a butch in a very upscale guard's uniform. She returned my stare with disdain. "Keep your eyes on the floor."

"Salinka," the Queen's voice echoed into the hallway. A pause ensued and I could feel everyone in the room getting nervous — finally, someone besides me. "Are you having problems controlling the slaves again?"

"No, your Highness. I, no, I . . . "

"Salinka, leave your slave with the guard and approach my throne." Her every word sent shivers down my spine.

"Your Highness, I, yes, your Highness." I heard Salinka's well-worn boots shuffling away from me.

"If this slave's face smells of you she'll be mounting you like one of my Dobermans. Guard, bring in the slave."

"No, ma'am, it's disgusting and filthy, don't, I'm sorry, I'm truly sorry."

The guard dragged me onto a red carpet

"Angelina," the Queen's voice changed to a purr, "sweetheart, put your face very near — but don't touch, my dear, because it *is* truly a filthy creature — put your face very near to this thing and tell me what you smell."

Angelina's name fit — a truly angelic face came into my vision. She had buttery toffee for skin, wore her curls naturally like a halo around her face, and her eyes were the color of a chocolate river. She put her cheek just an inch from mine and sniffed — just as I had at the door. Her seemingly innocent eyes narrrowed as she inhaled Salinka's scent. She curled an eyebrow at me, then moved out of my vision again.

"Your Majesty, she doesn't smell clean. She smells of dank places, a place I cannot name but which has been on my own fingers."

"Angelina cannot tell a lie, Salinka. Unfortunate for you." I appreciated her rhythm of speech: solidly delivered words punctuated by pauses to work our nerves and make us weak. I clung to the sound of her voice, for I still had not been able to see my Queen. "So," pause, "guard, pick up," pause, "this, this *thing*." Pause. "Let me see its face."

They dragged me and dumped me at her feet. I recognized the sleek, muscular lines and the perfectly painted toenails which commanded a pair of red patent leather high heels from behind red fishnet stockings. My first thought was to look up at June, the Queen, but a natural instinct took over and I found myself leaning forward to kiss her feet.

"Outrage!" *Thwack.* She hit the side of my head with a riding crop. "Not only did you violate my property, Salinka, but you didn't even succeed in training it! You pathetic excuse of a slavemaster. You master nothing but your own asshole and now I will master even that."

"No, your Highness." Salinka's voice wasn't a grovel or a plea but a statement. I remembered this was a game and wondered if June was about to cross some line.

"Look at me, creature."

I was immediately brought back to my role.

I let my eyes follow the trail of her crossed legs past the top of her thigh-high stockings, past the meeting of her delicate dark thighs. I noticed that she wore an elaborate gown split open to her crotch, piles of red fabric on each side like curtains that could be shut at any time. This led to a tight bodice, bulging cleavage, the throat that begged of sucking, and my Queen's face, framed by ringlets of hair falling down from a sparkling crown. I looked into her deep, hazel eyes only for a second.

"My Queen." I quickly bowed my head.

"Wrong! Do not address me. Ever. It is *I* who is examining *you*. Lift your head like a good sow."

I did as I was told, indignant that I didn't even seem worthy of worshipping her. That pissed me off. She poked my head side to side.

"It seems to have good bones and teeth. Let's see what else. Lean up on your haunches."

Yes, this is more like it, I thought. I leaned back to reveal my specially chosen cock, knowing she couldn't resist it.

"Hung like the court donkey," she said. This witticism brought peals of laughter and I suddenly remembered the voices I'd heard earlier. Quickly I looked around and saw that the room hosted ten or more others, all aristocratically dressed in gowns and tuxedos from various eras.

"Angelina, pull it out, my dear."

The girl gasped but did unbutton my shorts until my pride tilted out like a lowering drawbridge.

"Guards, bring Salinka. Everyone, let's have some entertainment, shall we?"

"Hear, hear!" Fans quickened, cigars puffed, and nails clicked.

"Guards, undo the shackles from the creature's wrists. You know the rest."

Just as my excitement for freedom rose it quickly crashed. The guards released only one of my wrists, then forced Salinka to stand with her back to me. They shackled her right wrist to my right wrist. I knew what they wanted. I grabbed her other wrist before she could wrestle it away.

"Fuck her, donkey. Fuck the filthy Salinka who likes to spoil my goods."

The crowd clapped and shouted with anticipation.

The Queen looked me square in the eye. "You can fuck her right up the ass, donkey, right up the ass."

"Bitch." Salinka's voice brought the applause to a halt.

The Queen slowly rose from her throne, leaned into Salinka's face and spat.

"Test me . . . my Queen," Salinka said slowly, and fought no more.

The Queen returned to her throne and flounced her skirts in the court's dead silence. Then she tilted her head back, smiling evilly. "Guards, prep the meat," she commanded and fell into laughter.

The guards stood on each side of us. One donned a latex glove and poured streams of lube into the deep crack of Salinka's fine ass. One guard pushed a hand into the crevice and worked in the lube. Salinka couldn't help but push back and grind her hips around. I just watched, my inner boner growing as my outer dick bobbed against her flesh, waiting for entry. The other guard rolled a condom onto my dick and shined it up with lube.

"Do it, donkey," the Queen said teasingly. The court chanted, "Do it, donkey, do it."

I teased her hole until she pushed back into me. The head of my dick glistened between her cheeks. *What a big dick for an ass, I hope she can take it*, I thought, as I sank the head into her darkness. "Oh baby," I muttered.

"Oh, yeah, I can take it, donkey, don't hold back. Oh yeah," she moaned, and pushed back into me. My dick slid until my belly pressed against her ass cheeks. I grabbed her wrists and used them like reins as I banged into her harder and harder.

The Queen squealed and yelled, "Look at Salinka's titties bounce as she gets plowed — plowed by a donkey!" and more peals of laughter arose from the court. I faintly registered their heat rising and their clothes dropping as the sounds of sex mixed in with their laughter.

"Bounce those titties, donkey, bounce those titties and plow that ass." I looked over Salinka's straining back into the Queen's face. From the height of her throne she could see everything. She smiled wickedly at me, then tossed her head to the side shouting more orders. "Angelina! My feet. Lick my feet, you precious slut."

Angelina threw herself at the Queen's feet and took up her task. The Queen's face soon softened so I knew the girl's mouth was working hard. I just kept fucking and Salinka kept fucking me back, moaning and egging me on. I grabbed her shoulder and growled into her ear, "Come like it's your pussy. You like me fucking your ass? Fucking your ass like it's your pussy? I bet you can come with my donkey dick up your ass, come like it's your pussy, slave . . . master."

The Queen looked drugged. She took little gasps of breath and watched us through heavy-lidded eyes. Angelina's head bobbed frantically.

"Oh, yeah, that's it, slave, that's it."

"Come like it's your pussy, come for me," I reached around, pinching her nipple with my free hand. She shoved her fingers in between her legs and jerked, coming on my dick. The Queen came too, screaming and writhing in her throne. I groaned from the pressure pounding back into my clit. Five seconds more and I could have come but Salinka pulled away from me and, forgetting the shackles, brought us both tumbling to the floor.

We lay panting; I was totally frustrated. I had a moment to look around and see people in all stages of sex: lapping, fucking, kissing, teasing, coming.

My head lolled to the side. The red-dressed feet stood there.

"Guards, unshackle them and have the maidens bathe the *thing*." I looked up in time to see only her retreating skirts. The guards dragged me from the lust-filled den and shoved me into a candlelit room with a hot tub. Angelina and another ethereal treat welcomed me. Angelina smiled sweetly and motioned me toward the bath.

"How blessed you are to be bathed in the palace. Here, let us help you. This is Dainty." Dainty's raven hair was piled softly on her head, her alabaster skin pale even against the white lace shifts they both wore. They undressed me, guided me into the hot tub, and soaped my back and chest. Then they sank down into the bath with me; their dresses melted into the wetness like clouds. They dropped gentle kisses like flower petals onto my neck, back and chest as their fingers reached under the water, soothing my thighs. Their softness lulled me into an altered state. Finally Dainty kissed me firmly on the mouth. Then Angelina, then Dainty. I turned my head side to side taking in tongues, lips and sweetness of girl. My edge returned, and I faced the two maidens. I grabbed them each by a nipple and took turns biting and kissing them.

"I think I am clean enough, girls, don't you?" I finally said.

Angelina led the way back to the carnal ballroom and Dainty followed. Both of them were now nude and covered in oil. I returned to my leather and had a clean cock again in my shorts.

Sounds of spanking and laughter rang out from the room. I knew the drill this time: When the door opened I kept my eyes to the floor. My clit and heart ached in frustration. I wanted to get close to my Queen the easiest way possible. I was willing to play by the rules . . . for now.

"Approach the throne."

I walked, without looking up, to her feet, where I knelt.

The court shuffled into silence. I wondered where their gowns were now.

The Queen stroked my face with her long, soft fingers. I pushed my cheek into her hand — her touch felt so good, so familiar and comforting. I hadn't realized how much I'd missed it.

She tilted my face up to meet hers and said softly, "You clean up nice." She raised her voice for the benefit of the court. "You have the opportunity to become my personal slave. My *personal* slave. All you have to do is lick my pussy adequately. But if you fail, your head will roll. You have a choice. You can be a slave of the court and keep your head or you can take a chance and possibly be mine. But remember, if you do not satisfy me then off with your head." She did one of her perfectly calculated pauses. "Notice, no others are beside me. No others passed the test."

The entire court stood frozen.

"They couldn't *give* head so they *lost* heads!" She laughed wickedly at her bad joke and the court laughed uneasily with her. How had I missed seeing this wickedness in June?

"Test me . . . my Queen," I said, and a hush followed.

"Your eyes may rise, slave," she said. "Everyone, fuck." She clapped her hands together. "I want to see fucking, now." They did as they were told.

She leaned back into her throne, pushing her hips to the edge of her plush seat. Her mouth curled into a sideways smile as she parted the curtains of her gown so I could see what was mine.

"Approach the throne," she said again, her voice now low and husky.

I crawled forward, reached out a hand to each of her thighs. My senses reported in slow motion. Warmth, softness straining through the sharp lines of the fishnet, then solid as I wrapped my arms around her legs. I pulled her pussy to my face. She gasped. I openly sniffed her moist hair and smelled her come, her sweat. I moved excruciatingly slowly, separating her soft, silky curls with my nose and letting my breath tease her clit. She moaned and writhed slightly. My tongue came down on her clit hood so slowly that I could feel the warmth of her on my tongue before I even touched her. She groaned as my tongue landed. I did full, rough doggy laps up the length of her cunt. She gasped and sank into me further. I tightened my grip on her and let my tongue do the rest. I dipped into her hole to taste the juices that had flowed during her foot-licking.

I pushed my nose into her like a puppy's. I teased and nibbled, tickled her lips with my tongue, and sucked at her clit. When I knew the teasing could settle into a beat, I sank my teeth into the base of her clit and throbbed my tongue with her rhythm. She groaned and writhed, ran her fingers through my hair, guided my head with her hands.

"Oh, God. My slave, my slave . . . " she bucked wildly into my face over and over, pulling my hair, pounding my face, screaming as she pulsed with wave after wave of orgasm.

I was resting with my face against her thighs when she grabbed my face between both hands and pulled me to her. We kissed ferociously and then she jumped on me and we fell to the floor. The Queen freed herself of duty and the whole place became an orgy. I finally got to fuck June until I came — my cock pounding into my clit, her body full in my arms, her screams ripping my ears as sure as her nails on my back.

There's the door; done just in time. I went to answer it.

"Hey, Jeanie, come in, I was just finishing a story. Listen, I couldn't wait to tell you: I reserved a little hut-like cabin on the beach and the curve of the beach at this place even resembles a lagoon! It looks exactly like Gilligan's Island. I already have Gilligan, the Skipper, Mr. and Mrs. Howell. I thought you would be just perfect as Mary Ann . . . if you're interested." I smiled mischeviously.

June's birthday is next month, and she's always had this *thing* about Ginger and the Professor.

Victoria Smith

First Call

The only rule was that she had to do whatever he said.

Startled from sleep by the ringing phone, she listened to his seductive voice whispering in her ear. "You're my little slut, aren't you?"

She loved to tell him no. It was a game she enjoyed playing, seeing how high she could get him. He loved it as much as she did, as long as she let him win. She never forgot that part, the part about who was really in charge. Whatever he asked her to do, she did — and she did it just for him.

She stretched, fighting off the morning, knowing she could not refuse him.

"Wake up and talk to me, sweetheart. I need to hear your voice. Are you feeling like a bad girl today?"

"No, I'm a good girl . . . a very good girl."

Instinctively, she caressed her bare breasts, rolling her nipples between her fingers. She squirmed as they began to harden.

In that luxurious place between sleeping and waking, she let herself be seduced by his words. It was like floating on a cloud. Lisa loved the sound of his voice, the things he said, the way he whispered in her ear until she ached for him. Her fingers began a downward journey, seeking the moisture between her thighs. As she slid a hand through her silken hair and across her clit, she sighed and spoke his name.

"Mmmm, Carl . . . "

"You sound good, baby. Tell me what you're doing."

She massaged her clit in tiny circles, ignoring his words, lost in the sound of his breathing. If she was very quiet, she could hear him stroking his cock, slow and steady. She closed her eyes and pictured his hand, moving up and down, spreading the wetness along his shaft. She imagined him standing over her, watching her, stroking his cock right above her face. She slipped two fingers into her warm, wet cunt, then brought them to her mouth and sucked them, knowing he heard every little sound.

In his sweetest, most reassuring voice, he said, "I really want you to tell me what you're doing, Lisa. I think — perhaps — you're being naughty. You *are* a bad girl, aren't you?"

He spoke to her like she was a small child, and she sounded childlike when she answered.

"No, Carl, I'm a good girl. You're the one who's naughty. You *make* me act this way for you. Please don't make me tell you what I'm doing."

His voice was sweet. "Are you a masturbator?"

"No." It came out as a whimper.

"I'm masturbating for you, Lisa. You know I am. Please tell me . . . "

"I can't . . . " She was already so far out there that she could barely form the words.

"Say it, Lisa. Tell me what you're doing."

Heart pounding, breathing like a child who'd been crying for a long time, she tried, her voice a broken whisper.

"I'm masturbating, Carl."

"Louder, I can't hear you."

"No, Carl, stop . . . I don't like this game." Lisa took a deep, ragged breath, rubbing herself furiously. She liked to make him wait. She was right on the edge, and ready to fall. Lisa tried very hard to be quiet, but her noises were animal-like.

Carl knew and loved the sounds she made when she came, and his cock grew harder in his hand. He heard Lisa groan as she lifted her hips to meet her searching fingers.

"You're a bad, nasty girl, Lisa. I know exactly what you're doing. I can see you and feel you and smell your fingers. Tell me . . . I want to hear you say it again."

"I'm masturbating, Carl, just for you." Barely breathing the words, she panted into the phone as her body began to shake.

"I want to hear you come, Lisa. I need to hear you. Please tell me what you're doing. I'm on my knees in front of a mirror, stroking my cock for you. If anyone found out, they'd think I was very nasty. You like it when I'm nasty, don't you?" He said it not as a question, but as a plea.

She had him right where she wanted him now.

"I'm not sure if I like it or not, Carl. Nice girls don't talk to nasty men on the phone."

"You like it, Lisa. Don't lie to me. Say it louder. Tell me you're a masturbator."

Trembling, she rode an orgasmic wave. She didn't want to talk, she wanted to listen to him tell her that she was his. She closed her eyes tightly and moaned.

"I'd do anything for you, Carl, anything to get you this high. I'm a very bad girl. I like talking to men I don't know and making them come."

"You're a nasty, naughty girl, aren't you?"

No answer.

"Say it!"

"Yes, Carl, I'm *your* nasty little girl — and I like the way it feels. You like it when I'm a little slut for you, don't you?"

His turn to not answer.

Inside her head she counted, making him wait, as she listened to the incredible sounds he was making.

Carl took a deep breath and started questioning her again.

"You want lots of men to watch you masturbate, don't you? You want them to watch you touch yourself and lick pussy juice off your fingers. You're addicted to this, Lisa. You need it. You need to be listened to and watched. Tell me you're addicted."

"I'm addicted, Carl. I'm addicted to the sound of your voice, to hearing you stroke yourself for me, to knowing you think of me all day long. I like knowing that I can get you off like this, it excites the hell out of me. Is that what you want to hear?"

She was getting closer and closer, getting lost inside herself. But he kept pulling her back, making her wait, making her pleasure last.

"I want you to come for me again, Lisa. I want to hear how wet your pussy is. Let me hear you."

"No, I can't. Not now . . . just talk to me. Tell me what you want me to do."

Lisa knew that Carl watched himself in the mirror, his swollen cock all red and purple in his hand, knew he wanted to come. She could hear it in his voice, he sounded so helpless. They took turns being in control, pushing and pulling each other right to the edge of passion, then stopping abruptly, changing the tone, trading places.

"Are you masturbating for me, Carl?"

"Yes, just for you. Tell me you are, too. Tell me you're touching yourself."

His words came out in one long, forced breath, and she imagined his hand pausing on his throbbing cock while he waited for her answer.

"I love to touch myself for you, Carl. I love the way it makes me feel. I want to lie here all day and feel like this. I want men to watch me, and I want you to watch them watch. I'll do anything you ask. What do you want me to do?"

She was so high now that she could barely stand it.

"Would you like to spank me, Carl? Listen . . . "

Smack! She slapped her own thigh, and rolled onto her side. Again, *Slap! Smack!* Hard, across her bottom.

"Did you hear that? Does it get you hot? It makes me very, very wet."

"You *are* a bad girl, Lisa, and I'm going to have to spank you. I'm going to put you across my lap, and then I'm going to spank your little ass for talking dirty on the phone. I know you talk to other men. I know how much you like to tease them, to make them stroke their cocks for you."

She heard the crack of his hand against his own skin.

"You like to make men come for you, don't you? Tell me you tease them." *Smack!* went his hand again, as another orgasm reached out and grabbed her.

"Again, Carl, harder . . . I want it."

"Tell me you're a masturbator."

"I'm a masturbator, Carl. I do it just for you."

"No, you're lying."

His tone was teasing now, his voice hypnotizing. She was completely under his spell.

"Not just for me, Lisa. You do it for lots of guys. I like knowing you fuck other men on the phone."

Her thighs were slick with her juices. She pressed them tightly together and bit her bottom lip. His words poured into her ear, smooth as honey.

"Listen very carefully, Lisa, I'm only going to tell you once. I want to see how many guys you can talk to today, and then I want you to tell me about it. All the details. I like to hear about what you do. Will you be a nasty girl for me today and see how many men you can fuck on the phone? At least ten . . . and I want you to masturbate with a woman, too.

"When we get off the phone, I want you to go online and go into a room and tell everyone what you just did. Tell them you masturbated for me, and tell them you want a lot of men to fuck you and make you come."

"Can I tell them you told me to?" She said it in her sweetest little girl voice. The idea was making her very hot.

"Yes."

"Can I go to a room full of guys and let them all fuck me right there? I want to do it in front of everyone, lots of them watching and stroking themselves. And they can do whatever they want to me."

His breathing had changed again — she had him back on the edge. She was his little whore, and she knew how to get him off.

She moved the phone away from her ear, and held it right above her parted pussy lips. Slowly, she slid her vibrator in and out, raising her hips to meet the thrusts. The sounds were incredible, squishy slurpy slippery sexy wet fucking sounds. As another wave washed over her, she moved it faster and faster, knowing Carl heard her moans in the background.

She knew the power of those sounds. This was the part she liked the very best, a man listening to her sweet wet cunt. Every man she had ever talked to had been totally blown away by it, begging for more. And it never failed to send her somewhere she had never been before, pure feeling and raw nerves mixed into a drug she could never get enough of.

She could picture Carl stroking himself harder, faster, furiously matching her rhythm. Her orgasm rose up and out of her, and she collapsed onto the sweaty sheets, unable to speak or move.

She was his, and she knew the rules. Fuck at least ten guys — plus a woman — on the phone. That would be tough, even for her.

Breathing deeply, Lisa smiled. It was going to be a wonderful day.

Cecilia Tan

Always

Morgan was always the one who'd wanted a child. Even when I first met her, before we got involved, before we got engaged, always the talk of motherhood with her, of empowering Earth Mother stuff and of making widdle baby booties. I, on the other hand, had always said I would never have children, was sure somehow that I would never decide to bear a child, and yet I had always thought about it, secretly. So when I fell in love with Morgan, and she fell in love with me, and we had a hilltop wedding where we both wore white dresses and two out of our four parents looked on happily, I figured I was off the hook on the parenting issue.

This was, of course, before John, and way before Jillian. But I'm getting ahead of myself.

Back up to the summer of 1989. New England. Cape Cod. Morgan and I are in a hammock in the screened-in porch of her aunt's summer house. The night is turning smoothly damp after a muggy day, cars hiss by on pavement still wet from the afternoon's rainshower, the slight breeze rocks us just enough to make me feel weightless as I drowse. I am on my back with one foot hanging out each side of the hammock; Morgan rests in the wide space between my legs, her spill of brown curls spread on my stomach and her knees drawn up close to her chest. The hammock is the nice, cloth kind, with a wide wooden bar at either end to keep it from squeezing us like seeds in a lemon wedge, not the white rope type that leaves you looking like a bondage experiment gone wrong. Morgan's hands travel up my thighs like they come out of a dream. It never occurs to me to stop her. Sex with Morgan is as easy and natural as saying yes to a bite of chocolate from the proferred bar of a friend. Before her fingers even reach the elastic edge of my panties I am already shifting my hips, breathing deeper, thinking about the way her fingers will touch and tease me, how one slim finger will slide deep into me once I am wet, how good it feels to play with her hair on my belly, how much I want her. With Morgan, I always come.

Imagine afterwards, lying now side by side, holding each other and sharing each other's heat as the beach breeze turns chilly, when I decide to propose to her. I am gifted with a sudden and utter clarity — this is the right thing to do. It has been six years since I came out as bisexual, three years since I began dating women, but something like ten years of getting into relationships with men and constantly trying to disentangle myself from them. It's not that I don't like men. I like them, and love them, a-proverbial-lot. But I've never been able to explain why it is I feel the need to put up resistance, to define myself separately, to have my foot on the brake of our sex lives, with a man. I always do.

But here, with Morgan, the urge to resist is not even present. Maybe it has nothing to do with men versus women, I think, maybe it has everything to do with her. She's the right one. And she says yes.

So we got married, that part you knew. Marriage for us did not mean monogamy, of course — rather we defined it as "managed faithfulness." We had our boundaries, our limits, our promises — but outside dalliances were allowed. When you're happily married, though, who has time or energy for all the flirting and courting and negotiating with someone new? Neither of us did for several years. And that's when John came into the picture.

A raw spring day in Somerville, me in galoshes and a pair of my father's old painting pants with a snow shovel, cursing and trying to lift a cinderblock-sized (and -weighted) chunk of wet packed snow off the walkway of our three-decker. On the first floor lives our landlady, one frail but observant old Irishwoman, Mrs. Donnell; on the second a new tenant we haven't yet met, a single guy we hear walking around late at night and never see in the morning. Hence me trying to shovel the late-season fall, two April-Fool's feet of it, because I'm pretty sure no one else will. Morgan inside rushing to get ready for work, emerging soap-scented and loosely bundled to plant a kiss on my cheek as she steps over the last foot of unshoveled snow onto the sidewalk (cleared by a neighbor who loves to use his snow-blower). She's off to catch the bus to her job downtown as facilities coordinator at the Theater Arts Foundation. I heave on the remaining block of snow with a loud grunt. Perhaps it is my grunt that prevents me from hearing the noise my back must surely have made when it cracked, popped, "went out," as they say.

I am hunched over in pain, cursing louder now and not caring if Mrs. Donnell hears it, when another person is there, asking if I'm all right. His hands are on my shoulders and he slowly straightens me upright. It is the new tenant, wearing an unzipped parka and peering into my face with worry. I tell him I'll be all right; he says are you sure? I say yes but I'm clearly not sure — it goes back and forth the way those things will until it ends up somehow with me in his apartment drinking some kind of herbal tea and then lying face down on his formica counter with my shirt on the floor while his thumbs and palms map out the terrain of my back.

In the theater world a backrub is a euphemism for sex ("Hey, come upstairs, I'll give you a backrub." "Oh, those two, they've been rubbing each other's backs for years.") So you'd think I'd know. But no, there's obviously no way that he could have planned my trying to lift too much snow. No, it was an honest case of one thing leading to another. Maybe a couple of resistance-free years with Morgan had dulled my old repeller-reflexes, and we . . . well, to be specific, after his hands did their magic with my spine, they strayed down to my ribs, and he planted a line of warm kisses down my back. He had longer than average guy hair, straight and tickly like a tassel as it touched my skin. I moaned to encourage him, my body knowing what I wanted before my mind had a chance to change the plan.

Morgan always says I plan too much.

My father's oversized pants slid to the floor and kisses fell like snowflakes onto the curve of my buttocks, feather light, and then a moist tongue probed along the center where it went from hard spine to softness. We got civilized after that, and went to the bedroom. It wasn't until we were lying back having one of those post-coital really-get-to-know-you talks that Morgan knocked on the door. No bus, saw your galoshes on the second floor landing, she explained at her seeming clairvoyance, to which I replied, "This is John."

John always says "How do you do?" and bows while he shakes two-handed when he's formally introduced.

Our first threesome happened right away, that night after dinner fetched on foot from the corner Chinese restaurant. On our living room floor, the white waxy boxes and drink cups scattered at the edges like spectators, the elegant curve of our bay windows standing witness to his hand between my legs, Morgan's mouth on his nipple, my lips on Morgan's ear, John's penis sheathed between us, my chest against his back while he buried himself in her, her tongue on my clit, his nose in my neck, my fingers in her hair, our voices saying whatever they always say, mmm, and ahh, and yes. I didn't know if this was going to be one of Morgan's experiments in excitement, or one of my few dalliances, or one of John's fantasies come true. What it was, which I didn't expect, was the beginning of something more solid, more intricate, and more satisfying than any twosome I had known.

John always buys two dozen roses on Valentine's Day, which he gives to Morgan and me one rose at a time.

Maybe a year later, when Morgan became director at TAF, the three of us talked with Mrs. Donnell about buying the building. The idea hit us at Christmas dinner, at Morgan's parents' house in Illinois, her mother on one side of her, me on the other, John on my other side, and all manner of relatives near and far spread down the two long tables from the dining room into the ranch house living room, in folding chairs brought along in minivans and hatchbacks. Turkey so moist the gravy wasn't needed, and gravy so rich that we used it anyway. Wild rice and nut stuffing heaped high on John's plate, shored up by mashed potatoes, his vegetarian principles only mildly compromised by the addition of imitation bacon bits on green salad. Family chatter and laughter, Morgan's father sometimes directing men's talk at John. Somehow the discussion turned to Mrs. Donnell and her plans to sell the house, and somehow our three hands linked in my lap, under the table, and John announced to everyone, suddenly, that the three of us would buy the house together, voicing the thought that was at that moment in all three of our heads, even though until then we'd never contemplated the idea.

I always clean the toilets and the sinks but I hate cleaning the shower and bathtub. John, who has a slight paranoia about foot fungi, loves to do the shower and tub. If only we could convince Morgan to do the kitchen floors.

If my life seems like a series of sudden revelations, that's because it is. The most recent one was watching Jillian walk her stiff-legged toddler's walk from one side of our living room to the other. I knew then what Morgan looked like as a child, what her exploratory spirit and her bright smile must have been like when she was knee-high.

The night we made Jillian we had a plan. We didn't always sleep together, or even have three-way sex together, but we knew all three of us had to have a hand in her creation. For months we had charted Morgan's period, her temperature. We cleared a room to be a new bedroom and put a futon on the floor, lit the candles and incense (we're so old-fashioned that way) and made ready. Imagine Morgan, her long brown curls foaming over her shoulders, her back against the pillowed wall, her knees bent, framing her seemingly round Earth Mother belly, watching us. John kneels in front of me, naked and somber-faced. I will not let him stay that way for long.

I begin it with a kiss. I kiss Morgan on the lips and then John and we pull away from her. I take his tongue deep into my mouth, my hands roaming over his head and neck, and he responds with a moan. My hard nipples brush against his; my hands on his shoulders, I continue to kiss and wag my breasts from side to side, our nipples brushing again and again. Then I am licking them, my teeth nipping, my hands sliding down to his hips, one hand between his legs, lifting his balls. He gasps and throws his head back. My mouth is now hovering over his penis, hardening in my hand. I reach out my tongue to tease.

Instinct begins to overtake the plan, his hands are reaching for me, he pushes me back, his mouth on mine, his tongue on my nipples, his fingers seeking out my hottest wettest places and finding them. He knows my body well, he slides two fingers in while his thumb rests on my clit.

Morgan watches, her belly taut, her hands clenched in the sheets.

He is slicking his hand wet with my juices up and down his penis, and then he climbs over me, my legs lock behind his back, and he settles in. Tonight there are no barriers between us. I let go with my legs and let him pump freely. If I let him I know he will grant me my secret wish, to make me come from the fucking, from the friction and rhythm and pressure and slap and grind. I am sinking down into a deep well of pleasure, his sweat dripping onto me, as he becomes harder, hotter, faster, tighter, his jaw clenched, and I become looser, and further away. The turning point comes, though, with a ripple in my pelvis, and then every thrust is suddenly bringing me closer to the surface, up and up again, drawing me in tighter, closer, until my wish comes true. I break the surface screaming and crying, and calling out his name, and thinking how good it is to have learned not to resist this.

His eyes flicker in the candlelight as he strokes my hair and jerks out of me — the plan is not forgotten after all. His penis stands out proud and red and wet and the strain of holding back is evident in his bit lip. Morgan's nostrils flare and she slides low on her pillows. I go to her, my fingers seeking out her cunt, my mouth smothering hers, our tongues slipping in and out as I confirm what we already know. She is ready.

I put myself behind her, my hands cupping her breasts, my legs on either side of her, as John lies down between her legs. My fingers sneak down to spread her wider, to circle her clit and pinch her where she likes it, while he thrusts slickly, my teeth in her neck, her hair in our faces, the three of us humping like one animal, all of us ready.

Morgan always comes twice.

There's nothing like a grandchild to bring parents around. So Jillian has six grandparents and none of them mind enough to complain about it. We always have them here for Christmas now, we've got the most bedrooms and the most chairs. Jillian will always be my daughter. John always shovels the snow. And Morgan always says we could make Jillian a sibling — that it could be my turn if I want. I don't know. I just know that I love them always.

Carol Queen

Being Met

We've had so many adventures together. It started out as an adventure. I was not looking for you, nor you for me: we were only looking for a story to tell later, a hot night, excitement. Now we tell it over and over again, the story of how we met. Mostly we tell it to each other, because I am your best audience and you are mine.

It was a party, a very particular sort of party, an erotic gathering for wild searching people. I had helped to plan it, hoping for an adventure, hoping that by bringing people together with plenty of latex we might strike a blow against the terrible fear of sex that pervaded so many hearts, the legacy of AIDS. I had only just met you; I'd invited you along.

In a part of town rarely visited after dark we met like a secret society of initiates to faded but still potent mysteries. A San Francisco night, the kind we have here on the edge of the land, with fog swirling between the buildings, shrouding then revealing a waxing moon. There you were, arriving just before me, pulling up before the warehouse whose address I'd given you.

The door of your little car swung open. Your foot hit the pavement squarely, your booted foot, black leathered ankle wound around by a silver chain. It mesmerized me. That was where it started, this wanting you. The silver chain on your black boot signaled me in a language I wasn't sure I knew. The left boot. It meant — perhaps — that you played with mastery, that you would know what to do with this desire that I was not sure how to show you.

We went into the dark building; inside it was light and warm and convivial, like a clubhouse. We worked together to set up the party. You charmed me, taught me a dirty limerick, helped me strew condoms around, looked up my skirt when I climbed a ladder to change a lightbulb; you flirted. How could I tell you what I wanted? Finally you took my hand and led me upstairs.

You smelled like family, from the minute I got close enough to you to touch. I wanted to reach for you, though I'd come to the party only wanting to explore, to be with other people who thought sex was important. But the minute you took my hand I started making plans — that's so dangerous, making plans! — lists of things I wanted you to do, ways I wanted to see you, things I wanted you to know about me, what I wanted to know about you. Where you came from. Why now, why here, when I had lived in this sexy city half my life, why were you here smelling like someone I'd known forever? So I kissed you, just to taste you — taste who you were — and since that second I have never for a minute stopped wanting you. When we are wrapped up in each other now, curled together under a quilt, feeling like we have never been apart, when we take each others' faces in our hands and come together in a kiss, I always feel an echo of that first one, the kiss I knew I'd willingly change my life for. That first kiss from you, with my common-sensical self still shouting, "But you don't even know this man!" I didn't care. I wanted you consumingly, wanted your hands on me, the want coming from a pool of desire so rarely accessed, and so precious, that trying to hold it back would have made me feel dead. You kissed me like you wanted to eat me in tiny, savory bites, you kissed me like we could start to learn each others' life stories there.

I shook as much from fear as from the electricity of that kiss. I was so afraid that I had tumbled off a cliff. That I wanted too

much of you. I was asking one kiss to carry so much, and I
scarcely knew you, and already my heart was ready to break for
losing you. It was crazy, I didn't even have you yet.

I get lost in kisses. I still get lost in yours.

You found us a place to sit, finally, after that kiss that seemed
to last an eon. You put me in your lap, do you remember? And
pulled long black latex gloves out of your pocket.

"Show me how you like to be touched."

No man had ever said that to me before. No other man has
said it since. You asked me to show you and it told me that my
pleasure was important to you. I showed you how I like it, how
to run your fingers into me and moisten them, to slide the
middle finger down over my clit and into my cunt a little, over
and over, each neighboring finger on either side of my labia,
pressing it all together, fucking me a little deeper each time

When your mouth was not on mine it was next to my ear,
whispering. You still talk to me that way when you're making
me come. Your words make me as hot as your hands do.

"Give it up to me, little one, little honey, that's right, give it
up, come for me, come in my hand . . . "

I had not been looking for you, but I was so deeply ready for
you. Your silver chain, the way you spoke to me. The way your
kiss made the floor under my feet turn to quicksilver. I wanted
your collar the way a straight woman wants a ring. But mostly
I wanted you.

For hours we sat and told each other where we came from, the
stories of who we were — though it felt to me that we already
knew. You held my foot in your lap, stroking it. I remember what
we wore, what we ate for dinner when we finally went out. You
dripped Thai peanut sauce onto rice while you looked into my
eyes and I nearly came. For weeks after that, every minute I was
on the edge of a broken heart: "What if this ever ends, what if

this ever ends?" That's the salt, falling in love, the salt in the wound. "What if I tell him I love him, what if I chase him away?"

We are both so complicated. I grew up thinking men were another species. I never thought I could learn men's bodies, so I just learned how to fuck. I always loved women, but besides the love, women seemed easier. I trusted my prowess. You were the first man I ever told I was scared. And your sexuality has so many layers. For weeks we didn't even fuck. We explored with our hands and our mouths; we invented games and personas. We told each other our fantasies, our deep arousals.

My pussy is easy. But my fright and heat and shame when you touched my asshole made me tremble. I have been masturbating that way, anally, in secret, since the crazy heat of puberty. But I'm tense and tight and another man tried to fuck me there once and hurt me

Now I know you won't hurt me, so I can divert the fear into fantasy. Sometimes that's what I do. I make up stories, I give my fear a context. Sometimes I pretend I'm you, a boy on my belly waiting to take it up the ass. Sometimes I pretend you've kidnapped me. Or that I'm a gay man in a bathhouse. Other times I'm only myself, and you are yourself, the only man I've ever trusted so much. Showing you that trust, that's what the collar means to me. It proves to me you want me enough to make it into a ritual. It tells me you're going to be focused on me. So many of my past lovers were nervous about my intensity, felt afraid of me. I never feel that from you. I feel like you want my intensity all to yourself, enough to give me the signal, "We are going to be each other's whole world until the collar comes off."

When you say, "You're mine," I get wet. My cunt starts humming and thinking for me.

I know how alone you were, thinking no one else wanted sex as much as you did. I used to masturbate and cry after my lover went to sleep. I used to wander around the house looking for things to fuck myself with. I felt alone, convinced I would never find someone who would want me as much as I wanted them — but it wasn't only *them*: it was the sex, the touching, the smells, getting high on each other. When you tell me how much you want me, that I'm yours entirely, I want to cry — from happiness, now, and because of how sad I used to be, convinced I'd never be *met*.

When you hold me down and fuck me, when you tie me down and pretend I'm your captive, you're proving that you want me and you're willing to show me. When we lie tangled together, holding each other fiercely, eyes locked, murmuring words to each other, your cock thrusting in and in and in, our hips pumping together, I pray the whole rest of the world will learn how to feel this way.

We're floating then. We're in the secret world we found that first night, even though we were surrounded by people.

We're brother and sister, veins running with the same blood. You're my good little boy, touching mommy so sweetly, making me feel so wonderful and loved. You're the best little boy in the world, honey, don't be scared, touch me again right there, oh, darlin', I'll teach you everything. It's how you give your vulnerability to me. Feeling like a frightened little boy. It's the way you fantasize being taken, seduced, letting me be the powerful one. Such a big man, turning into a trembling child in my arms . . . you are so open then, it makes me want to do sweet, forbidden things to you. Riding through the land of dreams with you, where we can be anything for each other, where we have a hundred ways to love each other, a thousand.

Where I have a companion even in the things I thought had to stay secret. Where who you really are is my lover. Through every adventure.

Susan St. Aubin

The Man Who Didn't Dream

Evelyn the dreamer married a man who didn't dream. Every morning she'd tell Hal her dreams as though she were giving him the harvest of her night. She always had at least one, usually more: dreams of tigers, of sailing through the air, of falling — a circus of images.

"Flying tigers?" he'd laugh. "Isn't that an airline?"

"Well, what do you dream, that makes so much sense?"

"I don't dream," he'd say. "Not since I was a kid."

"What did you dream then?"

"I don't remember."

Sometimes when her dreams woke her, she'd lean on one elbow and watch him in the dim light that showed through the slats in the blinds. She knew he didn't dream as he lay there, gray as a statue, because he never moved and scarcely seemed to breathe. She was active at night: In the morning she often found herself in a ball at the foot of the bed, or on her back when she clearly remembered falling asleep curled up on her stomach. Hal kept the same position all night — on his back, nose in the air, lips unmoving, snoring his half snore that was like the whistle of an interrupted sneeze.

One summer night she watched as he lay unconscious in heat that would have kept any normal person awake. When she touched him, his skin was cool and smooth as marble. She ran her hand across his chest and down his right arm.

She wondered if she could give him a dream. She put her mouth on his shoulder, so much cooler than his daytime flesh that she felt like she was seducing another man. She ran her hand down his side, following it with her tongue. Harold, as he called his penis, lay flat while he slept, as unstirred as the rest of him, dreamless until Hal awoke and willed him to rise and take the form Evelyn called The Herald. Hal was different from other men she'd known, whose cocks had dream lives of their own, pressing her hips and ribs while their owners slept.

Her tongue moved closer, licked Harold, moved away. She took him in her mouth and massaged his cool tip with her tongue; then he stirred, growing and hardening into The Herald. When Hal's mouth twitched at the corners, she let The Herald slide out and watched him loll against Hal's thigh, pulsing as he diminished into Harold.

The next morning when she asked Hal what he dreamed, he said, "You're the dreamer."

"Maybe you don't remember," she prompted. "Maybe you're hiding your dreams from yourself."

"No. I don't have dreams." He wrinkled his forehead. "I don't know if I want to. I don't miss them."

"I saw you smile in your sleep last night," she offered. "I thought you might have been dreaming."

"Could have been a muscle spasm." He frowned. "Maybe I had a headache in my sleep."

"The Herald rose up," she said.

His eyebrows lifted. "Men have erections in their sleep, but I don't think it's part of a dream."

"But there must have been some dream to arouse you," she insisted.

He shook his head. "Not necessarily. It's just a reaction. I don't remember anything. I'd like to remember that kind of dream, but I don't think there was one."

Evelyn began waking every morning at two, as though there was an alarm in her brain that forced her out of her own dreams to watch Hal lie dreamless, a blank slate on which she could create a picture.

A picture of what? What would he dream if she could get inside him? Would he dream about a lover? What would he want? She searched for props. At a garage sale she bought a riding crop — a short wooden stick sprouting worn leather strips from one end. She slapped her wrist with it as she walked down the street. What did people do with whips during sex? Threaten each other before? Spank each other after? Everything she imagined seemed like bad theater.

One night Evelyn knelt beside Hal with her hands on his scalp, her eyes closed, and invented a lover for him, someone who looked like a perfect version of herself, with dark hair cut in a curve along her cheek and tanned honey skin. This ideal self knelt beside him and took over the stroking of his hair, then let her fingers inch down his side, shifting him gently until he was on his stomach. With her palms she kneaded his shoulders like mounds of dough, then moved down to his ass, which she rocked back and forth with caresses. An ideal woman like this just might have a whip hidden at the back of her closet to bring out at the right moment.

He moaned, then mumbled, and seemed to be awakening. When he rolled over, his eyes were open and The Herald brushed her legs. "Hal?" She shook his shoulder; perhaps if she woke him right away, he'd remember a dream. "Hal, wake up, you're talking in your sleep, what are you dreaming?"

With one arm he pushed himself up, then shook his head. "No," he said, "I don't remember any dream. Something woke me, some noise — sounded like a crash somewhere. Something fell, didn't you hear it?"

"No," said Evelyn. "Nothing fell."

"You must have been asleep then."

"Are you sure you didn't dream it?" she asked. What about the woman rubbing your back, she wanted to say. Don't you remember her?

"I heard it," he said.

If she didn't hear a crash, he must have dreamed it. That was a start.

The next night she woke in the light of a nearly full moon. She thought she could throw something to recreate his dream crash, make love to him, and then tell him the next morning it never happened, he must have been dreaming. But what if he couldn't get back to sleep? He'd know he wasn't dreaming, unless she could convince him that not sleeping was also a dream.

She pulled off the covers to inspect his body, under her power, every inch but that brain, the unknowable part of him that refused to dream. She pressed her lips to his jugular vein and gave a light suck, then licked her way down his throat — the Adam's apple, the hollow, then across the chest. She was a mother cat cleaning a kitten, a growling purr low in her throat. She licked him to his toes, which were less clean than the rest of him, salty and slightly musty, like miniature cocks.

When his toes were clean, she paused for breath, then took poor limp Harold in her mouth, sucking and licking him until he was hard, like a Popsicle that would never melt. She willed Hal to dream; she tried to make her brain join with his. Dream this, dream it, she thought, but she couldn't find an opening into his mind. She sucked that Popsicle until The Herald quivered between her lips, becoming warm salt in her mouth. She saw Hal's eyelids flicker and open. Was he awake? No, the lids shut again and his quick breathing slowed. What would he remember?

Since the next day was Saturday, she could watch him all morning before she had to leave for the restaurant where she worked as a *sous chef*. He ground beans and made coffee — she thought the beans smelled rancid, but he didn't say a word. He didn't seem to notice she was watching him. He read the paper and ate an English muffin.

"I dreamed I was licking a yellow banana-flavored Popsicle," she said, "but no matter how much I licked it and sucked it, it didn't go away. I could devour it without eating it, and have it, and still suck it some more."

"That's a cook's dream," he answered. "Food as art, not nourishment. I've always hated bananas, though." He got up to make himself another cup of coffee, scratched one leg with his foot, and yawned. "God, I feel drained this morning."

He went into his study, where toasters with wings floated beside pieces of toast across the screen of his computer. When he sat down he stared at them, shaking his head. "I can't seem to get started," he mumbled.

"It's because you don't dream," she told him. "Maybe you don't really sleep if you don't dream."

"You think I'm abnormal, don't you? You're trying to make a big deal about my not dreaming."

She stood behind him, rubbing his shoulders. "No, everyone dreams. Some people don't remember, that's all."

"Oh, bullshit. You're saying two different things — first you say I don't dream, then you say everyone dreams. Which is it?"

She shrugged, dropping her hands to her sides, and stepped back. "Nobody knows," she said. "There's different theories.

Maybe you don't dream and maybe you don't remember."

"So, what difference does it make?" The toasters and toast were gone from his screen now; lists of words in squares filled it.

"None," she said, but he was no longer listening. She saw a book called *The Psychology of Dreams* under some papers on his desk. She left him, closing the door of his study.

Saturday night she came home late from the restaurant, slid out of her shoes at the front door, and crept into the bedroom, where he was already stretched out like fallen marble. She slipped off her clothes and lay down beside him, then reached under the thin blanket that covered him and ran a hand down the cool flesh of his leg. He didn't stir, but his lips moved.

She felt he must be dreaming. "What do you see?" she whispered.

"Mmmm," he answered, licking his lips.

"Tomorrow you won't remember," she said, stern as a teacher, "so I want you to tell me now."

"Mmmmm," he said.

She sensed he was very nearly awake, so she waited until he began to breathe through his nose in a light, steady whistle. She stroked his arm; he didn't stir. She crept her hand down his side and across his relaxed belly to Harold, whom she teased with her fingertips and draped across her wrist like a fat bracelet until he grew so hard she couldn't bend him anymore. When Hal sighed and stirred, she withdrew her hand again, watching her playmate The Herald soften and retract. This wasn't going to work if arousal woke him. But would he be conscious enough to know he was awake? He didn't wake up last night, but then he was so completely unaware, he didn't even think he'd dreamed. She wondered if a person had to be almost awake in order to dream.

She leaned over him, her mouth open, and licked Harold's tip.

It felt cold, so she blew on him, sucking him into the warmth of her mouth, where he warmed and hardened. Hal's breathing quickened but he didn't move. She slipped her mouth off The Herald and sat back on her heels. Hal's eyelids flicked open.

"This is a dream," she stated.

He stared beyond her.

"A dream," she repeated.

His eyes closed. "You're mine," she whispered.

She took The Herald in her mouth again, sliding him back and forth with her tongue while gently touching his balls with her fingertips. She felt heat rise from him. Again she withdrew and watched. Hal rolled to one side, moving his leg over the thick Herald, and murmured into his pillow. When she nudged his shoulder, he rolled onto his back again, The Herald on guard.

She sat up on her knees and straddled Hal, then lowered herself onto that alert Herald, still clean and glistening from her mouth. Hal opened his eyes and stared. She stared back, not blinking, holding her breath. He ran his tongue over his lips, closed his eyes, and sighed.

"Strawberries," he said.

Evelyn moved up and down, fitting The Herald into herself. She tried to remember when they'd last eaten strawberries. Strawberry shortcake last summer? A tart a couple of months ago? Strawberries weren't a great favorite of hers, nor of his, as far as she knew. They never ate bowls of strawberries and sugar, or strawberries on cereal or ice cream.

She was still until he went into a deeper sleep, when she began to move slowly. Leaning close to his face, she whispered, "Whipped cream. Whipped cream and strawberries."

His tongue flicked at the corners of his mouth.

"With powdered sugar," she said.

He rolled his head back and forth.

She balanced on her knees, touching nothing but The Herald, whom she massaged with her inner muscles. When Hal began to move, she stopped to be sure he was asleep. When he began chewing and smacking, she whispered, "Strawberries?"

He stopped moving his jaws, but didn't answer.

She moved again and he moved with her.

"Mmm," he said, "Mmmm."

He sighed and thrashed but she didn't want to stop; although she thought it might be dangerous to lose control and come herself, the man beneath her was irresistible.

She slowed down, contracting her muscles against The Herald to see how far she could arouse him while barely moving at all. Hal moved his hips faster, driving The Herald into her; he was like a runaway horse with Evelyn bouncing on top. His breathing became so harsh and fast she felt he must be awake, but she didn't care. They seemed to her to be together in another world, neither dream nor reality. She felt her cunt ripple as the pressure of pleasure spread from her cleft to her toes and fingertips.

She didn't want to ride any more, but The Herald wasn't finished with her yet. He churned beneath her, leaving her with no choice but to stay on as he ran. All the time Hal galloped he didn't say a word — his mouth was open, nostrils flared, eyes shut; he panted, and after awhile she began to pant, too. His eyebrows knit together. She wondered when his dream would end, or if it already had; she wondered if perhaps this was his dream or hers. Finally The Herald moved deeply inside her and shook with the effort of his proclamation.

Hal, as usual, was silent; only his quick, deep breathing gave him away. Sweat glistened on his forehead, where his damp hair clung to his skin. Evelyn collapsed on top of him, listening to the slowing thump of his heart. She was sure he must be awake because no one could have slept through that, but soon he began his soft snore. When she was certain he was asleep, Evelyn rolled off and lay on her side.

"Strawberries?" she asked again, but he was too far gone to react.

Sunday morning he said nothing. Harold lay limp on Hal's thigh; she stroked him and still he lay there.

"He's being a nerd today," Hal said, pulling away from her. "Give him a couple more hours of sleep." He rolled over on his side, his back to her.

"Did you dream last night?" Evelyn asked.

"No," he said.

"But I heard you talk in your sleep." She sat up.

He rolled over on his back again. "What'd I say?"

"'Strawberries,' which must at least be proof of a dream about strawberries."

Hal raised his eyebrows.

"You smacked your lips when you said it."

He shook his head. "I don't remember."

"Do you remember anything else?"

"Not anything that's a dream," he said. "I like strawberries. We don't eat them much because you don't like them, right? You're the cook, so you control what we eat." He laughed.

"We'll have them; I'll get recipes."

"We don't need recipes — I like them raw."

Her hands were in fists. "Rest up for tonight," she told him as she got out of bed. "I'll bet you remember some dreams."

He laughed again. "What are you trying to do, control my dreams, too? Bake them in a quiche?"

While Hal was in the bathroom, Evelyn rummaged in the back of the closet until she found the riding crop. She took the smooth wood in her right hand and slapped her left wrist with the leather, twice, hard, with a whooshing snap. He *will* dream, and remember, she promised as she stuck the crop under her side of the bed.

Late Sunday night she woke to find Hal on his back, breathing his whistle that was almost but not quite snoring. The Herald stood upright, a promising sign.

"Nocturnal beast," she whispered into The Herald's eye. "You will make him dream."

She reached under the bed, found the riding crop, and climbed on top of Hal, gliding The Herald inside her cunt, already wet at the thought of the ride to come.

The smooth wood of the whip fit her palm as though she'd been born with it in her hand; the strips of black leather drooped from its top. With a snap of her wrist, she flicked them against her pillow as she began to move up and down on the Herald. She tickled Hal's nose with the leather tips, which made it twitch. If he sneezed, he'd wake up. She moved up and down faster, clutching the riding crop, ready to convince him he was asleep and dreaming. Had he ever seen her with a whip before? No; therefore, he must be dreaming.

She rode him slowly, imagining her steed trotting into an ocean, over the waves, while she bounced on his back. He moved under her now in an independent motion that became so strong she was afraid he'd throw her. She steadied herself with her knees. His heart thumped beneath her, and his eyes were wide open, staring up at her. She brushed the leather fringes of the riding crop across his eyebrows, which made him blink.

"Sleep," she whispered. "You're asleep."

This time he answered, "No, I'm awake."

She raised her whip above his head. "See this? You can't possibly be awake because I don't own one of these. I don't even ride horses. But if you're awake, I'll use it until you sleep." She brushed the leather across his forehead, shaking the handle in his face like a threat.

He closed his eyes and sighed, continuing to bounce her along on his rotating pelvis.

She bent and whispered in his ear, "If you're good, I'll buy you some strawberries for dinner tomorrow."

He licked his lips. "Good."

When she lifted herself up on her knees, he rose with her. She tightened her legs around his flanks.

As they rode together, she whooshed her riding crop in the air over his head. He panted hard and rose until she was sure he'd throw her off the bed, and then with a groan he was still.

She had forgotten herself. Rider without a mount, she'd have to walk. She waited until she heard a faint snore, then stuck the handle of the riding crop into her cunt and walked her fingers down her belly into the swamp of her fur, wet with his jism and her juices.

Her fingers slid around her hard and swollen knob, the key to all the secrets at the center of her body. She pressed on it with one finger while with her free hand she moved the riding crop up and down, letting the leather softly slap her ass. At first she moved in time with Hal's slow breathing, and then faster, leaving him behind as she galloped across hills rippling with grass and lupine and poppies until she dropped, exhausted, into a soft field, where she pulled the whip out and flung it away before she slept.

In the morning he woke early, went into the bathroom, came out brushing his teeth, went back in. She lay with her head under the pillow, peeking at him. Monday was her day off.

He sat on the bed beside her. "Hey." He shook her shoulder. "Pretty good last night. I liked that."

"Liked what?" She lifted her head from under the pillow and stared into his eyes, making herself not blink because only a liar would break eye contact for even a second.

"What you did last night. Getting on top of me like that and waking me up."

"What are you talking about? I went to sleep as soon as I came home."

He smiled. "Come on. Where's your whip?"

She raised her eyebrows. "What whip?" Where had she thrown it? Far under the bed, she hoped. "Are you talking about some *dream*?" Now she was up on her knees. The whip was out of sight.

He shook his head. "I don't think so. It was very real."

"Well, what do you think dreams feel like? Mine are real."

"No, they're not. You fly, you see monsters. That's not real."

"But it always *feels* real, that's what matters."

"Well, this *was* real. Sex is real."

"Sex? Tell me more."

"You were there," he said. "What do I have to tell you?"

"Well, what about this whip? Have you ever seen me with a whip before?"

"No, but just because I've never seen it doesn't mean you don't have one."

"So how long was this whip? Six feet? Did I slash it around like a big black snake?"

He stared at her. "Well, you know, it was this stick with leather strips at the top."

She gazed at him steadily. He looked away.

"Like a riding crop?" she asked. "Like for horses? Do I ride horses?"

"Well, it was sort of like a fantasy." He was smiling at her now. "A dream. Of course. Now it seems like a dream. You could be right."

"Tell me about it," she murmured. "I'd like to share it with you."

"I'm not sure I want to," he said. "It's mine. I might not have another if I tell you about it."

"We could really do it the way we did in your dream," she said.

"Do you want me to dream, or not?"

She lay down again, exhausted from the effort of the past few nights. *All right*, she thought. *The next dream better be his because I can't keep this up forever.*

He put on his shirt, pulled on his pants, buckled his belt. "A dream," he said. "I'll be damned."

Susannah Indigo

Shadows on the Wall

There was never a problem of trust between us. Yet I promise myself every night that I won't do it. I will not go near that wall. I will light the two tall emerald green candles on top of the upright piano. I will play my music out, trying to let the memory of Jack pass through the dissonant chords and disappear into the shadow of the flames.

I start with "Going Out of My Head." Jack loved it after I told him about winning a fifth grade talent show with this song. I'm not sure it sounds any better twenty years later, but it does make me feel like a little girl again. Before I play, I lift my skirt as he always required, placing my bare bottom on the velvet-padded piano bench. I spread my legs as he liked; I rarely use the pedals anyway. He called me his little girl, he called me his pet, he called me his kitten. "Play for me, kitten . . . dance for me, kitten," he would say.

Most of the lights are off, but the special track lighting that he had installed for me is on. He would often turn the lights toward me playing or dancing. "You're on my stage, kitten. Entertain me. You're all I need. Let me watch you."

I will not go near the wall tonight.

I dress every morning for him, even though he's not here. I look at my closet and see the style he brought to my life. When I moved in, he threw out all my pantyhose and restrictive underthings.

"A body like yours needs to be free, kitten," he said. He didn't touch my dance clothes, since I use them to make a living. He told me the things I should wear. It was control, but he was right, and it was beautiful. My closet is full of short skirts, and thick belts to show off my waist. The colors are mostly black or red, some white, and some emerald green, his favorite color.

I felt him watching me this morning as I got dressed. I slid on black thigh-high stockings, a longish black wraparound dance skirt, and a white silk shirt tied at my waist. I put on the black Chinese pierced earrings that represent the symbol for energy. Jack liked to put my earrings on for me. The first time he slid a long steel post through the tiny hole in my earlobe was one of the sexiest moments of my life.

Next I play "As Time Goes By," my own favorite song. Jack's picture sits on the piano in a brass frame between the candles, but I don't need to look at it. I see him and feel him every minute of the day. His dark eyes and warm smile are emblazoned on my soul. I always teased him that he looked like Sam Shepard, but of course I wouldn't even look at Sam Shepard if Jack was in the same room.

A couple of weeks ago I was playing this song over and over again, and the guy named Michael who lives below me came up to tell me how much he liked it. I think he was a bit drunk, we just stood at my door and looked at each other, wanting to say more. I found him very warm and attractive and I wanted to invite him in. But I couldn't.

I turn the track lights off for now. Jack owned my life for almost a year before the motorcycle accident. It was so like him to be prepared for his death, even though he was only 44. He left me instructions, and I followed them perfectly. His headstone says "While alive, he lived." He trusted me. He is controlling me from the grave and I don't know how to get away from it.

The wall is painted a deep emerald green.

I move to the sofa and try to read, after putting on a Van Morrison song — "heart and soul/body and mind/meet me/on the river of time." When I opened the box of letters full of instructions, I cried. How could he have known? When did he do this? The first letter said:

My kitten,

I'm writing this under a strange and very frightening premoni-tion. I feel like I will not be with you for long, as silly as that sounds as I write it. I suppose it's because of my father dying of a heart attack when he was just forty-five. I guess if you're reading this, my fears are right. I know you can't live without me. I could not live without you. We belong to each other. You are so young and so beautiful. I don't want you to be lost and crying without me. I will always be with you. Feel me on you right now. Touch yourself for me. Close your eyes and run your hands up your thighs just like I would. Thank you, kitten. I've written these letters to be opened one a week. I know you will obey this. I trust you implicitly to do everything that I ask. I don't know how many letters there will be. Do not read ahead for any reason. Your only instruction this week is a simple one. Know that I am with you and that I am watching you. Mourn me with love and respect and sensuality. Do not withdraw from the living. This is what I want you to do: Read this letter every morning for a week before you get out of bed . . . .

At that point the letter went into great detail about how I was to stroke myself to orgasm for him every night for a week. Where I should sit or lie each night, what I should wear, what I should think about. I never thought I could do it. But I did. With my eyes closed, I could feel him watching. I don't believe in spirits. I don't believe in God or heaven. But yet I follow these letters just as though Jack can see me.

I played the piano at his memorial service. My ass was bare on the piano bench underneath my full black skirt, as he requested. I played "Amazing Grace" for him, and I know that he smiled as I sang the second verse, his favorite, to myself:

'Twas grace that taught my heart to fear
And grace my fears relieved;
How precious did that grace appear
The hour that I first believed

Some days I think of telling the man downstairs my whole story — I know he's a writer, and I need someone to talk to. But I don't.

I turn the lights back on and shine them on the wall.

We lived in harmony. Perfect equals in the outside world, perfect lovers inside our home. We lived a life of what people call "dominance and submission." I can't talk to anyone about it, because people have this image of women in chains and leather being abused. That's not what it was at all. It was about an exchange of power, about our agreement that we wanted to do this, about love and passion and a depth of sexuality I'll never know again.

I arrange myself in the big black leather armchair as he has instructed me to, the same way I did when he was here. I always wear skirts, never jeans. I lift my skirt, spread my legs over each arm of the chair, and relax back. Sometimes we would both just sit and read this way, with me available to him. It was in both of us, a very intense sexuality just under the surface no matter what we were doing. Tonight I lift my black dance skirt up above my hips.

I opened the second letter and it was rather spooky. I found a tape with it. I put it on the tape player as instructed and cried all the way through the first time. Then I rewound it and listened more carefully. There was laughter, he read a favorite story for me, and there was a lot of music. There was also sexual talk, the kinds of words that have always made me blush. Then there was that music, the music that will haunt me the rest of my life no matter what happens. And the instruction to get up and dance for him.

I dance for a living with the Black Oak Dance Project. It seemed to entrance him; he could watch me practice my dance for hours. He would just watch me dance whatever routine I was practicing. Then he started asking more of me. The first time I stripped for him I was buzzed on a couple of glasses of wine. I'm not a stripper, I'm a modern/jazz dancer. It took me forever, and I know by the way he fucked me that night that it turned him on as much as it did me.

The wall beckons me, and somehow I know I will go to it yet again.

After discovering the creativity in my stripping, he moved on. He started to control me as I danced. Not just asking for something, but setting up requirements, usually sexual. At first it was fun and challenging. Then I started to get scared. The control he has over me takes me into a space where I'm flying and completely vulnerable. I don't think he could have known the impact these letters would have on me.

It's been almost six months now. Twenty-four new letters. Sometimes I dread opening them, sometimes I can't wait. The letters have gotten shorter.

The fifth letter started in about the wall. It was something he made up for me one night long ago. It began mildly, dancing in the shadows. He would sit and watch me and often stroke his cock. We would fuck like crazy afterwards, like animals in heat. I don't know what you'd call what we were doing, not exactly dancing, not exactly sex. Just another world, a special moment of power in our own private universe.

I think about Jack so much that sometimes when the phone rings I'm sure it will be him. Yet when I see Michael from downstairs go by my window, I often wish that he would come and save me and make me normal again. I know no man can save me, but that doesn't stop the desire.

I untie my shirt and slide it off my shoulders. The heavy silver heart that Jack gave me dangles between my bare breasts. My nipples are hard. Every time I open a letter now, I half hope it will talk about my future, about the possibility of another man. But he doesn't write of it, and I still dance my heart out for him every night. I rise from my chair, start the exotic Indian music, and head slowly toward my wall.

#5

My kitten, I'm rather enjoying writing these letters, much to my surprise. If nothing ever happens, we can share them some day and laugh over my silly fears. This brings out my creativity like nothing else ever has, except for the hours I spend painting you. I try to picture you in our apartment alone, without me, reading this, dancing for me, staying sexual for me. I try to think of what you will need. I have several hard things to ask of you, but I also want to take care of you. You know that I left all of my paintings to you, with instructions to keep them in storage for now. We both know how much I love my art, hobby though it is. And we both know the most gorgeous work I've ever done involves you as my model. You also know that James had a standing offer to me to put on a show in his gallery. I not only want you to do it, I want you to be there as the guest of honor. You can do it. You may destroy the hundreds of photographs if you like, but I want the paintings shared. James has the instructions on how I want it done. It's to be called "Visions of Juliana." All you have to do is call him. It's always your choice. Your submission to me was always the choice of your free will.

What he didn't mention in the letter is what the paintings are.

Naked, half-dressed, stroking myself, lost in ecstasy, on the wall, bent over the chair. He painted them beautifully. I think he painted me through a haze of love, because I don't believe I've ever looked like that in my life. They are all dreamy, massively sensual, and I would die before I'd let anyone else ever see them.

This fifth letter went on —

I want you to dance on the wall for me tonight, kitten. Do you remember the things you submitted to there? I remember the first night we got past the play of dancing in the shadows. You were like a beautiful butterfly pinned to a board for me. I could have kept you there forever. But nobody else is watching you now, not like before. I know you haven't moved any of the equipment. I hope you never will. Dance for me there tonight. Put your wrists where they belong, the lights as they should be, and see me in the shadows . . .

I stood before the wall that night as I do now. It's all still here. The glossy deep green paint, the black velvet cords hanging down, the octagonal mirror on the opposite wall, the leather box in the corner. There used to be a dining table in this part of the room, but we moved it out a long time ago.

Sometimes we'd laugh and joke about "our wall." He'd even say we might not do it anymore. But when we got here there was no laughter, there was only music and power and sex. It obsessed both of us after awhile, wondering what could possibly be next. I teach dance and gymnastics to small children in my off-season. How could I ever explain this to anyone?

I press my bare back against the green wall. He would ask me to decorate my body before I started. The leather box holds many choices for decoration, and most of them hurt. My body is still permanently decorated for him, but these are all temporary. I slide my skirt off, leaving nothing covering me but my black stockings. My hands caress my marks: the tiny ribbon-shaped tattoo just above where my pussy hair would be if I didn't still have it waxed off for him. The ribbon says only "kitten." A matching tattoo with his name just above the top of my stocking, on the inside of my thigh very close to my pussy. And, of course, the tiny gold ring pierced through the hood of my clit, the gold ring that shows up clearly in so many of his paintings.

I never thought I'd let a man do any of these things to my body. But each act of marking turned out to be desperately sensual and erotic. He had his friend James come to our home and do each one at different times. Jack would get me high on submission beforehand and then hold me down tightly while James did his work on my body. I remember having an orgasm during the piercing of my clit hood. Jack never let me forget it.

Go to the leather box, kitten, and choose a decoration for your body. Remove all of your clothing except stockings if you're wearing them. Wait, let me choose for tonight. I want you to put on the gold filigree chain that threads through your clit ring and up over your ass and around your waist. Then put on the nipple clamps that match, the tiny black ones with the matching chain . . . .

The thing that people miss sometimes from reading things like *The Story of O* is that real S/M is not about force at all. It's about love and power and desire. It's like my ballet training when I was a young girl: It's a tradition of ritual, sacrifice, pain and beauty, all at the hands of another. Jack introduced me to all his devices of power, but I would beg for them if he didn't initiate them. We were like two pieces of an interlocking puzzle — he was dominant and power-driven, and I am submissive and driven by the need to be controlled. Discovering that I could live this way and still be in the world saved my life.

I reach up and slide one wrist through the black velvet restraint. He liked me to do this to myself while he watched. The cords are long enough to give me a full range of motion. He would start the same music every time, give me that look, and say, "Tie yourself up for me, kitten," and I would. Real bondage is in the mind, not the knots.

My other wrist is tied. How can I do this without him? He made me feel safe. I don't feel that way now.

The gold chain around my waist shimmers in the lights. There are other restraints, but I can't do them all myself. Everyone who comes to our home thinks the black cords draping the green wall are a work of art.

Jack forgot one thing, and that's why this is so hard for me: he didn't realize I would transcend reality even without him here. Afterwards I need him to take care of me, to bring me down, to bring me back.

Remember the things we did there, kitten.

The night of the feathers. The night of the examination. It all makes me soaking wet to remember. The night he mastered how to lift me off the ground against the wall with the combination of cords. When he said I should be nothing but a work of art and kept there forever. The night his friends came over and he showed them everything. He let them touch me, he let them command me. He never let them fuck me. The pictures. The first night I asked him to take me to the wall. The small black suede whip. The music. The music.

I dance.

This is not something to do alone. I will go mad. I have to stop. I turn and face the wall the way he required.

I love it.

It makes me wet.

My nipples are hard against the cold wall.

I hate it.

I slither against the wall, making love to the wall and to myself as he would want me to.

I miss him. I need him. I need his voice telling me it's all going to be all right, telling me to go wherever it takes me and he will be here to bring me back.

I turn and twist and rub my gold clit ring against the wall and I am coming for him and our love and our past and his power. I start to shiver. No more. I will free my wrists and put my shirt back on and begin to find a way to tell my story. I am alone, and I will learn to live without him.

Contributors

Red Jordan Arobateau has been writing and self-publishing since the early 1970s and is officially on the bookstore shelves with *Lucy & Mickey, Dirty Pictures, Boys Night Out, Rough Trade, Satan's Best, Street Fighter, The Black Biker, Where The Word is No,* and *The Nearness of You/Sorrow of the Madonna.* She has acquired something of a cult-like following among many working-class dykes.

Deborah Bishop is an award-winning romance writer who lives in southern Indiana with her husband, two step-children and three unruly dogs. When she isn't writing she enjoys reading, gardening and rebuilding computers.

Kate Dominic is a Los Angeles-based writer who is addicted to sexy stories because they're so much fun. Her work, mostly fiction, has been published under various pennames in various periodicals and anthologies. Under this name, her credits include honorable mention in *Libido* magazine's 1997 fiction contest. A graduate of the University of Wisconsin, Kate considers writing erotica to be her solution to the quandary of "what do I do with an English degree besides teach?"

Diva Marie is an active, out, happily married pansexual leather player and professional dominatrix currently residing in New Mexico. When she's not teaching or writing, she can usually be found at national SM/leather conventions looking for virgin boys who need debriefing of any kind.

Nancy Ferreyra is a disabled lesbian living in the San Francisco Bay Area. "After Amelia" is her first published short story. She is currently finishing an erotic novel, *Slip*, about a disabled lesbian's journey of self-discovery through an affair with a married man.

Mel Harris is a freelance writer who has only recently discovered how much she enjoys writing erotica, especially humorous erotica. "Neighborhood Round Robyn" is her first erotic story based on a favorite fantasy. She has also contributed to *Sex Toy Tales* (Down There Press). She lives on the Gulf of Mexico in Northern Florida with her Miniature Pinscher Maya.

*Susanna J. Herbert's words have lived via TV, films, theatre, magazines and *Herotica 4*. Thanks to Marcy Sheiner for her support. "Three Note Harmony" is dedicated to the Brown Bear boys, the lads from Shepherd's Bush, and Alan — who is too much of a gentleman to peek at my notes.

Susannah Indigo is a systems consultant and writer, and the mother of two young boys. Her fiction has been published in a variety of magazines, including *Libido* and *Black Sheets*.

The only thing **Shelley Marcus** likes more than writing gay porn is reading it, so she couldn't be happier to see the genre flourishing. Shelley is currently single, but is not opposed to seeing that situation change some day. A writer since childhood, she lives and works in New Jersey.

Maria Mendoza was born and raised in Texas. A college graduate in journalism from the University of Texas at Austin, Maria's main love is fiction writing. "Mourning the Peasant" is her short fiction debut. The 24-year-old resides and works in New York City.

Mary Anne Mohanraj has published her first book, *Torn Shapes of Desire*. Her work also appears in *Sex Toy Tales* (Down There Press) and in *Best American Erotica 1999*. She moderates the Internet Erotica Writers' workshop, co-moderates the newsgroup soc.sexuality.general, and edits the erotic webzine www.cleansheets.com.

Laural Fisher lives, loves, and writes in Denver in the company of one knight in slightly tarnished armor and an odd assortment of critters and motorcycles.

Lisa Prosimo lives in Southern California and entertains dreams of living in Northern California. "I like to think my characters are alive before they enter my stories and will continue to live after they leave." Her erotic fiction has appeared in *Sauce Box Journal, XStories*, and Lonnie Barbach's *Seductions*. She has a novel under construction.

*Carol Queen's first novel, *The Leather Daddy and the Femme*, was released in 1998. She is also author of *Real Live Nude Girl: Chronicles of Sex-Positive Culture* and *Exhibitionism for the Shy* (Down There Press), and co-editor of the Lammy award-winning *PoMoSexuals,* as well as *Switch Hitters* and *Sex Spoken Here* (Down There Press).

Shar Rednour wrote *The Femme's Guide to the Universe.* Her short stories appear in *Best American Erotica 1996, Leatherwomen III,* and *Once Upon a Time: Fairytales for Women.* She publishes *Starphkr.* Jackie Strano, lead singer of The Hail Marys, is Shar's true love and eternal inspiration.

*Marcy Sheiner is editor of *Herotica 4* and *5,* as well as *The Oy of Sex: Jewish Women Write Erotica* (Cleis). She writes fiction, journalism and erotica, and is the author of *Sex for the Clueless* (Citadel).

Victoria Smith lives in central California, dividing her time between the desert and the coast. Her stories, poetry and sexuality articles have appeared in many venues, including *Carnal Knowledge, SEXlife,* and *Moondance.* Victoria's current projects include a market guide for writers of erotica, and two novels.

*Susan St. Aubin's erotica has been published in *Libido, Yellow Silk, Erotic By Nature, Fever, Best American Erotica 1995,* and the *Herotica®* series. She believes her dreams, even when they don't come true.

*Michelle Stevens lives in Los Angeles with her wife, Chris, who wants everyone to know that "Lesbian Bed Death" is purely fictional.

*Cecilia Tan is the author of *Black Feathers: Erotic Dreams* and the editor of numerous erotic science fiction and fantasy anthologies for Circlet Press. Her short stories have appeared in *Best American Erotica 1996* and *1998, Best Lesbian Erotica 1997,* and many other anthologies and magazines.

*Joan Leslie Taylor is a writer and accountant who lives in the woods of northern California with a large dog and a small cat. She is the author of *In the Light of Dying,* a book about her experiences as a hospice volunteer. In *Herotica 2* her story appeared under the name Maggie Brewster.

*Contributors to previous *Herotica®* collections.

The *Herotica*® series

Published by Down There Press

> *Herotica*, Susie Bright, editor (1988, 1998)

> *Herotica 6*, Marcy Sheiner, editor (1999)

Licensed to Plume

> *Herotica 2*, Susie Bright and Joani Blank, editors (1991)

> *Herotica 3*, Susie Bright, editor (1994)

> *Herotica 4*, Marcy Sheiner, editor (1996)

> *Herotica 5*, Marcy Sheiner, editor (1998)

Audio editions licensed to Passion Press

> *Herotica*

> *Herotica 2*

> *Herotica 3*

> *Herotica 4*

All titles are available from your favorite bookstore, or by calling (800) 289-8423.

To Order Down There Press Books:

_____	Herotica® 6	$12.50
_____	Herotica®: A Collection of Women's Erotic Fiction, _Susie Bright, editor._ The spunky original in the best-selling series.	$11.00
_____	Sex Spoken Here, _Carol Queen & Jack Davis, editors._ Passionate prose and vibrant verse from San Francisco's Good Vibrations.	$14.50
_____	Sex Toy Tales, _Anne Semans & Cathy Winks, editors._ Tasty tales incorporating a multitude of imaginative accessories.	$12.50
_____	I Am My Lover, _Joani Blank, editor._ Artful duotone and black & white photos of 12 women pleasuring themselves.	$25.00
_____	First Person Sexual, _Joani Blank, editor._ Women and men write about the joys and taboos of their masturbation experiences.	$14.50
_____	Femalia, _Joani Blank, editor._ Thirty-two stunning color portraits of women's genitals by four photographers.	$14.50
_____	Anal Pleasure & Health, rev. 3rd edition, _Jack Morin, Ph.D._ This is the classic, definitive guide to enjoying anal stimulation and well-being, with a new chapter on power dynamics.	$18.00
_____	Exhibitionism for the Shy: Show Off, Dress Up and Talk Hot, _Carol Queen._ "...a sexual travel guide...." _Libido_	$12.50
_____	Good Vibrations: The Complete Guide to Vibrators, _Joani Blank._ "...explicit, entertaining...." _L.A. Times_	$6.50
_____	Good Vibrations Guide: Adult Videos, _Cathy Winks._ Everything you wanted to know about X-rated flicks.	$7.00
_____	Good Vibrations Guide: The G-Spot, _Cathy Winks._ Demystifying the ultimate pleasure spot and female ejaculation.	$7.00
_____	Sex Information, May I Help You?, _Isadora Alman._ Behind the scenes at a sex information hotline.	$9.50
_____	Erotic by Nature, _David Steinberg, editor._ Luscious duotone photos with polished prose and poetry, elegantly bound.	$45.00
_____	The Playbook for Women About Sex, _Joani Blank_	$4.50
_____	The Playbook for Men About Sex, _Joani Blank._	$4.50

Catalogs — free with purchase of any book, else send $2

_____	Good Vibrations. Sex toys, massage oils, safer sex supplies — and of course, vibrators!	
_____	The Sexuality Library. Over 300 sexual self-help and enhancement books, audios and videos.	

Buy these books from your local bookstore, call toll-free at **1-800-289-8423,** log on to _www.goodvibes.com/dtp/dtp.html_ or use this coupon to order directly:

Down There Press, 938 Howard Street, San Francisco CA 94103

Include $4.50 shipping for the first book ordered and $1.25 for each additional book. California residents please add sales tax. We ship UPS whenever possible; please give us your street address.

Name _____

UPS Street Address _____

_____ ZIP _____

Mastercard/VISA/Discover/AMEX _____ Exp. Date _____